SEASON'S SCHEMINGS

A HOLIDAY HOCKEY ROM COM

KATIE BAILEY

Character cover art by
CINDY RAS

ELEVENTH AVENUE
PUBLISHING

1

MADDIE

July

"This isn't working."

A camera rolls closer to me, zooming in on my face as I wipe a smudge of flour from my cheek with the sleeve of my novelty Christmas sweater. I flip off the mixer and turn to look at my boyfriend, Adam, who's standing next to me at the counter, stirring food coloring into a vat of royal icing.

"Maybe add another drop or two of color?" I advise as I pick up a spatula and start scraping batter off the edge of the mixing bowl. The camera looming ever closer to me is serving as a very clear reminder that there's no time to waste—we only have two hours to produce 200 cookies for the judges, with no less than three different flavors and Christmassy designs on them. "If we want to do a Santa cookie, the color has got to be really rich and vivid."

"I know how to make frosting, Maddie," Adam retorts, pulling at the collar of his own itchy holiday sweater, and I hear it immediately: the thinly disguised contempt in his tone.

He's been using that tone a lot with me lately.

Because he's stressed, I reassure myself.

And he really does know how to make frosting... better than me, that's for sure. We're both bakers at heart, but I usually focus on healthy ingredient substitutes for traditional baked goods, whereas Adam's the pastry chef at a high-end restaurant in metro Atlanta. He's been making some strides towards opening his own place: a dessert emporium where he'll create luxurious confections to cater to the most upper-crust and refined of sweet-toothed cravings.

It was my idea for us to apply as a couple's team for the Food Network's *Behemoth Holiday Baking Bonanza!* I thought the television exposure might do him good. That the publicity might help him get on his feet. Even if it did mean putting my own budding career on pause for a hot second. Or more. I'm not sure anyone's going to want to hire a nutritionist known for peddling butter, flour and sugar in gargantuan quantities, but I'll worry about that later.

I also thought it might be a nice way for us to spend more time together. Adam's been hard at work trying to make his business dream a reality, and we haven't seen much of each other lately. Which is rather unusual. Adam's been in my life almost as long as I can remember—his dad and my stepdad are criminal defense lawyers at some fancy law office downtown, and when my Mom married my stepdad, she became friends with Adam's mom, too.

As a couple, we just made sense. While other high-schoolers spent their weekends partying and illicitly drinking, Adam and I would make cookies together. Until Adam graduated a year before me and moved on to culinary school, creating soufflés and choux pastry and leaving me to lick snickerdoodle batter from the bowl alone on Friday nights.

But having a dessert emporium is Adam's dream, and I totally respect all the work he's put into it. Including frequent meetings with Elizabeth Carberry, business advisor extraordinaire. And really, really pretty.

2

I know, because I've visited her website. Numerous times.

I was a little suspicious for awhile... but then, I found the ring in his sock drawer.

Adam's finally going to *propose*.

And I'd bet money that he's planning on proposing this Christmas. My family has spent every holiday season with Adam's family at their cabin in Aspen for years. It was at that cabin that Adam asked me out for the first time, and though it was over a decade ago, I still remember it like it was yesterday. It would be the *perfect* place for him to propose. Bookend our relationship. Christmas is only a few months away now.

That has to be why he's been so stressed and distant lately. Planning a proposal for your girlfriend of over a decade while also trying to start your own business has to be a *lot* of pressure. And on top of that, I had this idea for us to do this nationally televised baking show together.

But a nagging, unsettled voice in me wonders if I have it wrong. Maybe this whole thing—making 200 novelty holiday cookies for a TV show—is beneath him and his luxurious dessert brand.

Maybe he's only taking part in it because *I* wanted us to?

I suddenly feel a bit guilty. Guilty enough to smile and soothe his snapping tone.

"You're right, I'm sorry," I say gently as I put a hand on his arm, trying to ignore the cameraperson who's currently getting all up in my face. Which I'm sure is beet-red and sweaty as all hell. I feel like I'm about to melt into the floorboards. Why do they have to film Christmas shows in the height of summer when it's literally a hundred degrees out? "I'm sure you know better than me how to fix the frosting."

"I'm not talking about the damn frosting." Adam's jaw tics and he yanks his sweater off. His glasses get stuck in the process and go flying, skidding across the counter.

He blinks at me, all squinty.

"Oh, let me get those for you!"

I can't even take a single step before he grabs my arm.

In-my-face cameraperson is now literally so close, I can see my tiny, surprised, red-cheeked reflection on the lens. In the corner, the judges have taken notice of the commotion and are looking at us with interest. Another camera materializes right next to us. And another.

Apparently, our little tiff is more interesting than the grannies at the next station happily whipping up fruit cookies.

"Mads," Adam says, looking at me through unfocused eyes. His eyesight has always been terrible, and contacts never agreed with him.

"Just let me get—"

"I mean *this* isn't working." He gestures from himself, to me. "Me and you."

I sigh. Adam is highly competitive. I want to win this thing, too; it's a trait we share. But if we want to have a shot at claiming that W, we need to put a pin in this convo. Stat.

And if I know Adam at all, I know that the only way to end a squabble is to roll over and let him believe he's right. So instead of telling him to pipe the hell down and focus on getting his Santa-red right, I smile. "I'm not as skilled a baker as you, but if I'm being a crappy teammate, you can take the lead and assign me grunt work—"

"Our relationship!" He half yells, and for the first time, I notice the thin sheen of stress sweat dotting his forehead. He only sweats like that when he has something on his mind that he doesn't want to say, and I know that because... dammit, I know everything about this man after being with him for the past eleven years.

"What?" I blink at him. Camera one is so up in my face, I suddenly feel like a goldfish in a very, very claustrophobic bowl.

He sighs. "I don't want to do this with you anymore, Madelyn. Us. Our relationship."

I blink again, not comprehending.

"It's over," he adds for good measure, really twisting the pastry knife.

"B-b-but... the ring," I stutter, my vision blurring at the edges as hot tears prick the corners of my eyes.

Now, it's Adam's turn to look confused. "What ring?"

"I found it in your drawer," I mumble, blinking up at a shiny decorative Christmas bauble suspended above me.

"Oh. That's not for you."

It's then that I notice that the studio is quiet. Too quiet. The only thing punctuating the silence is the tinny blast of that "Deck the Halls" song coming from the speakers. Camera four is now also focused on Adam and me. The grannies to our left have stopped adding raisins to their oatmeal dough. The steam-punk bakers to our right have paused piping their neon-pink-and-black-skull sugar cookie stockings. Gina DeLaurier, beloved host of *Easy Peasy Lemon Squeezy Meals For One*—and today's guest judge—stands up, concern worrying her pretty features.

But I can't focus on any of that. Because Adam's words are sinking in like acid on my skin.

"Wait... you're breaking up with me... so you can propose to someone else??" My voice has taken on the harpy, almost hysterical quality of a too-tight violin string.

Adam swallows, his unfocused eyes darting back and forth like a metronome. He, at least, has the decency to look bashful. "I've fallen in love with Elizabeth."

"Elizabeth," I repeat dumbly.

Adam frowns. "You know... *my* Elizabeth? I didn't mean for this to happen, but..."

I tune Adam out as a rush of blood floods my eardrums, roaring like the ocean in indignance.

His Elizabeth. Elizabeth Carberry. Business advisor extraordinaire. Really, really pretty.

And apparent go-to girl for an affair.

Ha.

It's the third round of the competition. We were only *one step away* from making the finals. And my cookies in the form of jolly little Santa Clauses sipping hot chocolate were going to knock it out of the park today.

But now, Adam has Elizabeth, and Elizabeth is going to have a ring, and all I have is some red frosting that is totally the wrong color because Adam mixed it wrong, for frick's sake.

"So, I think you'll understand that this is for the best for everyone," Adam concludes blinkily as his voice comes back into focus.

He puts his hands on the counter and starts to pat around blindly.

And so, I do the only thing that a reasonable, sane, mature, twenty-five year old woman who's just been dumped on national television would do:

I reach up, grab the back of his head... and dunk his stupid blind-bat face in the vat of wrong-color-red frosting.

Fa la la la la la la la la.

2

MADDIE

November

"You can do this, Madelyn. You got this. Everyone will take you seriously and nobody will laugh at you." I smooth down the front of my favorite long-sleeved black blouse—the one with the flattering but demure V-neck and all the tiny buttons down the front—and nod at my pale, freckled reflection.

I'm talking to myself in the mirror in the public restroom of Atlanta's brand-new RGM arena, in case you're wondering.

It's not a habit I indulge in often, but trust me, it's helpful when you're in a pinch. Like I am today.

I'm about to start my new job for the Atlanta Cyclones NHL team. They're currently third in their division, and though it's still early in the season, there's already lots of buzz around them potentially making the playoffs for the first time in nine years. All thanks to their new star center. Number 19, Sebastian Slater.

Who, as an aside, is quite possibly the hottest man I have ever laid eyes on.

And when I say "laid eyes on," I mean that Adam once pointed him out to me on TV as his favorite player.

Not that it even matters if he's hot—if he's Adam's favorite player, he's probably a massive douche. And anyhow, I have been a man-free zone since *The Incident*, in that I am forgetting men exist entirely and am instead throwing myself into my career.

Evidenced by the fact that I did a whole lot of job research before today.

In my former life, Adam was the hockey fan, and I didn't give a damn about sports of any kind. He took me to a game once, on a date, and I snuck in my Kindle to keep me entertained.

But now that a hockey team has given me a job, I am *alllll* about hockey. Miss Number One Hockey Fan over here. I'm super interested in all things pucks and sticks and slapshots and wrist shots and... why are all hockey terms so innuendo-laden?!

Michael Scott would have a *that's what she said* field day with this sport. Or rink day, I guess. (Can you tell I read an entire hockey lingo book to prep for my first day at work?)

I should also clarify that my new job has nothing to do with actual hockey. Thank goodness. I'll be doing mostly meal prep, working under the team's chef and head nutritionist. It's an entry-level position, but this is a perfect place for me to get more experience in the nutrition field. Hockey players follow a very strict, high-protein and veggie-heavy diet, and I know how to make a mean green smoothie and can transform protein powder into a variety of surprisingly-edible sugar-free, flour-free desserts.

In fact, it's all I've been doing on my new TikTok channel: showcasing ways to make treats healthier and more nutrient dense.

Starting a TikTok was a great way to distract myself after the breakup. It was also something I've been wanting to do for a while—combining my love of baking with my education on nutrition so that I can help people create healthy treats they can enjoy.

Adam would've probably thought it was stupid, but if I'm honest, I think it's what landed me this job. The hiring manager saw my videos, and apparently hockey players are a big, hungry bunch who want lots of taste and variety, but also need like a million grams of protein per day. And despite the fact that I know—*knew*—next to nothing about sports, I couldn't exactly say no. It's not like I was drowning in job offers after my holiday baking show stint.

So, hockey it is.

"Yay, sports. Or something," I mutter aloud, grabbing a wad of paper towels and blowing my nose, loudly. The sound echoes around the bathroom.

I'm just hoping that my new boss will let me be creative and might eventually use some of my recipes as part of the team meal plan.

And while I'll be relegated to the industrial kitchen that's part of the team's training facility—and so, will have absolutely no interaction with the actual players or be required to attend the actual games—it's almost laughable that I've landed a job working for Adam's favorite NHL team.

But I don't laugh. Because I don't think of Adam anymore. At all. Ever.

Thinking of Adam makes me want to cry, and I've only allowed myself three pity cries since *The Incident*:

1. After my mother called to tell me that she'd heard the news of our breakup from Adam's mother, and she wanted to know what, exactly, I'd done wrong and how I planned to make it up to him.

2. Last week, when the first *Holiday Baking Bonanza* episode aired and I, like a true masochist, watched the entire episode, including the little intro about each team where Adam

gushed about how much he loved me. Which was false. Because he'd already bought a ring for Elizabeth at that point.

And last but not least,

3. On my way into the arena this morning—with impeccably terrible timing that had me fleeing to this bathroom in the first place—because the Instagram post I've been dreading finally popped up on my feed.

Adam and Elizabeth are engaged. And I doubt that the timing is a coincidence—he kind of *had* to get that ring on her stupidly slender, long, perfect finger before *The Incident* episode airs in just over a week. *And* according to that same post, he—*they*—recently opened his new dream dessert emporium, too. So the happy couple have more than one thing to celebrate.

Of course everything came up smelling like roses for Adam, while I'm standing in a smelly public bathroom, crying before my first day on my new job as a kitchen lackey.

"I'm fine, though," I tell the girl in the mirror, who's staring back at me with only slightly red-rimmed green eyes. I smooth a strand of my light brown hair back into place and sniffle. "Totally fine."

Behind me, a toilet flushes.

I spin on my heel to find a man lumbering out of one of the cubicles. He's wearing the uniformed red polo shirt that all the hotdog and popcorn slingers at the snack kiosks wear. He's also got on a slightly terrified expression. I blink at him in full confusion for a moment.

"Um, I'm glad to hear you're fine," he says meekly. Cautiously. "But... I'm pretty sure this is the men's restroom?"

"No," I say staunchly with a shake of my head. "This is definitely the..."

And that's when I spot the urinals.

Great. So not only was I talking to myself aloud in a public restroom, but I was talking to myself aloud in the *men's* restroom. While a man was trying to take a quiet poop in stall three.

The guy follows my eyes towards the urinals, then hops from one foot to the other before appearing to make a split-second decision and bolt for the door.

Without washing his hands.

Ew. That's got to be a public health violation in the extreme. But I can hardly blame the guy—he was clearly fearing for his life. Still...

Note to self: never buy a hot dog at the RGM arena.

I clearly need to get the hell out of here ASAP, but before I go, I decide to wash my own hands as a gesture of goodwill, hoping to spread the antibacterial vibes in his direction.

As I'm lathering up with soap, the door creaks open, and for a moment, I actually think I've voodoo magicked him back in here.

But no, Hot Dog Boy is not back.

Instead, standing in the doorway of the restroom—pretty much entirely filling it with his big, hulking frame—is the Atlanta Cyclones' new star center. Number 19. Sebastian Slater.

Who might be even hotter in real life than on TV.

And who I'm currently meant to be making lunch for.

Oh, for puck's sake.

3

SEB

I might look like a dumb jock.

Hell, I might even *be* a dumb jock.

But the first thing that springs to mind as I stare at the woman in the men's bathroom—who's scrubbing her hands while sporting raw, red, teary eyes—is that scene in *Macbeth* where Lady Macbeth goes off the rails. Proof that I did listen in class once in a while. Man, my high school English teacher would be proud.

My second thought is that this will teach me for drinking so much Gatorade on the way to practice that I have to duck into the arena's public restrooms before I can even get to the locker room. Because here I am, staring at a woman who's staring back at me with wild eyes as she clearly experiences some sort of a crisis of the highest order.

"Hi!" she squeaks, her eyes roaming over me as her cheeks color scarlet like they've been painted. "I'm just finishing up in here, I'll be right..." She shoves her hands back under the running water a little too fast, and a jet of liquid sprays all over her shirt. "Out," she finishes dejectedly, staring sadly at her soaked top.

I open my mouth to ask if she's okay. Ask if I can help. Do something to assist her.

And then, I take in the unique celery-green tint of her eyes. The stick-straight light brown hair. The freckles dancing over the bridge of her button nose... A *familiar* button nose.

Frick.

"This is perfect. Absolutely perfect!" The lady sounds a touch hysterical now. She sniffs, then takes a paper towel and dabs at her wet eyes before taking it to her drenched shirt and scrubbing it as roughly as she was her hands. "Of course Sebastian Slater walked in here and this is happening right now!"

My internal panic button starts to flash. Though I'm not one to usually acquaint myself with hysterical women who lurk in men's restrooms, I have definitely seen this particular woman before... I just can't remember *where* I've seen her.

Please, *please,* tell me this isn't a Puck Bunny I took on a date or something.

And if it is, what in the name of all that is holy is she doing in the men's restroom at the RGM?

I wrack my brain, trying to remember the women I've dated since I was sold by the Edmonton Wolverines to the Atlanta Cyclones and moved to Georgia this time last year. But I come up empty. All of my flirtations here have been brief. Unremarkable. Well, they've been like that everywhere, given that for a long time now, I've been committed to nothing and nobody but the sport I love.

Those eyes of hers, though. I feel like I'd recognize those strange eyes anywhere.

But the fact is, I don't really know anyone here in Atlanta except my teammates and the women I've dated.

Plus, she's looking at me like I've ruined her day.

My panic button segues into alarm bells as I stare blankly at a woman who I may or may not have had a romantic dalliance

13

with, while I may or may not have been suffering a brain hemor-rhage and/or temporary amnesia.

I *should* ask if she's okay.

Should ask if I can help her.

Should ask for her to remind me of her name so I can remember, and maybe apologize, for whatever I did.

But apparently, I really am a dumb jock. Because instead, I blurt, "You missed a spot on your pants!"

Then, like the gentleman and scholar that I am, I turn on my heel and bolt, and the bathroom door slams closed behind me.

※ ※ ※

"Who do you think would win in a fight—a narwhal or a unicorn?"

I look up at Jimmy Jones-Johnstone, AKA Triple J, from where I'm unlacing my skates on a bench in the locker room. He beams back at me, like he's just asked an actual, legitimate question.

"You do know that unicorns aren't real, right?"

Triple J considers this for a moment as he removes his jersey. "But neither are narwhals."

For the second time in a matter of hours, I find myself putting my high school education to good use. And you know, my general non-absolute-idiocy. "Yes, they are. They live in the Arctic Circle."

"Sure, and Santa's elves ride them to work every morning." He sticks out his elbow in a little *nudge, nudge* gesture, then starts wheezing with laughter.

Is he serious right now? Sometimes when I talk to Jimmy, it's like he's tuned into a totally different frequency than the rest of the human population.

"I always imagined that Santa's elves would be super hot, if they were real." Dallas Cooper—famous for being one of the best defensemen in the NHL, and for having a roster as long as his arm—pipes up.

"But sadly, they're about as real as narwhals," says Aaron Marino, our alternate captain and the world's biggest softy despite looking like a real-life Gigachad.

I am surrounded by idiots.

And yet, as my teammates traipse off to the showers one by one, I can't help but smile. Because honestly? I don't hate it here.

At all.

In fact, I like it a whole lot more than I thought I would.

When the Edmonton Wolverines dropped the bomb that I was being traded and would be going to the Cyclones, I wasn't exactly delighted—I viewed the Cyclones as a relatively unexciting franchise who didn't have the best track record.

Like... the team hasn't even made the first round of the playoffs for years.

Despite my reservations, my agent, Mike Ambrosia, was sure that joining the Cyclones was going to be the best move for me and my career. Give me a chance to be the hero and lead a team in a dry spell to glory.

And I wanted to do anything I could to further my career.

So, I decided to give Atlanta a chance. A *calculated* chance. I had Mike negotiate my initial contract to only be for a year's duration instead of the standard five years so that I could bail if things didn't work out the way Mike predicted, and there was better opportunity to advance my career elsewhere. My agent wasn't pleased, but he did say that the silver lining to my decision was that we could revisit negotiations regarding salary, bonuses, etc.—which *I* cared about much less—after the team's management saw my performance on the ice for the franchise.

Which has been pretty stellar so far, if I do say so myself.

Last season—my first season with the team—we came fourth in our division, missing playoffs by only a few points. This year, we plan on going all the way.

And I say "we," because it turns out that Mike was right... I have no desire to go anywhere else.

I want to stay here in Atlanta for a long while. Make a name for myself on the Cyclones, and lead them to the playoffs, and eventually, to the Stanley Cup. I can feel it the same way I can feel when my stick hits the puck *just* right, this is the team, the place, for me. It's hard not to notice the whiff of victory in the air—and all of us can smell it to the point that we're ravenous.

The Cyclones' head coach Tony Torres has carefully curated peak camaraderie and brotherly vibes among our team. It's nothing short of *Ted Lasso*-worthy. My teammates—despite their general idiocy and lack of wildlife biology knowledge—are really good guys. Guys who look out for each other. They immediately accepted me as one of their own and looked out for me.

And I, in turn, have each of their backs. To the point where I recently got three stitches removed from my upper lip for coming to the aid of Colton Perez—left winger and one of the guys on my line—after that dickhead on the Hawks illegally crosschecked him.

Boy, was *that* a brawl and a half.

After I finally get my skates off, I head to the showers, but before I get undressed, I check all the stalls for any more rogue women covered in soapy water. Which is not something I'd normally be averse to finding in the shower, but after my restroom encounter earlier, I'm on higher alert than usual.

Who *was* that?

When I'm sure that the coast is clear, I get in and wash myself slowly, savoring the scalding water on my bruised body. My ribs are purple and black from where I took a huge hit in our last game, but it was worth it, because we won.

By the time I'm done, the locker room is quiet. I imagine my teammates have all piled into the player's lounge to devour whatever protein- and veggie-rich dish Stefani, our nutritionist, has come up with today.

For once, I'm not particularly hungry, so I change into sweatpants and a faded gray hoodie emblazoned with the maroon Cyclones logo, and then pull a baseball cap over my damp hair. I'm absolutely beat, and I can't wait to get a few hours of sleep...

But first thing's first—we have a whole lot of game tape to review.

We have two home games this week against Charleston and D.C., and then next week we're off to Vegas to face off against the High Rollers for a Thanksgiving Day special—a tradition established a few years back between our two franchises that's always highly anticipated... and competitive.

I'm ready. I know we can beat them. Coach Torres has already gone through hours of tape with us, and I know exactly where their goalie's weaknesses lie.

On my way to the media room, I swing by the kitchen. I'm hoping that Stef has a spare smoothie or two whipped up that I can grab. The smoothies aren't my favorite—they always taste vaguely like chalky protein powder—but I can't complain. I know what a privilege it is to have someone take care of all my nutritional needs and calculate my macros for me.

We guys don't tend to go into the kitchen very much—it's Stef's domain—so I call out a "hello" before sticking my head into the room.

And for the second time today, I find myself looking at a short, green-eyed woman washing her hands frantically. Only now, she's wearing an apron with the Cyclones logo on it.

Her eyes pop when she sees me, and her mouth pops open to match. "Uh... hello again, Slater. Um, Sebastian. Sebastian Slater."

17

Despite my confusion as to what the hell the restroom lady is doing here, I can't help but grin. "Seb usually works fine."

"You don't look like a Seb." She frowns. "You look like a Sebastian Slater. Number 19. Center. Leading scorer in your division."

"Hockey fan?" I ask warily. Why didn't I consider earlier that she might be a crazed hockey lover/borderline stalker?

I had one of those once, back in Edmonton. I'm certainly not in the market for another.

I'm vaguely wondering whether I should be calling security right around now when she surprises me by replying, "No. Hockey's never been my thing, if I'm being honest."

Color me officially intrigued. Maybe I'm still experiencing that brain hemorrhage, but I'm beginning to think there might actually be a reasonable explanation for Lady Macbeth's presence in our team kitchen.

"So, we meet again..." I stroll into the room and lean on the industrial metal counter, then wait for her to fill in the blank.

"Maddie."

I smile. Cute name. Suits her.

"So we meet again, Maddie." I nod in her direction. "And you're scrubbing your hands again. Please tell me you didn't commit a murder."

She hops from foot to foot before turning off the faucet and grabbing a hand towel. "Well. Not *technically*."

"That's an ominous response if I ever heard one, *Maddie*. Is that short for Madison? I want to get it right for the police report."

"Madelyn. And no police report necessary." She crinkles her nose. "Unless an epidemic of e-coli spreads through the arena and bodies start dropping like flies. Then I'm most likely to blame. Albeit indirectly."

My eyebrows shoot up when I see that she's totally, 100% serious.

I'm still confused as all hell, but I have gleaned one thing for certain: I know her from somewhere, but this is no Puck Bunny, nor a former flame. This girl is... funny. In the weirdest good way possible.

I open my mouth, but then quickly shake my head. "I'm not even going to ask." Now that I'm (mostly) certain that the girl's sane, and might actually be a staff member here—and not just an apron thief on top of being a restroom lurker—I hold up my hands. "But I do need to apologize."

"What for?"

"For running away earlier like a coward."

She snorts. "I don't blame you. I'd run too if I was minding my own business, trying to enter a bathroom for a pee, and came across a crazy lady crying at the sinks."

"Still. I should've asked if you were okay."

She finishes drying her hands and hangs the towel on a hook. "Oh. Well, um... thanks."

"Are you?"

"Am I what?" She looks at me blankly.

"Okay?"

She seems to consider this for a long moment. "Yes, actually. Yes, I am."

"Good. Well, I'm sorry we got off on the wrong foot. Have you been working here a while?" I examine her face, wondering if we've been passing each other in hallways for months and I've simply made a huge deal in my head about literally nothing.

"First day. I'm Stef's new assistant. I do food prep, etc. Which I know doesn't sound ideal given the aforementioned potential e-coli outbreak."

"It does not." I chuckle. "But given how many times I've walked in on you washing your hands today, I'll give you the benefit of the doubt and say congrats on the new job. Despite the maybe mass murders."

"And don't forget the crying in the men's restroom."

"Quite the eventful first day." I smile at her.

I could swear her cheeks tinge the slightest bit pink, and she turns away quickly. "Anyway. Can I get you anything?" Maddie-Madelyn frowns suddenly, her green eyes widening. "Assuming I can find it in this massive kitchen... I'm afraid some of Stef's kitchen orientation is already slipping my mind."

I give a little snort. "Kitchen orientation, huh?"

"Yup." Her expression is entirely sincere. "It's all very official, kitcheny business."

"Sounds like it. But I am actually on the hunt for a shake or a smoothie... Are there any in the fridge?" She pauses for a moment, looking a little deer-in-the-headlights, and I quickly add, "If not, don't worry about making anything new, I was hoping to grab something quick on my way to the media room."

"Hmm, yeah, I think we're fresh out." She taps a finger to her chin, and then her expression brightens. "But I *did* whip up some greek yogurt and berry parfaits on Stef's request, in case anyone wanted dessert later. I can grab you one and sprinkle some nuts and seeds over the top for fat and protein."

The light in her eyes is all it takes for the penny to finally drop.

"I know where I know you from!" I exclaim. "You're on that Christmas cookie show!"

My grandma is an absolute fiend for those shows—the ones where people compete in outlandish baking challenges. The holiday themed ones are her favorites, and I used to watch them with her back home, propped up at her butcher block countertop after school. I'd be doing my homework as she cooked dinner, the ancient TV in the corner filling the room with pleasant, sugar-sweet background noise.

Years later and thousands of miles away, I still watch those shows. Usually reruns late at night as I'm drifting off to sleep. Not because they're boring, but because they're soothing. Familiar.

They remind me of the people I love that I haven't seen in way too long.

I look at Maddie triumphantly, glad to have finally figured out my mental puzzle, but I'm surprised to find that the light in her eyes has extinguished. Like someone dumped an entire bucket of water over a single flame.

"I didn't take you for a *Food Network* type of guy." She places a hand on her hip and smiles, but it's flimsy, and her voice is slightly strained.

I clearly made some sort of misstep. And wanting to bring the tone back to the light bantering it was a few minutes ago, I waggle a finger at her. "Never judge a hockey player by his cover, Madelyn."

She raises a skeptical brow at me.

"We are sensitive souls under all our muscle and bruises," I continue. "Sensitive souls who binge-watch cookie shows. While eating cookie dough."

"To be honest, that just sounds like you have PMS."

"I believe the term you're looking for is IMS—Irritable Male Syndrome."

This makes her grin round out substantially as she walks over to one of the big, stainless steel fridges that line one of the walls. "Well, either way, I call BS, Mr. Hockey Man. You look like you haven't eaten cookie dough in years."

"Thank you." I pat my abs.

"Not a compliment. Plus, I bet you watch nothing but *Braveheart* and *Saving Private Ryan* and... *Die Hard*."

"Like I said, never judge on appearances. But yes, *Die Hard* is a solid Christmas movie."

"You're proving my point." She sets a parfait down in front of me and opens a tupperware full of nut and seed mix. "And not a Christmas movie."

"Agree to disagree?"

"Absolutely not."

21

I grab a spoon from the stack of utensils in the basin on the counter and dig into the parfait.

Ho-ly it's good. Like, ridiculously good.

"What's your favorite Christmas movie then, Madelyn?"

"Easy: any and all of the Hallmark movies."

"Oof," I say, taking another huge spoonful of yogurt. And another. I don't know what she's put in here, but I'm not ruling out crack. This shiz is almost weirdly delicious. "You make great-tasting yogurt snacks, but your taste in movies is all wrong. The correct answer is *Home Alone*."

She puts a hand to each of her cheeks, imitating Kevin McAllister from the movie. "I'm beginning to wish you'd stayed home alone today, too."

"The feeling is definitely not mutual." Now that I know for certain that she's not a stalker or an ex, I'm free to let my natural flirty flag fly. From what I remember on that baking show, she's got a boyfriend, so it's all harmless and in good fun anyway. I wink at her, then walk to the fridge and load two—actually, make that three—more parfaits into my arms before heading for the door. "It was genuinely wonderful to meet you. Thanks for feeding me."

"You're welcome."

"I guess I'll see you around the kitchen and the men's restrooms then, Lady M."

"Lady M?" She frowns, even as her cheeks turn pink.

But I'm already out the door, laughing all the way down the hallway.

Never a dull moment here at the Cyclones.

4

MADDIE

"I feel ill," I moan as I pull a blanket over my head. I'm on my stepbrother Jax's couch—where I've been living like a little hobbit since *The Incident*—with his rescue dog, Rick Astley, curled up at my feet.

It's Thursday night, and we're watching the airing of episode two of *Holiday Baking Bonanza*, which perhaps confirms that I am, indeed, a masochist at heart. Because on the screen in front of me, a previous, rounder-faced, more naive version of myself is smiling at the camera and gushing about how Adam and I are high school sweethearts, and he's my first and only love of my life.

Beside me, Jax tugs the blanket off of my head with one big calloused hand and fixes me with a look that tells me I have chocolate all over my face.

"I recommend you stop eating that, then." His gray eyes are dubious. "It doesn't look right."

I hug my bowl of vegan caramel and dark chocolate chia seed pudding tighter to my chest. "It's not the pudding making me sick. Or even Adam. It's *her*." I point at myself—or I should say my very dumb, former self—on the screen. "How was I ever so stupid?"

"Not stupid." Jax gives me an only slightly awkward pat on the shoulder. "How were you to know?"

Jax has been my brother since I was six years old and he was eight; when my mother married his father. The fact that we are not blood related is glaringly obvious—I'm short and freckled and pale, with smooth hands from all that time I spend baking in warm, cozy kitchens, while Jax is tall and broad, with a weather-beaten perma-tan from all that outdoorsy stuff he likes to do. Camping and hiking and fishing and the like.

Weirdo.

However, Jax and I are as close as a biological brother and sister. Have been from around the time we both realized that, despite our obvious differences, we were firmly united on one thing: our parents' marriage was a total sham, and the two of them would be much better off going their separate ways.

Almost twenty years later, they're still married and still very much not in love. I think my mom likes Richard Grainger's platinum credit cards, and Rich likes having a trophy wife by his side who makes him feel, well, *rich*.

But I can't complain too much. My real dad was out of the picture, and Richard was a decent stepdad in that he taught me how to ride a bike and was always happy to give me twenty bucks when I asked for it. Jax, on the other hand, has a serious disdain for his father. He will never accept a cent from him. Or be anything like him.

Case in point: rather than trying and failing at relationships, Jax simply opts not to have them. Ever.

"I wish I could be more like you and swear off love forever," I tell him.

"No, you don't."

He's right. While Jax looked at our parents' loveless marriage and decided he didn't want marriage at all, I looked at it and decided I wanted marriage very much—but a loving one. I wanted to put love on like a sweater, feel it all over my skin and snuggle up into the warmth and security of it.

So I did.

And every day for a decade, I did everything I could to keep that sweater fitting me.

But my work was in vain. Adam pulled a loose thread and unraveled the whole thing anyway.

Which means that, at some point—when I'm ready to acknowledge that men exist again—I need to begin the work of knitting a whole new sweater. An unbreakable one, this time.

"You're right, I don't," I tell him. "And I also don't need to sit here wallowing any longer. It's freaking Christmas, dammit."

"Stop with that," Jax grumbles as he sets his beer down on the coffee table. "It's freaking November."

"Thanksgiving is next week and then it's officially Christmas. The best of all the holidays, back to back."

And my first of each in over a decade without Adam.

I push down the sour thought and wipe my mouth with my sleeve.

"Enough of this!" I declare and flip the channel... only to find myself staring at a close-up of Sebastian Slater. Number 19. Leading scorer in his division. Loves *Home Alone* and my yogurt parfaits.

Jax laughs, mistaking my ogling at my bathroom buddy for me taking actual interest in tonight's game against the D.C. Eagles. "Four days of working for the Cyclones and the sports-hater is a hockey fan?"

TV Sebastian Slater is skating backwards, looking absolutely dashing in his maroon and white jersey—even as he's yelling something to the guy on his left.

I nod at the image, thinking it weird that the guy on my TV screen currently has a bellyful of wild rice and monkfish I cooked for the pregame meal this evening before my shift ended. "I met him on Monday."

"Slater?" Jax snorts. "Was he a jackass or what?"

"Kind of." I remember him fleeing from the men's restroom in horror, but then, I think of his apology in the kitchen... before we had an actual, albeit very weird, conversation. Like, we talked about freaking Christmas movies together. No idea why he was calling me "Lady M" though. *Lady Maddie?* That would be weird. "No, he was nice enough."

Definitely not the monster I half-expected Adam's favorite player to be. And, surprisingly, even more handsome in real life. Those glinting blue eyes and full, smirky lips were nothing short of... well, hot.

"I thought you said you don't really see the players."

"I don't. I haven't met anyone else, but Seb came into the kitchen on my first day looking for food because he missed lunch."

"Oh, it's *Seb* now, is it?"

"He told me to call him that," I mumble down at my hands.

Jax grins. "Well, I'll make sure to drop *Seb* into the conversation if I have the displeasure of running into Adam anytime soon."

"Ugh, I hope you don't. Did you hear that Mom and Richard had dinner with Mr. and Mrs. Plumlee last week and Adam was there with Elizabeth?"

"Yeah, about that..." he grimaces. "Don't shoot the messenger, but your mom also told me that Adam invited them to the engagement party on Saturday night."

"Of course he did." I snort-laugh. This isn't a huge surprise —like I said, our families are best of friends. "I bet they'll go. Also, when were you talking to Mom?"

This earns me an eyeroll. "She dropped by the bar yesterday."

By "the bar," Jax means the uber-cool, industrial-looking bistro downtown where he's a bartender. Jax is the kind of guy who works to live, rather than lives to work—again with the

26

trying to be nothing like his dad. He's super content working night and weekend hours so long as he gets to take off in his campervan during the week whenever he pleases.

"She came in for dinner?" I ask, surprised. Mom favors tablecloths, multiple place settings, and frilly napkins at the establishments she frequents.

"Absolutely not. She came by to drop off a bunch of supplements and self-help books for single ladies for you."

"What?!" I demand. "What did you do with them?"

"Threw 'em all in the trash."

"I knew you were my favorite family member."

"And you're the only family member I tolerate." Jax smirks, then turns the volume up on the TV. "Now. Shall we watch your new buddy Seb crush the Eagles or what?"

"Watch hockey?" I make a face and grab the remote from him. "No way! Let's see what's on the Hallmark channel. Christmas movie season is well underway, you know."

Jax groans and puts his head in his hands. "I love you... but I can't wait until you move out."

❀ ❄ ❀

I have Friday off, then work over the weekend, and before I know it, I have one week down at my new job... and I have to say it's flown by in a nice, mostly testosterone-free way. I do not think of Adam, nor do I look at his Instagram once (progress!).

I also have no further run-ins with number 19 or any other numbered jerseys, much to my relief.

And, if I'm being entirely honest, a little to my disappointment. Only because he seemed to like my yogurt parfait so much, of course.

Stefani is a nice boss. She's a few years older than me, with round cheeks and long, dark hair that she always wears braided.

She's basically everything I want to be when I grow up—working a job she adores, commanding the respect of everyone she works with while still being universally liked. On top of this, I never feel stupid when she explains things to me. And she lets me play Christmas music in the kitchen, even though it's only mid-November.

I have to say, for the first time since Adam and I broke up, I'm starting to feel somewhat... normal again.

The team will be traveling to Vegas later in the week for their Thanksgiving game and Stef is planning to travel with them. Meaning I'll get the holiday off. I plan to spend it as busy as possible to distract myself from the fact that *The Incident* episode of *Baking Bonanza* is due to air the night of the holiday itself.

I've agreed to go hiking with Jax on Thanksgiving, which is probably not my smartest move. But I'm also going to try to perfect my new gluten-free, dairy-free, refined-sugar-free Snickers bar recipe, which I'm super excited about. If I get it right, I might even ask Stef to take a look at it to consider for the team "treat" menu. Jake Griswold—who's a notorious fighter and wears a permanent scowl—apparently has an incurable sweet tooth.

After our hike, Jax and I are going to brave turkey dinner with our parents. I'm glad he'll be there when my mother inevitably comments on how much ham I've eaten, and talks about how svelte Elizabeth looked at the engagement party, which she and my stepdad *did* end up attending (called it).

Some people would think that maternal loyalty would come into play in a situation like this one, but those people have not met Kaitlyn Grainger.

Speaking of which—we're obviously going to gun it out of the parentals' place before the episode airs later in the evening so I can avoid a bloody World War III taking place all over the living room of my mother's pristine home.

28

All in all... I don't think it's going to be the entirely awful Thanksgiving I envisioned after the breakup.

And so, I'm in a relatively cheerful mood when I walk into the kitchen on Tuesday morning and crank up "Santa, Baby." I wash my hands, put on my apron, and get to work slicing papaya, pineapple and watermelon for the gut-friendly açai bowls that are on the menu for today's late, post-skate second breakfast.

I'm so lost in my humming and chopping that it takes me awhile to notice that Stef is late.

Very late.

I'm about to call her when the team's HR and Scheduling Manager, Adrienne, bursts into the kitchen. "There you are!"

I'm not sure where the hell else I would be at 11am on a Tuesday, but I smile at her anyway. "Just getting breakfast prepped. Stef isn't here yet, though."

"I know!" Adrienne cries, throwing her hands up. The woman certainly has a flair for the dramatic. Which I can appreciate. "She slipped this morning. She's gone to the emergency room."

My knife falls out of my hand and clatters on the countertop as I gasp. "Oh, no. Is she okay?!"

My mind is whirling, immediately going to all of the worst possible places, when Adrienne yells, "NO! She is not okay. She has a fractured thumb. Thumb!" she repeats the word, apparently for good measure.

Or maybe she thinks I'm a bit slow... which I might be. Because if I'm hearing Adrienne correctly, Stef *isn't* on death's door?

"Oh," I breathe in relief. "Is that all? That's all right."

"Of course she's not all right!" Adrienne bellows. Her volume is rather impressive given her waify disposition—Adrienne is tall, blonde, slim, and incredibly pale. She doesn't look unlike one of the elves in those dreaded *Lord of the Rings*

29

movies that Jax watches purely for the scenery. "How is one supposed to cook with her thumb in a cast?"

"Umm…"

"She's out of commission for at least a week." Adrienne points at me with a perfectly manicured finger. "Which means you, my dear, need to pack your bags."

"You're firing me?" I squeak.

Adrienne clicks her tongue impatiently. "Keep up, Madelyn. You're coming to Vegas for Thanksgiving."

5

SEB

The ice beneath my skates feels slick as I race down the rink, the puck gliding effortlessly with the guidance of my stick.

A breakaway. *Finally.*

I love playing in Vegas. Their arena is always buzzing with energy and noise, but for today's Thanksgiving Special, it's even more electric than usual.

And it's turning out to be quite the game. We're tied 2-2 and there's just under one minute left in the third period. The outcome could be squarely in my hands. The crowd roars, but their voices fade into the background, white noise shimmering in the distance as my focus hones in on the net that's fast approaching.

Pressure has never been a problem for me.

I freaking thrive on it. And after a year together, me, Mal, and Colton make a pretty great line, playing effortlessly as a unit, in total sync with each other.

And right now, thanks to a perfect pass from Colton, I have no intention of doing anything that isn't scoring. I have one of the best slapshots in the entire league, and I finally have a chance to put it to good use this afternoon.

I tear down the ice faster, my thighs pumping, my skates

sliding across the ice with perfect precision. Adrenaline flows through my veins and I feel the tension in my gut, the focus of my entire concentration as I swing back my stick, and strike.

It's a good shot. Exactly where I want it.

I look on as the puck sails past the goalie's outstretched glove and into the top right corner of the net.

GOAL!

The arena erupts with a mixture of boos from the Vegas fans, and cheers from ours. My teammates pounce on me, yelling and pumping their fists. I love it when games come down to the wire like this. Reminds me of playing junior league hockey in grade school, how my dad would always be in the stands, ready to give me a secret little thumbs up when I sought him out in the small crowd of parents when my nerves threatened to get the better of me, silently letting me know that he believed I could do it.

Today, in the middle of the jostle of bodies and yells and helmet smacks in an arena filled with almost twenty thousand, I glance around at the sea of screaming fans. Another nice thing about playing in Vegas—there are so many visitors in this city that, at any given time, the likelihood of the away team having more of their fans in the crowd is higher than when we play an away game anywhere else. And the cheers coming from thousands of maroon-jersey clad spectators are plentiful.

I'm soaking it all in. And then, for some reason, my eyes zero in on an unexpected familiar face...

Lady M.

AKA Maddie.

I've barely seen her since our kitchen and bathroom run-in at the beginning of last week. But I've sure heard her. On the flight out here, she sat with one of the physios, Georgia, and talked her ear off for three hours. Right now, she's on her feet, a few rows behind our bench, cheering. Her hair's in a sloppy braid, her cheeks are flushed apple red, and one hand is gesticulating wildly in a gesture I can't decipher as she...

Talks into a phone?

I almost laugh. For a moment, I thought she was cheering for the goal alongside everyone else in the arena. Like a normal person watching hockey would do.

But nope, she's on the phone.

Strange one, that girl.

"Nice shot, Sebby my man!" Colton smacks me on the back. I return the gesture, strange girls long forgotten as the rest of the guys on the ice surround us and we all slam into the corner with shouts of victory.

Because we *won*. And even though American Thanksgiving is in an entirely different month to Canadian Thanksgiving and they have extremely questionable yam toppings for their holiday dinner, I am feeling very, very thankful right about now.

After the final buzzer blows, I skate off the ice on a high. Sweat is dripping from my brow and I'm sure my whole body is going to hurt for the next week, but I'm happy as I pile into the locker room with all the guys.

"I'm talking mashed potatoes. Roast potatoes. Sweet potatoes. Potato casserole. Those thinly sliced potatoes with that cheese sauce on them. Potato salad, even."

"Jimmy?" Dallas says with a startlingly sweet smile.

"Yeah?"

"Shut the hell up about potatoes."

"But they're the best part of Thanksgiving dinner! Everyone knows that." Triple J puffs out his chest and glowers at our teammate. "It's my Irish blood, makes me love the things. Can't get enough of 'em."

Jake Griswold, another of our stellar defensemen, takes a seat on the bench next to Dallas, rolling his eyes. "Binge-watching Collin Farrell movies while you eat Lucky Charms doesn't make you Irish, dumbass," he grouches.

"I dress up for St. Patrick's day, too," Triple J responds, defensive.

I swivel from where I'm removing my shin guards to peer at him. "What the hell do you dress up as for St. Patrick's day?"

He shakes his head at me like I'm incredibly stupid for asking this. "A leprechaun, of course."

Dallas grins. "Surely you don't even need a costume for that one."

Everyone cracks up at this. Even our usually somber goalie, Lars Anderssen, is laughing. In response, Jimmy throws a bottle of Old Spice body wash at Dallas, and I collapse into laughter as it bounces off of my teammate's skull perfectly, as if in slow motion.

"Ouch!" he yelps.

"Nice reflexes, D." I snort.

Before Dallas can snap back at me, Malachi Holmes—our team captain who plays right wing with impressive power and finesse—cuts in. "Okay, children, enough fighting. Can we get back to the matter at hand and decide where the hell we're going for food? I'm starving."

"Caesars Palace buffet, fo' shizzle," Jimmy says.

"Nah, I heard the one at the Bellagio is better," Dallas responds immediately. I get the feeling the guy hasn't heard a damn thing about any buffet—he's just salty about the Old Spice hit.

"No way, I—"

"Don't we have to eat what Maddie has planned for us?" I interrupt.

"Who?" Aaron asks, rubbing his bare shoulder, where a large purple bruise is beginning to bloom from when an opponent's high stick whacked him during the game.

"Duh, the new team nutritionist who's on this trip with us?"

The assistant captain bugs his eyes at me. "Well, sorry I didn't know her name was *Maddie.*"

"And you two are acquainted how, exactly?" Malachi joins in, waggling his eyebrows.

I flick my towel at him. "Not in the way you're thinking, that's for sure."

My teammate taps his nose knowingly. "Well, seeing as you know her *so well*, you should be aware that we all have a dietary Hall Pass tonight. Holiday tradition."

"I don't know her well at all," I reply as I wrap my towel around my waist. "But great news about the Hall Pass. I'm so freaking hungry right now."

Twenty-five minutes later, all nineteen of us Cyclones who traveled to Vegas are assembled and ready and looking (mostly) presentable. "Mostly" because Jimmy is wearing a knitted sweater with a belled-up turkey on the front. And there's Colton and Aaron, who keep bickering about something, shoving and ribbing each other like they're five-year-olds at a waterpark deciding who gets to go down the big slide first. Lars is the only one of us who appears semi-normal, watching over the group from a slightly removed position like a sentinel.

We don't have another game for five days, so I think I'm going to take this rare opportunity to hit up a buffet with this bunch of goons. Stuff my face with cheat meal food alongside the men I think of as both teammates and brothers.

Because really, the Cyclones are like a big family who have welcomed me as their newest member. And bumbling and dysfunctional as said family is, I'm happy to be part of it.

We're on our way out of the locker room when I spot a familiar figure in the corridor. Suit, sunglasses, cellphone permanently attached to his skull. I pause in surprise as my eyes meet his, and he gives me a wave.

"Mike!" I walk towards my agent. "What're you doing here?"

Mike lives in Boston, working with the majority of his athlete clients remotely. I assumed that he'd be spending this

Thanksgiving holiday at his condo in Palm Springs, golfing. The last place I expected to see him was here, in Vegas, standing right in front of me.

"Hey, Sebastian." He scratches the back of his neck, seeming almost nervous. Which is very out of character for him. "Tony and I were hoping we could have a word."

I make a face. "Torres wants to talk to me... now? With you?"

"Dennis Lieberman, too."

"Actually?" If that isn't the oddest request. Why would my coach, my agent, and the Cyclones' freaking GM all need to see me? On a holiday, no less.

"Yeah. They're waiting for us."

I give a nod, a little disturbed by the twist in Mike's mouth. I turn back to the team. "I'll catch up with you guys in a bit."

Then, I follow Mike in the other direction, towards the Coach's room, while the voices of my dysfunctional pack of brothers fade behind us.

6

MADDIE

Ahh, Christmas in Las Vegas.

Well, to be precise, Thanksgiving Day in Las Vegas.

But everyone knows that those two holidays practically blend into one. The second the witches and ghouls and pumpkins pack up, it's one big festive season through to January.

And even though it's about a million and ten degrees as I step out of the arena and onto the Vegas Strip—where I shed my Cyclones hoodie and tie it around my waist so my skin can sizzle in the late afternoon sunshine like a fried egg—the entire place is buzzing with holiday cheer.

There are lights strung up everywhere, an abundance of 40-foot trees covered in glittery ornaments, and many, many sexy Santa Clauses milling about as I start to walk aimlessly, taking in the sights, smells and sounds of the holidays, Vegas style.

I take a deep breath, and realize I'm... content.

All things considered, it's been a very good Thanksgiving so far.

This morning, I woke up early and ordered nutritionally balanced, personally customized breakfasts to be delivered to each player's hotel room before their morning skate. Apparently, I don't even have to do any cooking while I'm here, simply order

37

food based on each of the guys' macros. Which I probably could have done from Atlanta, but hey, I'm not complaining about a free trip to Vegas.

Plus, traveling with the team automatically got me out of today's dinner with my parents (not to mention venturing into the great outdoors with Jax). And so, I ordered a ton of boring chicken-and-wild-rice-themed dishes for the boys' pregame lunches, and then I mightttt have hit up a behemoth Vegas buffet, where I gleefully stuffed ham n' yams in my face without my dear mother or ex-boyfriend to make comments on how much food I was ingesting.

After consuming about a million fat and sugar calories that shattered my inner nutritionist's "everything in moderation" mantra, it was time for the game itself. It was an afternoon event so the arena was packed with families, which made the atmosphere very wholesome indeed. Save for the woman three rows up who kept trying to flash her bra at the players, and the drunk guy sitting behind me, double fisting plastic cups of beer and screaming "Go on Soupy! HIT HIM, SOUPY!" the entire time.

Goodness knows who Soupy is.

Anyhow, it was a much more entertaining event than expected. And the Cyclones won the game, thanks to Seb's incredible last-minute goal. That man's focus is like a laser beam when he's out there on the ice. I might not be a hockey fan, but even *I* could tell how good he is. How much his head is in the game when he plays.

He scored at the exact moment my mother called me for the fifth time in a row. I may or may not have jumped up from my seat and cheered (because it's part of my job, of course) as I answered, because clearly Mother Dearest was hellbent on ignoring my "I'll call you after the game" texts.

Needless to say, I couldn't hear a thing over the noise in the arena. And now that the game is done and I'm outside, I know that I should call her back... but I'm enjoying a few moments of happy solitude first.

Thanksgiving has been great. Maybe my first Christmas in years as a singleton won't be so bad, either.

Adam who?

As if on cue, my phone rings, popping my little bliss bubble.

I wince, take a deep, gulping breath in, then answer. "Hello?"

"There you are, Madelyn." My mother's voice is sharp. Not unlike the screech of skates coming to a quick stop. "And at a normal decibel level. Finally. First, you abandon your family to jet off to Vegas for Thanksgiving, and then you add insult to injury by screaming at me like a banshee."

"I didn't 'jet off.'"

"You took a jet, did you not?"

Serves me right for telling my family about the team plane. I pinch the bridge of my nose with my thumb and forefinger. "I'm here for work, Mom. And I was at the game when you called. It was loud."

"Well what did you expect, being somewhere as uncouth as an ice hockey arena." Mom sniffs.

I shake my head and jump on a subject change. "How's your holiday going, Mom? Are you and Richard having a nice day?"

First rule of handling my Mother Dearest: when in doubt, make the conversation about *her*.

"I'm having a lovely day, actually." Mom surprises me by saying. I was expecting another guilt trip. "After you decided to abandon us for Vegas, Jaxon canceled too and took off to the mountains for the weekend. Said he was going on one of his strange wilderness survival thingies to do... whatever he does out there."

"You mean, he went on a backcountry camping trip?" I supply as I step around a couple taking selfies on the street.

39

Mom tuts. "It's not good for a man to spend all that alone time without a female body to keep him warm."

"Mom. Gross!"

"I'm just saying. That brother of yours needs a good wife so he can stop taking off on these strange little adventures."

"Backpacking is a pretty normal hobby for those who are outdoors inclined."

i.e. Not me.

"I would never go so far as to call such a thing *normal*, Madelyn." Mom is silent for a moment and I picture her shaking her head and sighing about her wayward children. "Anyhow, your father and I are effectively childless for the holidays, so I thought it was hardly worth making a turkey dinner for two people. Especially with your father's cholesterol..."

"Mmm," I hum in noncommittal agreement as I'm momentarily distracted by an array of showgirls walking past, waving their feathered costumes like they're exotic birds.

"So we ended up having a delicious lunch at the Plumlees. I wish we could've stayed longer, but you know how your father feels about footba—"

I tune back in. "Wait, what? You went *where* today?"

Mom lets out an exasperated sigh. "Keep up, Madelyn. We were at the Plumlee's house. You know that Alicia always puts out quite the spread."

Yes, I do know.

"Mom, why on earth did you go over to the Plumlees?"

"Well. Just because Adam and you have parted ways doesn't mean that we can't honor tradition. When you said you weren't coming, this felt like a natural solution." Mom says this with finality. Like no further explanation could possibly be warranted. Then, she goes on to twist the knife a little. "Elizabeth was there with Adam, you know. Such a *glamorous* woman. Very well put together. She was wearing this positively striking cream pantsuit, and I had to ask where she got it. She told me—"

"Mom, why are you telling me this?" I interrupt, a little irked by all the singing-of-Elizabeth's-praises.

"Because you should've been there, too." Mom's voice rises slightly. "I was the only person at the lunch without her children present. But fortunately, Alicia Plumlee has invited us again for Christmas this year, so you and Jaxon can make up for your no-shows then."

"What?" I stop dead in my tracks, almost causing an entire family of German tourists in matching anoraks to fall like dominoes.

"Schiesse!" one of the blond giants exclaims as he springs left with surprising grace for such a substantial man.

"Sorry, sorry. My bad," I mumble as the rest of the colorful anoraks scatter around me. I address my mom again, "What do you mean she's invited us for Christmas?"

"I mean she's invited us for Christmas," Mom repeats with exasperation. "The same way she's invited us for years. I'm not sure how much clearer I can make myself."

"I assumed that since Adam and I aren't together anymore..." I trail off, realizing that I have, of course, made an ass out of myself by assuming anything when it comes to my mother. I clear my throat. "You said no... right, Mom?"

Silence.

"Mom?" My voice sounds vaguely strangled.

"I said we'd be delighted." Mom sniffs. "Why would I say no to Christmas in Aspen? It's tradition for us by now. What else would we do?"

"Um, maybe *not* go on a vacation to my ex's family cabin for the holidays!?"

"We were friends with Alicia and Paul before you dated Adam," Mom argues.

"Well, then I hope you and Richard have a lovely time, but I will not be attending." No matter how warm the Vegas air currently is, I feel cold from the inside out on this positively frosty phone call.

"Indeed you will be." Mom's response is calm. Measured. "You dated Adam for over a decade, and obviously, he was lacking for something in your relationship. So what you need to do is turn up and show him that you've changed." She pauses for a moment to take a long, labored breath. "Prove that you're not wallowing in misery without him. I mean, you must have lost at least ten pounds since the breakup. Couple that with a new haircut and some highlights—I'll happily book you in with Pablo, my treat—and you'll be able to make him reconsider, at the very least. I'd like this to *not* be the last time we get to enjoy the Plumlee cabin for the holidays."

Ahhh. This isn't just any regular guilt trip call...

This is a *vengeance* call.

"So, let me get this straight," I say, surprisingly evenly. "You're saying that it's *my* fault that Adam dumped me on national television and that it's therefore *my* obligation to win that absolute douchebag back?"

"No," my mother replies curtly and I breathe a short sigh of relief. Until she adds, "I mean, not in as many words. I'd never use language like that."

I almost laugh—more so at the fact that I gave her the benefit of the doubt than anything else. My mother would put a Disney stepmother to shame. "I have to go, Mom."

"Only five weeks 'til Christmas!" She adopts a falsely cheery tone, like the argument we just had was fabricated in my own mind.

I hang up. Then, because clearly all sense and reason has left the building, I kick a trashcan.

A metal trashcan.

Owfreakingouch.

I rub my throbbing foot and swear. So much for walking up

and down the Strip this evening. My mother has managed to ruin my better-than-expected, first-time-solo Thanksgiving celebrations with a quick ten-minute phone call.

Because somehow, since our breakup, I have been sleeping on a couch and making yogurt parfaits for hockey players, while Adam has gotten the perfect job, the perfect woman, and the support of my own dear mother. And I now get the privilege of watching him get all cozy with his new fiancee over the holidays.

Schiesse, indeed.

With a sigh, I hobble off towards my hotel. If I can't take in the sights of Vegas tonight, I can sure as hell drown my sorrows in the hotel bar.

"Mmm."

I take a big gulp of my third Lover's Leap cocktail (ironic, I know, but the bartender assured me it was less full of love and mostly full of tequila) and sigh happily. My body feels pleasantly warm right now despite the hotel's powerful air conditioning. And my poor trashcan foot is more tingly than sore.

"That's good," I draw out the S like a snake. I take a few more gulps 'til I've drained half the glass. "Even better than the last one."

"Good to hear, ma'am." The bartender nods at me a tad stiffly. I think it's because I tried to be suave and slide him a folded twenty across the bar to keep 'em coming, but my money turned out to be an old stick of gum from the bottom of my purse.

Could've sworn I had a loose twenty in there.

I take another sip and hiccup slightly. I *may* be a touch intoxicated. Luckily my room is just upstairs, so I can get myself to bed later. Assuming that I can find my way to the elevators. The fancy casino on the ground floor of this hotel is an absolute riot of colors and sounds and piped-in air conditioning that kind of makes me feel disorientated and lost even when I'm one hundred percent sober.

I prop myself up on my elbows and lean forward. "I'm working, too. On Thanksgiving. We're both working right now."

"Oh, um." The guy looks me up and down and shakes his head. "Thank you for the offer, but I'm not really in the market for that. I have a girlfriend."

For some reason, I find this hysterically funny. "Nonononono, I'm not selling sex. I'm in the NHL."

Wait, that's not right.

"I mean, I *work* for the NHL. A team. NHL team. I am working for hockey."

In response to this, the bartender blinks at me multiple times, looking a touch concerned for my mental wellbeing.

"I feed the hockey players," I add helpfully, then break off into peals of laughter again.

Wow. I don't remember the last time I was this drunk. Words are hard, but at least my brain is happy. Finally.

Took me multiple drinks to drown out the memory of my mom's voice, going on and on about Elizabeth's stupid pantsuit.

Who does she think she is, anyway? Hillary Clinton?

"Harassing the bar staff, are we, Lady M?"

The deep voice comes from behind my right shoulder, and I jerk my head around to see Number 19, Sebastian Slater, slide onto the barstool beside me. Despite my drunken haze, I notice two things: one, he's wearing a *very* nice shirt that he's filling out *very* nicely. Two, he looks freaking pissed.

"Hello Mr. Hockey Man." I hold up my glass and toast him. A bit too vigorously, apparently, as a slosh of sticky pink liquid splashes down my arm. I grab a handful of napkins and start dabbing at my forearm. "What are you doing here? And I still

44

can't figure out why you call me Lady M. Why do you call me that?"

He ignores my questions. Instead, he flattens his palm on the bar, and smoothly slides what looks to be a one hundred dollar bill to my bartender friend in one slick motion. "Jack, neat. And keep 'em coming."

I watch, suitably impressed, as the bartender snaps up the bill and his whole body snaps to attention. "Right away, sir."

That's how it's meant to be done. Clearly.

The bartender places a glass of dark amber liquid on the bar and Seb immediately downs it. Another one appears like magic, and he drinks that, too.

"Celebrating your big win?" I ask with a smile that feels soft and blurry around the edges. Come to think of it, the room feels soft and blurry around the edges, too.

He scoffs, then gestures for another drink, his jaw clenching. His whole beautiful face is drawn, his brows lowered right down to his eyes and his lips pursed. He seems stormy. Not unlike a... *cyclone?*

I snort with laughter at my own internal monologue. Seb simply raises a brow at me.

"Doing okay over there, Lady M?"

"I am thriving, actually." At this very inopportune moment, my stool twiddles and I have to grasp onto the bar.

The mustachioed bartender looks at me wearily, then turns to Seb. "You two know each other?"

I nod manically. "Sure do."

Seb, meanwhile, cracks the first smile I've seen this evening as he stares into a brand-new drink that's magically appeared in front of him. "Watch out for this one. She likes to lurk in men's restrooms."

"WHAT? Not true!" I throw up my arms... and almost topple off my stool again.

"Whoa. Easy there, drunky." Seb steadies me. The

45

bartender gives us both a flat look and then walks away to serve another customer.

Once I'm seated and balanced back on my stool properly—like a *lady* (my abundance of class is why Seb calls me Lady M, perhaps?)—I pick up my drink and swirl my straw. Number 19 has returned to full-on glowering at the amber liquor in his glass.

"You're my ex's favorite hockey player, you know," I blurt. For whatever reason.

I should probably take a selfie with him.

Yes! Great idea, Maddie. Take a selfie with the big, clearly angry hockey player, and then, you can send it to Adam and make him jealous!

I'm about to propose this incredibly smart and sophisticated revenge plan to my new friend Seb (*see, Mom, I'm not the only one who can conduct a little phone vengeance!*) when he says, "Was."

"Was what?" I ask. At least, that's what I want to ask. It comes out sounding more like "Wathwart." Which, incidentally, sounds like my Harry Potter name.

Despite the hard lines around his eyes and his tense posture, he laughs.

"I *was* your ex's favorite hockey player." He polishes off his glass, then slumps forward in his chair. "But I'm not anyone's favorite hockey player now that I can no longer play."

"HUH?"

Maddie's decibel level isn't unlike one of Alvin's chipmunk pals—i.e. high enough to be earning us a ton of *looks*. But Lady M doesn't care about that. She's drunk off her face and wobbling around on her (entirely sedentary) stool like it's a mechanical bull she's attempting to ride, and failing. Badly.

"How much have you had to drink?" I raise a brow at her.

She makes a big, theatrical gesture in the direction of the empty whiskey glasses that now line the bar in front of me. "Pot, meet toaster."

"Wrong appliance."

"Don't change the subject." She hiccups. "What do you mean, you're not playing in the NHL?" Hiccup. "I heard you were one of the best ones."

Despite myself, I smile. For the second time in two minutes. What is it about this crazy little green-eyed drunkypants that's making me grin even in this most dire of circumstances?

"Visa issues," I say gruffly, literally feeling the smile fall off my face with my words.

"Hmmm?" She sways.

"I'm Canadian," I tell her. The word usually feels sweet as

maple syrup on my tongue, but it now tastes bitter. "So I need a visa to play in the States."

"Okay... so?" Maddie tilts her head.

It means I was very shortsighted on insisting on a one-year contract when coming to work in another country.

"Well... I just found out that my work visa has expired. Which makes me unable to play for a US franchise until I have a new one."

What I don't add is that, when I told Mike at the beginning of this season that I wanted to stick around in Atlanta for longer than the one year my initial contract was for, I didn't bother to think about it again. I'd made a decision to stay with this team, Mike was taking over negotiations with the Cyclones on my behalf, and I was totally caught up thinking of what this season had in store for us.

Unfortunately, my one-track mind ended up backfiring. While Mike and the Cyclones management were hashing out details, my old contract quietly expired. Which usually wouldn't be a big deal, but what slipped through the cracks in this case was that my work visa expired with it—and from what I understand, applying for a new work visa is going to take time... if I'm even able to get it, given how late in the year it is. Turns out, only a certain amount of these types of visas for athletes are issued each year by the US government. Of course.

There's a very long stretch of silence before Maddie blinks slowly.

"Well... damn."

"Damn is right," I agree.

"What're you going to do?" Those pale green eyes are huge, slightly smudged mascara rimming the edges as she peers at me with what almost looks like genuine concern.

Likely inspired by the cocktails she's been chucking back. Not that I can talk.

"No idea," I reply, reaching for my sixth drink. Or is it

seventh? Whatever number it is, my brain's starting to feel a little fuzzy. Static-y, like an old radio. I check my phone screen, then flip it back over and sigh. "I'm waiting on my agent to text me. He's trying to throw some kinda Hail Mary, see if there's a legal loophole that allows me to play while they're sorting this visa stuff out. But it ain't looking good."

Maddie slurps through her straw. "Bummer, dude."

I smirk at her word choice. "Something like that."

After I got the news, I couldn't bear to go out with my teammates. How on earth was I supposed to sit there and look them all in the eye over pecan freaking pie, knowing that I was about to get benched for who knows how long? And all due to my own lack of foresight.

That's the thing with team sports—you have to think about other people, not only yourself.

I take another slug of whiskey, then shake my head. My brain feels softer than usual, slower. I rarely drink, and I can feel the effects of the whiskey I've consumed already. Which was the plan, I guess. Drown it all out.

"On the bright side, at least your mom isn't making you spend Christmas with your ex and his new fiancée," Maddie offers from around another slurp of the pink liquid she's guzzling.

"Oof." I turn to her. "Same ex who likes hockey?"

"Loves *watching* it." She rolls her eyes. "He'd probably get flattened like a pancake if he ever tried to play it."

"But at least you have a new boyfriend?" I ask gently. She screws up her nose at me, apparently not comprehending. "You know, the guy you're on that baking show with."

At this, her face falls. "Nope. That's the same hockey-watching ex. He breaks up with me in the next episode."

"What?! Like on the show?"

She nods. "The ultimate public dumping. Turns out, there was someone else. Episode airs tonight actually." Her voice sounds perky, nonchalant, but the wobble of her lower lip doesn't escape me, even in my drunken haze.

"I'm sorry."

She snorts. "Don't be. I dunked his head in a vat of frosting after I found out."

A startled laugh bubbles out of me. I may not know much about Maddie—and I know even less about her awful-sounding ex—but I can't *wait* to watch that go down.

"Nice." I hold up my hand to her, gesturing for a high-five.

She smacks it with gusto, her little palm dwarfed by my big, callused one. "It definitely felt good at the time. I signed us up for the show originally to help promote his career, even though it compromised mine." She swirls her straw in her drink and stares down at the little whirlpool she's created in the glass. "I mean, what kind of person wants to hire a nutritionist who's participated in an all-sugar, all-butter, all-*everything* baking challenge? But at the time, I was happy to do it for him. Happy to see him happy. And now... well, now I'm scared to face his smug happy face again."

She goes on to explain that she'd been with her ex since high school—her family is friends with his family. And her mother is now, apparently, putting her friendships before her daughter's feelings by insisting that they keep their tradition of spending Christmas together this year, even after everything that's transpired.

At a loss of what to say to that—short of *what the hell kind of mother does that?!*— I turn to the bartender. "The lady needs another drink."

"And so does Sebastian Slater," Maddie adds.

"Seb," I correct.

"S-e-b." She over-enunciates, her lips smacking together. Then, she gives me a kind smile. "I hope your hockey stuff gets sorted out."

"Me too. But in the meantime, I've got a lot of free time on my hands. So, if you want me to rough up your ex a little..."

Maddie throws her head back and cackles loudly. "That's a *way* better plan than mine. I was gonna say that we should take a selfie together and send it to him. Hashtag leveled-up."

"Done." I reach across the bar and pick up her phone, then click the camera icon. I hold the phone in front of us and put an arm around her, pulling her into my shoulder. She leans into me, and I find myself reciprocating the movement—to the point where I'm not sure who's propping who up.

Boy, I am really feeling that whiskey. As a pro athlete where conditioning my body is part of both my job and my lifestyle, and has been for years, I don't drink at all during the season. I barely touch the stuff on the off-season either.

She inhales through her nose and smiles dopily. "You smell good, Seb Slater."

"Right back atcha," I say, because the girl snuggled into me smells like vanilla and cinnamon... with strong undertones of tequila.

I snap a few photos of us and hand her the phone again.

"Thanks." She flips through the pictures. "We look good together. Well, you look good for both of us."

"C'mere." I make a gimme motion so I can look at the pictures myself.

She's smiling wide in all of them. Clearly a little intoxicated —you can tell by the flushed cheeks and slightly dazed expression—but she looks cute. Hot, even, with those damned sparkly green eyes and full pink lips. The tight tanktop she's wearing definitely doesn't hurt, either.

"You look good, Mads." The words come out low, almost husky.

Her cheeks tint a deeper shade of red and she tilts her head at me. For a moment, her eyes clear and she looks totally lucid.

"You're nicer than I thought you'd be," she says.

"And you're saner than I thought you'd be."

This makes her smile turn wicked. "You mean, when you found me lurking in the men's restroom like a lavatory Gollum and then ran away like a little hobbit?"

I sit up to my full height and loom over her. "Hey. Who you calling little?"

"You, Slater. 'Coz the way you ran out of that bathroom, you looked like a frightened little girl." She tilts her chin up at me in challenge. "I might've looked crazy, but you have, like, a foot and a hundred pounds on me. What was I going to do, bludgeon you to death with a toilet plunger?"

This girl, I tell you.

"Okay, okay. I have a confession." I scrub a palm over my eyes, then down another gulp of my drink. I'm sure that the alcohol is the reason my lips are so loose right now, but somehow, I don't really care. "I ran away because I thought I knew you."

"What?"

"I thought you were, um, a woman I knew. And that you were there to see me."

She's silent for a good few moments, before sputtering. "So what I'm hearing is... you thought I was a woman you'd dated and I was stalking you in a public bathroom?"

I nod sheepishly. "I'm aware of how crazy that sounds."

"How many women do you date that you could make that mistake?"

It's a good question that I don't have a good answer for. So, I shrug.

"Wow." Maddie laughs and tosses back the rest of her drink. I mimic her. "And you ran away because you were scared. Of me."

"Precisely."

She wheezes with laughter and I give her a playful little

shove. Her bare shoulder feels soft and warm. Small in my hand.

Oh, jeez. I'm at that handsy point of drunk, aren't I? You know, when you have one too many and suddenly feel the need to invade other peoples' personal space?

Yeesh.

I yank my hand back. "In my defense, I had a stalker once."

She claps her hands in glee. "You did?!"

"Why are you so excited by that prospect?" The laugh that escapes me sounds far away. "Haven't you ever listened to a true crime podcast?"

"YES! And now, I know someone that's actually experienced it. Did they sneak into your house at night and cut a lock of your hair off while you were sleeping?"

"That was weirdly specific. And no. But she did sneak into our team locker room at my old training facility and fill my locker with her underwear."

Maddie's laughing so hard, she's practically falling on the floor. "How terrifying for you."

"I'm not joking. There was even a photo of her entire extended family with me photoshopped in."

Maddie wipes a tear from her eye with a happy little sigh. "Well, there's an idea. If the selfie doesn't piss Adam off, I'll photoshop you into *my* family Christmas photo and pretend that you're my new boyfriend." Her eyes light up like two glowing, beautiful Christmas trees. "Actually, screw that. I should put my stalker knowledge to good use, kidnap you, and make you come to Aspen with me to rub it in Adam's face in person."

"If you put enough underwear in my locker, maybe I'd come with you of my own accord."

"Yeah, and how did it work out for the last stalker who did that?"

I smirk. "Restraining order."

"Hmm. Well, that would mean kissing my job goodbye or I might've actually tried it for funsies." She lets out a long sigh. "You'd be a *way* more exciting addition to the line-up than *Elizabeth*."

"Who?"

"Evil Ex's new fiancée. The one he was cheating with. He proposed to her."

I wince. "Ouch."

"I'll say." Maddie sighs. She has clearly had quite the year—in fact, her problems kind of make my grumpy "I can't play pro hockey for a couple months" spiel seem a little self-centered.

At that moment, my phone vibrates on the bar. I pick it up and the screen's a little blurry—whiskey glasses, for sure—but my vision clears so that I can see that the incoming call is from Mike. *Finally.*

"Scuse me a sec, I gotta take this." I slide off my stool (which is a little more difficult than usual, not gonna lie) and answer as I step away. "Mike?"

"I'm sorry."

Well, those aren't good first words... I down the rest of the drink I'm clutching in my other hand. I don't think I've been this intoxicated since, well, ever.

"I did everything I could, Seb. It'll take a while for the lawyers to get your visa paperwork in order." He gives a long, painful sigh. "You can remain in the country, but you can't work. So, no ice time 'til this all gets sorted out."

No ice time. No Cyclones.

No hockey, period.

I lean against a wall, my head spinning. "How long?"

Mike sighs. "Long enough that it might impact the team making the postseason."

"There's really nothing we can do?"

Mike laughs humorlessly. "Well, short of you being married to an American citizen, no. We just gotta wait this one out."

Married to an American citizen...

54

My head swivels towards Maddie, who's currently fishing the ends of her hair out of her drink. She studies the wet strands for a moment, then puts them in her mouth and sucks on them. She has to be the strangest woman—person—I've ever met in my life. And yet, also somehow so damn cute you can't help but smile around her. Like she's a little hobbit, herself.

A hobbit who needs a boyfriend for the holidays. Someone to put that absolute donkey's ass of an ex in his place...

"*Married* married?" I echo, my drunken mind suddenly galloping.

"Yeah." Mike laughs humorlessly. "Why, you got a secret wife stored somewhere?"

I don't reply. I'm already making my way back to the bar.

MADDIE

"Hiiiiii," I sing as Seb slides back into the stool next to mine. "I got us more drinks. Shots!"

I gesture to the bar, where four Slippery Nipples are lined up. The bartender did not look pleased when I requested them —this being a classy hotel bar establishment and all that jazz— but I insisted. I have absolutely zero idea what's in them, but I wanted to say the name out loud.

I think I *miiiiiight* be a little—a lot—drunk.

"What are those?" Seb eyes them cautiously, but luckily, he doesn't wait for an answer. He throws back two of them, then winces. "Urgh."

"That bad?" I raise an eyebrow at the big ol' Hockey Man getting his cute little panties in a twist over a couple of teeny shots, but then I shoot one myself. "Ewww, you're right. Yuck, yuck, yuck." I flap my hands and grimace. "That'll teach me for ordering nipples."

"Nipples?"

"Don't say nipples."

"You said it first."

"Yeah, but it sounds obscene coming from your mouth."

Seb considers this for a moment, then nods. "Fair." He

wipes his mouth, takes a huge breath like he's working up the courage to do something, then looks me dead in the eye. "Maddie, I have an idea. A crazy one."

"I like crazy."

"I know. Hence why I'm asking you." He smiles. "You know the way you said I should come pretend to be your boyfriend for the holidays?"

"Ha. Yeah." I dreamily create a beautiful mental fabrication of Elizabeth drooling over the absolute hunk that is Seb as she scrapes Adam's jaw off the ground for him.

"What if I actually did that?"

I blink, sure that I've heard him wrong. "Sorry?"

Seb's gorgeous blue eyes are wide... and a little wild. Hazy. "We could help each other out."

"How would you pretending to be my boyfriend in front of my annoying family and even more annoying ex help *you*?" I raise a brow. "Are you looking for a Good Samaritan project for Christmas or something?"

Seb frowns, then leans forward and puts a big hand on each of my arms. "You are not a charity case, Maddie."

The way he says this, all growly and firm and low—coupled with the delicious feeling of his warm, callused palms moving along my bare skin—stirs something deep in my stomach. "You're going to have to explain what you mean then."

"You want to stick it to your ex, right?"

I really, really do. Spending Christmas with stupid, smug Adam and stupid, stunning Elizabeth is going to be miserable. Unless I can somehow hoist myself up out of the discard pile and onto their hellish playing field.

"And I want to keep playing in the NHL. Keep playing for the Cyclones, specifically."

I shake my head, entirely confused. "I don't see how these two things are connected."

"What if we didn't go to the cabin as boyfriend and girl-

57

friend..." Seb takes a deep breath and his eyes lock on mine. "What if we went as husband and wife?"

I'm not sure how I'm meant to react to this statement, but even in my drunken haze, I know the wrong thing to do is choke on my own spit.

"Whoa, there." Seb claps my back a few times. "Breathe, Maddie."

I sputter a few more times. "Sorry, sorry. I think I'm horribly mistaken. Because I'm pretty sure I just heard you say that we should get married."

"Temporarily."

"How drunk are you, exactly?" I demand.

"Very," he replies.

I stare blankly at Sebastian Slater. Number 19. Leading scorer in his division. *Asking to be my temporary husband.* "Well, there's no such thing as a temporary marriage. That's the point of marriage. It's forever."

Seb rolls his eyes. "And how often does that actually happen?"

I think of Adam, who gave me a promise ring when we were seventeen, and then chose someone else to wear an *actual* engagement ring. My mother, who was left by my biological father while she was wrangling a toddler. Jax, who has sworn off romance because of all the crap he's seen in his life.

Crap that I've seen too, but have simply... chosen not to pay attention to.

Seb reads my silence as agreement. "Exactly. Now, you need a level up—your words, not mine—to help you get through the holidays. Being married to a hockey player is the biggest level up you can get when your ex is into hockey. And besides, it's *me*." He smiles cockily. "And in return... I need an American wife so that I can continue playing hockey."

"A wife," I repeat dumbly.

He nods. "You're an American citizen, right?"

"Yes." I cough. "But this is crazy! Surely taking a bit of time off to wait for your new visa won't make too big of a dent in your career. I assume you make enough money not to work for a month or two."

"It's not about the money."

"What is it then?" I study his face. Watch his blue eyes flutter before he sets his jaw.

"I don't want to let my team down."

"And that's the only reason?" I challenge.

"Hockey is everything to me. Without it, I don't know who I am. I have to play." He chews on his lip, his face still hard. "I was brought to the Cyclones to help them out of their dry streak in the playoffs, and I intend to do it. Without me, there's no way we'll keep this winning streak. They need me."

"That was weirdly entirely egotistical and entirely selfless at the same time."

He looks at me with a simple shrug. "It's the truth."

"I wish I had your confidence."

He smiles. Flirtily, I think. But that could be the nipple shots talking. "Imagine how confident you'd feel going to Aspen for Christmas with me."

"It would almost be worth it just to rile up my mom." I can only imagine Mother Dearest's reaction if I showed up with a huge hunk of hockey man and derailed her plans for me to grovel at my cheating ex's feet.

"And if he's as big a hockey fan as you say he is, Eugene would freak," Seb adds.

"Who?"

"I don't know your ex's name, so I called him Eugene in my head."

I break into (what must be exceedingly unattractive) snorting laughter at the thought of Adam's face. Showing up married to his favorite hockey player, Sebastian Slater, would be way better level up material than simply sending him a selfie of us.

In fact, it would be the ultimate level up.

"That's amazing."

"I can't remember what he looks like from the show, but I'm imagining a bald spot. And that he smells like deli meat."

I cackle harder. "Are you trying to butter me up? Because it's working. To the point where I feel like this might actually be a good idea."

He smiles again. Holds out a hand.

I take it.

"Madelyn... wait, what's your last name?"

"Grainger."

"Middle name?"

"Louise."

"Madelyn Louise Grainger, will you temporarily marry me?"

I smile back at him. Not only because it's absolutely endearing that he used my full name. But also because this is beginning to sound hilarious, and also smart.

"I mean... why the hell not?" I throw my head back and laugh, feeling warm and fuzzy and altogether gleeful at the mental images of Mom freaking out and Adam scraping his jaw off the floor at his gorgeous cabin in Aspen.

It's genius.

A foolproof plan for a pair of drunken fools.

"So how do we do this?" I ask excitedly. Because right now, ridiculous, vengefully childish excitement is bubbling up in me with all the force of the Bellagio fountains. And I have a feeling that we are in for quite the show.

Seb chucks my chin. "Have you forgotten where we are?"

"Oh my gosh!" I squeal, almost sliding off my stool again. "We're in Vegas, baby!"

9

SEB

What the hell have I done?!

I pound on the door again and again, my head throbbing in tandem with the banging.

Eventually, I hear a groggy, pissed-off, "OKAY, OKAY. Jeez, I'm *coming*."

The door swings open, revealing Malachi Holmes in nothing but a pair of boxer shorts with pink candy canes all over them.

"Slater?" He stares at me incredulously for a moment before he follows my gaze to his underwear, sees my smirk, and scowls. "What? They're festive. Chantal gave them to me. And what the hell is this very uncalled-for wake-up call about?"

I blink at him. I wasn't sure what to do when I woke up this morning, but a visit to my steady and wise team captain seemed like the place to start. Short of throwing myself off The Stratosphere. "I have a bit of a situation on my hands. Can I come in?"

For the first time, his brown eyes focus on my face. His scowl deepens, frown lines marring his forehead. "You look like hell, dude. Worse than the time that puck hit you in the nose and you had a potato face for a week."

I walk past him and into his room without being invited,

flopping down on a large, impossibly plushy cream couch that seems to take up almost half the room.

"Come in, please, make yourself at home," Mal mutters sarcastically as he follows me into the room, slamming the door shut behind him. He pulls on sweatpants over those candy cane atrocities, and sits down on the end of his bed. "What's going on, Seb? And where were you last night?"

I shift uncomfortably. I'm still in yesterday's clothes, and in dire need of a shower. And Advil. And about twenty-five million gallons of water. "It's a long, crazy-ass story," I say on a sigh.

"I got time. Now, spill," the captain says.

I hesitate. It's probably best that I keep totally silent about all of this. But then again... I'm sure I can trust my captain not to blab. And I need to talk to *somebody* right now. Someone who takes hockey just as seriously as I do, and therefore *might* understand exactly how terrible my predicament is.

So I spill. Tell him about my visa issues, and the conversation I had with Mike, Dennis, and Tony after the game, and how I'm looking at being benched.

Mal listens intently, the sleepy fog clearing from his expression as he focuses on what I'm saying. Only when I'm finished speaking does he let out a long, low whistle, along with a curse.

"That sucks." He grimaces but gives a nod, the picture of a put-together captain. "We'll get through it, though. Sure, it'll affect our rankings, but we might still make the playoffs. Depending on how long the whole thing takes, that is. And if we don't, there's always next year. We can use the time to..."

He's lying. There won't be a next year for Mal—this is his last year in the NHL before retirement. It hasn't been officially announced yet, but everyone knows it. This is his last chance to win the Stanley Cup, to finish off on a literal career high.

"I sorted it out," I cut him off.

"What?"

"I kinda took matters into my own hands last night and tried to fix the problem." I rub the back of my neck uncomfortably.

Malachi narrows his eyes. "By doing *what*, exactly?"

"You have to swear on your life not to tell anyone."

"What are we, twelve? Tell me, Slater."

I cross my arms. "I need you to swear not to tell a soul."

He rolls his eyes. "Fine, whatever."

"Swear." I sound like a broken record, but I'm not a complete dumbass. This could affect Maddie as badly as me if this got out. Worse, in fact. Because I'm pretty sure I've just had her commit a crime.

"I swear. Now, talk."

"I got married."

"You... got married?" Malachi repeats, his mouth opening and closing like a goldfish.

I have a sudden flash memory of a drunken Elvis grandly declaring this last night. And then, the look on Maddie's face— her smile wide and lazy, her cheeks pink, her eyes at once slightly dazed and totally glittery. I remember feeling... *excited*.

I shake it off.

"Temporarily. So I can play. It's a loophole, apparently. Spouses of American citizens can work while their marriage immigration paperwork is pending. We could stay married until that all cleared, then we could go back to moving on with our own lives."

"Whoa, whoa, whoa. *We*? Do you hear yourself right now?"

I shake my head. "I know it sounds crazy."

"Damn right it does! I mean, what you're saying is that in the fourteen hours since I saw you after the game last night, you got benched, found someone willing to freaking MARRY you, and then ACTUALLY married them?"

"Yup." I hold up my left hand, complete with a gold wedding band, as proof.

Mal's mouth is still opening. Closing. "You are a madman.

An actual madman." He clears his throat. "And who, may I ask, is your madwoman bride?"

"Her name is Maddie."

And she's not a madwoman, I'm pretty sure. Despite her restroom-lurking tendencies and her very specific stalker knowledge, she's... nice.

Funny.

Hot.

Not that I should be thinking like that. The last thing I need right now is to find my new wife—who looked strangely alluring in her bedsheet-toga wedding dress last night—attractive. Which is a very weird thought altogether.

"Please tell me you didn't find her on Tinder."

"No. You know her, actually. She's Stefani's new hire. The assistant nutritionist."

An incredulous squawk of a laugh bubbles out of Mal's mouth. Apparently at a total loss for words, he shakes his head at me.

"I know, I know." I sigh. "And that's why I'm here. I need your advice."

"On what? Marriage counseling? Because I met my wife the normal way—i.e. I didn't commit international fraud with a freaking Cyclone's staff member—so I doubt I can assist you."

"International fraud?" I wrinkle my brow. "Do you think that's what it's called?"

"Sebastian, I don't *know* the actual term for it, because I am *not* an expert on marriages that occur overnight. Mostly because THIS IS NOT SOMETHING NORMAL PEOPLE DO!"

"Okay. In my defense, I was drunk." It's a poor defense, at best, and I'm aware I must sound like an idiot right now.

"Oh, good Lord. Was *she* drunk?"

"Yeah... but don't worry, nothing happened."

"I wasn't even worrying about that until you said it!" He throws a pair of balled-up socks at me, and I'm too slow and hungover to even try to stop them bouncing off my head. "You, my friend, are a class A idiot."

Great. Now he's actually calling me an idiot.

Maybe because I am one.

"I know. And I just..." I trail off. How do I say that I woke up this morning feeling like death warmed up, sprawled out on one side of a California King bed, while my new freaking bride snored softly on the other, a piece of cheese pizza bent over her neck like a scarf?

Bit by bit, I started to put together the pieces of last night: the crazy drunken proposal in the hotel bar. Maddie actually saying *yes*, her eyes hazy and glowing. The two of us running around Vegas like a pair of absolute lunatics because Maddie wanted something old, new, borrowed and blue to make it "official."

I remember buying her a vintage sapphire engagement ring from a pawn shop on the Strip—the only store selling jewelry that was open at that hour—to check off the new, old and blue boxes at once (how in the hell do they allow people in our states of drunkenness to purchase expensive things?!). And I remember Maddie laughing 'til she cried when I stole a traffic cone and swore I'd return it later, for our borrowed item.

We rushed into a little white chapel which was filled with *way* too much pink inside (I'm talking pink curtains, pink flowers, even the carpet down the aisle was pink), signed the papers, and minutes later, Elvis pronounced us man and wife.

And then, the fleeting skim of her lips on mine... my stomach fizzes (not unpleasantly, given my current state) at the memory.

That, at least, feels warm and fuzzy.

The rest feels like a fever dream sequence from a bad movie. A bad movie that I've gone and dragged a sweet, unsuspecting woman into. Turns out that "harmless" flirting is not so harmless, in that it can net you a brand-new wife.

"I guess I feel weird about it all," I finish.

Mal's jaw is working, clenching, as he takes in all this information. At least he isn't processing it all through a pounding whiskey hangover headache. "Well," he says eventually. "That's actually kinda sweet. I didn't think you had feelings about *anything*, save for hockey."

I sigh and push my hair back. "I don't, usually. But last night, I was so pissed off, I wanted to find a solution. ANY solution. I didn't even think through the implications of this; how badly this could go for *her* if we get found out. Obviously, the whiskey didn't exactly help with making a judgment call."

Mal's lips quirk a little. "Wow. He has feelings *and* he's worrying about someone else."

I throw the balled up socks back at Mal. He catches them easily. "Guess an old dog can learn new tricks?"

Mal chucks his socks to the side and then nods his head, his eyes turned towards the window where the rapidly rising sun is making my entire head feel like it might explode. Could also be because I'm facing the consequences of the insanely crazy thing I did last night. A little head explosion might serve me right.

Finally, the captain leans forward, his jaw set. "Look, man. This is insane, but it happened. For better or for worse, you're married right now. Of course I want you to play, and I assume Maddie had her reasons for going along with it."

I screw my eyes up, considering this. From what I gleaned last night, we made this arrangement with the intention to benefit us *both*. Strictly business, so she could get payback and I could keep playing hockey.

And as long as I keep it straight—AKA stop noticing how cute and/or hot Maddie is, and instead focus solely on what's really important here, and what my goal is (that being hockey)— maybe this will all be fine.

"She did," I reply, then clear my throat. "Last night, she did..."

He frowns. "Well, if she feels like she made a drunken mistake this morning, pretty sure you guys can get the whole thing annulled—no harm, no foul." Malachi stares at me quizzically. "*Have* you talked to her about it in the light of day? Where is this wife of yours, anyway?"

Wife of mine. Woah, hearing the words is gonna take some getting used to.

"Um, she was still asleep when I left to come here."

At this, Mal stands up, walks over to me, and smacks me upside the head.

"Ouch!" I protest.

"You left her asleep by herself, in your room, to wake up *alone*?"

My eyes widen as my soggy brain finally clues in. I left Maddie by herself, in a random room in Vegas, after a full evening of shenanigans together that resulted in our nuptials. Shenanigans which were completely insane. But also... I don't think I've laughed so hard in my entire life as I did last night.

And I might not know my new wife very well, but I'm pretty sure she wouldn't have left me to wake up alone today. "Well, when you put it like that..."

He smacks me again. "Go!"

I leave.

MADDIE

This morning, I am two things I was not yesterday.

First, I am a meme.

Second, I am married.

I think.

I have no idea if drunken chapel weddings where the groom is wearing a traffic cone on his head and the bride is draped in a hotel bedsheet are actually considered legal.

And I have no idea where my apparent new husband is so that I can clarify this with him.

I also have no idea why I'm so calm about this. Maybe it's shock. Maybe I'm still intoxicated.

Or maybe, it's because I'm more preoccupied by the fact that the most humiliating thing that has ever happened to me is currently pasted all over the internet.

Basically, I woke up a few minutes ago in a strange bed (fully clothed, thank the Lord), but also wearing pizza and cuddling my new husband's traffic cone (which is not what the meme is about, also thank the Lord). That was all a little startling, but then... I fished my phone out of my bag, and my day got a whole lot crazier.

It's a snapshot of me with my hand on the back of Adam's head, plunging him into a vat of red frosting.

It's everywhere.

And like the masochist that I am, I can't stop looking at it. Captions accompanying the photo range from "Taylor Swift fans when someone cheats on her" to "When people hang their Christmas decorations in September" and "When my boyfriend asks me if I'm on my period."

There's even a GIF version, with a super slow-mo of me committing the dunking offense and the word "Noooooo!" written above. Which is, coincidentally, what I currently feel like screaming.

I wasn't planning on watching the episode of *Baking Bonanza* that aired last night—I didn't want to have to relive *The Incident*. But now, I'm going to be forced to look at it everywhere on the freaking internet.

I'll also have to ignore my mom's relentless phone calls from here until eternity.

I don't realize I'm crying until the door opens.

Seb's standing there, looking much more disheveled than I've ever seen him. His hair is standing straight up, his clothes are rumpled, he has purple circles under his eyes, and there's lipstick smudged on his cheek (mine?!?).

He lingers in the doorway for a moment, clutching a tray of takeaway coffees and a bag of what I'm praying is baked goods.

"Maddie, hi. I didn't mean for you to wake up alone. I picked up coffee. And tea. And a hot chocolate. I wasn't sure what you drank. I also got croissants and breakfast bagels and..." He seems perturbed as he gingerly walks towards me—like I'm a chained-up dog with a biting habit—and sets down the tray of drinks. Then, he finally looks at me. "Oh, I am so sorry, I didn't mean for this to happen. Please don't cry, I can fix this."

His words are coming fast and a little panicked, and my

69

brain—in its current molasses-thick state—groans as it struggles to catch up.

I reach across the bed for a tissue and hurriedly wipe away my tears. I'm sure my eyes are entirely panda-fied by now. "I'll take tea, please. And a breakfast bagel. Sorry about the crying." I hold my phone out to him. "Evil Ex and I are a meme and I'm feeling a little humiliated. My delicate hungover state probably isn't helping."

He looks at me carefully for a few moments, like he pities me but he's trying not to show it. "I forgot, you said that the episode aired last night... Are you okay?"

I smile wanly. It's sweet of him to ask. Sweet that he brought me breakfast, too. Sebastian really does seem to be genuinely nice beneath all that flirty hockey-player swagger of his. "I'm fine. I'm a big girl and Eugene deserves no more of my tears, so I should reel in the waterworks."

Seb gives a small, encouraging nod, but his face is pale as he sinks down onto the edge of the bed. He passes a cup to me, his hand shaking slightly so that our fingers brush when I accept it. He then hands me a wax-paper wrapped bagel that smells like literal heaven—wafts of bacon and melty cheese that are making my mouth water—before saying, "Just to check... you sure you're not crying because of this?" He gestures between himself and me.

"Well, I mean, I probably should be. Have you seen our wedding pictures?"

"There are pictures?" Seb's handsome features relax slightly as he reaches for a coffee and takes a sip.

"Open at your own risk." I hand him a manila envelope. I found the "Complimentary Photos of The Happy Couple!" package under my butt when I woke up, and boy oh boy, it's a sight for sore eyes. Well, the bridal half was. The groom, meanwhile, somehow managed to pull off (literal) traffic-stopping orange and look like a top model.

It should say a lot that these are easily *not* the most embarrassing photos I've seen of myself today.

I watch Seb's face as he examines the pictures, his eyes creasing at the corners. "I can't believe we actually did this."

"Me neither. When I dreamed of my fairytale wedding, I certainly never thought *this* was an option."

The mood in the room suddenly shifts, and his eyes turn guarded as he looks at me—still holed up in bed and tucking into my bagel like a ravenous bear after a long winter of hibernation. "Now that we're more, um, sober, I need to ask you: is this something you actually... wanted?" He bites the inside of his cheek. "I hope you didn't feel pressured into something you didn't want to do."

He looks at me with caution, like he's terrified that I'm about to burst into tears again. I have to admit, it's nice to see that he's concerned about me. Even though *he* is the least of my concerns right now.

My *marriage* is the least of my concerns right now. Unbelievably.

"It takes two to tango," I say with a shrug. "We were both drunk and ridiculous, but I remember saying yes to this, Seb. I'll admit, the later the night gets, the blurrier my memory becomes, but you didn't pressure me into anything." *In fact, I'm the one who kissed you when Elvis gave us our cue. You were a perfect gentleman, waiting for my lead.* "You were as drunk as I was, and I'm pretty sure nothing, erm, physical happened between us. Save for, you know, our wedding kiss."

At that moment, a piece of pepperoni falls from my forehead onto the bedspread between us, as if to punctuate my point that, indeed, nothing could *ever* happen between a sexy pro athlete like him and a mere mortal like myself.

"Of course, it didn't," Seb confirms. Firmly. Almost too firmly. But I am, quite literally, Pizza Face right now, so I cannot blame the man for not wanting to ravish me. He sucks in a breath through his nose and releases it before continuing, "But I'm a little concerned that I asked you to do something life-altering when you were, you know, in a mind-altered state."

"It's not like you dragged me kicking and screaming to the altar."

"We got *married*, Maddie." His blue eyes—which look almost a bluish-gray in the morning light—glitter with all kinds of things I can't decipher.

"Temporarily," I supply with a jokey smile. "I can always have my dream wedding with my next husband."

"It's still a big ask." He's playing with his coffee cup, twisting the plastic lid back and forth. "And we could get in trouble if we get found out. *You* could get in so much trouble." He looks up at me quickly. "We can get it annulled before that's even an option. I can get a lawyer on it right away."

I consider this.

And then, I imagine showing up to the Plumlee's cabin in Aspen alone, while Adam and his perfectly pantsuited Elizabeth wax on about their engagement.

The family pariah who nobody can help because she's beyond help.

I'll be a laughingstock. A joke.

Meme Girl.

My chest pinches and I jut my chin out. "I'd say yes again if you asked me this morning, Seb."

This must surprise him, because he suddenly twists his hand and a jet of dark coffee spills out of his cup, soaking his wrist. He winces, swears under his breath, and sets the cup down. Turns to me. "I would never want to do anything you weren't one hundred percent on board with," he says seriously, his blue eyes laser-focused on mine. "I want to play, badly, but I want *you* to be sure of this even more."

"As long as *you're* sure that you're okay coming to Aspen and spending Christmas with my ridiculous family."

"I get the 23rd to the 26th off and I have no other Christmas plans. Will that timeframe work?"

"Sure. Any longer and I'm sure we'll both want to electrocute ourselves with the Christmas lights."

"Sounds like a festive way to go."

I grin. "The festivest."

"Not a word."

"Agree to disagree."

"Well, okay..." he says slowly. "I guess, this is happening. I promise to keep things professional—after last night, no more drinking. I'll let my agent and lawyer know that we're married, but ask them to keep it on the DL as much as possible, so we don't make a spectacle. In return, I'll come with you to Aspen. Make a great impression on your family, make your ex jealous, whatever you like."

I give a little nod before he goes on with a resolute expression on his face.

"Then, after the holidays are over and I have a clearer idea of what's happening with my immigration, I'll get us both out of it the second I can." He glances down at the meme girl on my phone quickly, and then back up to my face. "And I'm happy to go along with whatever breakup story you choose."

I frown, thinking it all over. I'm not a complete newb, I've seen this type of thing play out before. And sure, it was entirely in romcoms and Hallmark movies, but I have to ask. "Won't the media have a field day if they find out you got married in Vegas?"

Seb shakes his head. "Nah. It's unlikely to make it beyond the sports blogs, at most. The mainstream media don't really care too much who pro athletes date... unless you're dating Taylor Swift."

Well, I'm certainly no Taylor Swift. Despite my appearance last night across the entire freaking Internet.

"I'm in."

The words are out of my mouth before I have to think about them. Because even in the stark light of day, this remains my best option to make it through the holidays alive. And after having my breakup be broadcast on TV and becoming a meme, being temporarily married to a gorgeous hockey player doesn't sound like the worst thing to ever happen to me.

Seb shakes his head, looking from me, to the trainwreck of a wedding picture in front of him, and back again. "So... we're doing this?"

I take a deep breath. "We are."

"In that case, I'd better call my agent." His eyes focus on my cheek.

"And I'd better get cleaned up." As I say this, I swipe at the spot he's staring at, and come up with a rogue mushroom. Just the way I always imagined waking up the day after my wedding... not. "May I use your shower?"

Seb looks at the mushroom now on his comforter. His expression turns almost wary. "Uh, sure," he says. Though he very obviously means, *don't you have your own room with its own shower you can use, you crazy, topping-covered woman?*

"Didn't want anyone to see me sneaking out of your room looking like this," I explain. "Not very wife-like to do what appears to be a walk of shame."

A smile replaces his slight frown. "Oh, yeah. Good thinking." He gives a little laugh. "Sorry, I'm not really used to being in relationships, so this whole marriage thing is gonna take some getting used to. You have full permission to point me in the right direction when I go astray."

My mind immediately tumbles back to our conversation last night, when he admitted that he originally thought I was a prior conquest of his, and I smile wryly. "Right, I forgot. You normally go through so many women, you can't even recognize or keep track of them when you come upon them in unexpected places."

"No, I didn't mean it like that—" Seb starts, but I'm already striding to the bathroom as confidently as one can possibly stride when they look like they should be sprinkled with parmesan and served at an Italian restaurant.

I didn't get much of a chance to explore my own room in the hotel, but I know for a *fact* that my bathroom isn't nearly as nice as the one in this suite.

Or neat.

I take my time in the bathroom, helping myself to the toothpaste and mouthwash on the counter before cranking up the shower as hot as it will go. Then, I lather my body with every single bottle of free hotel toiletry.

The scalding water feels like atonement, and I imagine it washing away all of my crazy decisions from last night... but when I step out of the shower, I find that nothing has washed away at all.

In fact, I'm hit with the full weight of said crazy decisions.

I *married* Sebastian Slater. Number 19. Center. My ex's favorite player. And the man who has clearly never let a girl stay at his place long enough to even shower.

Which is not ideal. Because in order for our scheme to work —and for the story we're spinning to actually benefit either of us —we'll need this marriage to look real. We'll need to sell it, so that people will actually buy it.

In other words, we need a solid plan, or we're entirely screwed.

I throw on a plush white robe and rush out of the bathroom to find Seb pacing around the room, phone in one hand and his other hand pinching the bridge of his nose. His expression is dark and frowny, but when he sees me, he face becomes apologetic as he mouths "sorry, one sec." He then proceeds to pace faster, saying "uh-huh" and "mm-hmm" multiple times, with the odd "mm-kay" thrown in for good measure.

When he finally hangs up, he turns to face me.

"We need to make this believable!" I blurt at the exact same time as he says, "I don't think Mike believes me!"

We look at each other, wide-eyed and frozen for a few seconds, before we both laugh.

"Guess we're on the same wavelength," he says, his eyes quickly skipping over my robe-clad form as he sinks to a seat on the edge of the bed.

I push a wet strand of hair behind my ear shakily. Even his fleeting gaze on my body—which suddenly feels very naked under this hefty robe—brings all the blood in my face to the surface. I'm sure that I'm glowing like a neon-red beacon right around now.

"Yup," I say crisply, trying to sound as business-like as humanly possible. I hug my robe around me and take a seat by the desk—AKA as far from the bed as I can get, as space is definitely of the essence right now—and nod at my new husband. "If this is going to work, we need to be convincing."

Seb nods in agreement. "Mike said that he could ask the Cyclones' lawyer to file a change of status for me right away, but I need to see that lawyer the second I get back to Atlanta. And he said that the lawyer will need to be pretty... convinced about the marriage to continue with the paperwork." He starts scrolling through his phone. "According to Reddit, we'll need photos of us together as a couple, mail to the same address, and family and friends to vouch for us."

"Well, we do have photos together," I say, gesturing vaguely towards our wedding pictures featuring traffic cone and Elvis. "As for the other stuff..." I worry my teeth into my bottom lip, pondering. "My family will obviously know, and we can get more pictures over the holidays. Are you going to tell yours?"

He shrugs, looking more than a little uncertain all of a sudden. "I'm not sure. I hadn't gotten that far..."

"Maybe we can start by telling your teammates and the other Cyclones staff."

"Good idea," Seb agrees. "Okay, what about this: we could say that we've been dating in secret for awhile and didn't want to tell anyone because you were going for—and then got—a job at the Cyclones?"

"Ooh, yes! That's good." I play with the hem of my robe, thinking. "And I can get some mail sent to your address to cover that part..."

"Or you could move in with me." Seb looks up suddenly. "I have a spare room that you could stay in. And I mean, it'd be super convenient for you as I live close to work."

My eyes grow wide. "Oh, I couldn't. I—"

"Didn't you say last night that you've been sleeping on your brother's couch ever since your breakup?"

I did say that, didn't I? Stupid loose drunky lips. "Yes, but—"

"So. No wife of mine is going to sleep on some dirty old couch."

"Who said it was dirty?" I demand, throwing up my hands. Then, I remember that I'm wearing a bulky robe that isn't super snug around my upper torso region, and I immediately wrench my hands back in, grasping at the neckline and pulling it tight.

Seb watches this entire debacle with a little smirk playing on his lips. "That's just how I was picturing it."

His tone is dangerously close to flirty, and I give him a glare. "Okay boyo, I think we're going to have to set some ground rules here. Rule number one: no using the word 'dirty' when describing anything to do with me."

"Boyo?" He's trying not to laugh. Failing, too.

"Yes, *boyo*. Rule number two: no conversations while we're not both fully dressed." I look down at my robe, then back up at Seb. "Obviously, that rule kicks in after this current conversation comes to an end and I get dressed."

His mouth twitches. "Naturally."

"Rule number three: I will come and live in your spare bedroom, as I believe this will be best for appearances' sake. But, and I can't stress this enough, there will be *no* hanky panky of any kind."

"But that's my favorite kind," he protests, now full-blown grinning.

"What's your favorite kind?"

"All of the kinds. I like all variations of hanky panky, as you so sexily refer to it."

"Well, dear husband of mine, get used to having *no* variations of any of it."

"Hmm. This is the least fun honeymoon I've ever been on." He pouts, but I can tell by the way his eyes glint and his cheek tics that he's joking.

I also can't help but notice for the millionth time how almost painfully attractive he is. Like, I never, ever believed I'd even be in the vicinity of a man this attractive, never mind married to one.

But that is, of course, an entirely unhelpful train of thought as this marriage of ours is in name only. Sans hanky panky.

As *I* just decreed it.

Dammit.

"So..." I venture. "This will mean you'll have to reign in your girl-of-the-moment tendencies. You know that, right?"

"Huh?" He blinks at me, looking genuinely confused.

"Going through so many women, you don't even recognize them...?"

Light dawns in his eyes, and he snorts. "Madelyn Louise Grainger Slater, I believe you have yet another misconception about me."

"Do tell."

"Look, that's not who I am. Dallas, maybe. Me? It's not like that. I don't do serious relationships because hockey is my first— my *only*—priority. Not because I'm against girlfriends as a principle or have some ridiculous roster of women. I've never gotten serious with anyone because I don't have the time or the energy to put into a relationship."

I'm... surprised. Pleasantly so.

And his smile tells me he knows it.

"So, to recap." Seb's tone is teasing again as he holds out a hand to count down on his fingers. "We've been dating for a while, eloped last night, you live with me, and we're one of those married couples who never, ever have sex or anything close to it." He pauses. Smirks. "I mean, we'll have to have *some* physical contact or nobody will buy this."

"We can hold hands," I say primly, like I'm some kind of buttoned-up spinster-type with a million cats. "And hug."

"What if someone breaks out the mistletoe at Christmas?"

I level him with a *look*, and he laughs. "What? I'm just trying to be a good Boy Scout and be prepared for anything."

My mind instantly replays that thrilling moment last night when his lips brushed mine, and I find myself relenting. "A *quick* kiss. *If* there's mistletoe."

"Is butt-grabbing permitted during said mistletoe kiss?"

Yes... wait, why am I thinking that? "No!"

"Hmmm." His eyes travel over my burning face. I could fry up some eggs for brunch on these cheeks right now—FACE cheeks, not butt cheeks.

Frick. Now I have butts on the brain. My poor, hungover self cannot cope with Mr. Flirty Flirt over here, smiling at me with his incorrigible charm and making my imagination run wild.

And unfortunately for me, his smile only grows. "Let's jot that one down as a 'maybe', huh?"

What on earth have I gotten myself into?

Hello.

It's Seb

Sebastian

Slater

Your new husband

Wow.

The late afternoon Vegas sunshine streams through my hotel window as I stare at my phone screen, then smack my head back against my pillow. I've been married for exactly thirteen hours, and I have already lost all my smoothness.

To ensure that I do no further textual damage, I throw my phone across the bed, then rotate my shoulders, relishing in the feeling of the stretch on my sore muscles.

When my alarm went off earlier today—in the midst of a very logistical (and frankly, unexpectedly fun) discussion with Maddie wherein I made her blush about once every five seconds —I had no choice but to say goodbye to her at my hotel room door and then sprint my hungover ass all the way to the City National Arena where the Cyclones had scheduled ice time for noon.

And let me tell you... practice today was *difficult*. On many levels.

I'd almost forgotten about it in the chaos of the utterly bizarre sequence of events that were last night and this morning. And given that my recent nuptials mean that I am no longer warming the bench for the foreseeable future, it was a practice that I should have been throwing all my effort behind.

By the time I got down to the arena, it was clear that Mike had already briefed Tony and the other coaching staff on my surprise news. Needless to say, my agent was a little stunned when I called him this morning to tell him I was married. But he took it like any good agent would, tuned out the ridiculous details, and focused on the crux of the matter: I could still play hockey, and that was what mattered.

My coaches, however, seemed to be much more amused. Andy Fitzpatrick, an assistant coach who looks exactly like a boiled egg wearing glasses, was practically frothing at the mouth when he saw me.

I shouldn't have been all that surprised when the coaches divided us up to run drills and Fitzpatrick hollered, "Okay, let's have married guys on my left, unwed on my right."

Which, of course, made all of the guys scratch their heads as they split up to their sides... until I wearily skated to coach's left, and all freaking hell broke loose.

Even Torres looked amused by the guys' howls as I was forced to spill the beans that I had, indeed, gotten hitched last night. Add the crippling hangover to the equation, and let's just say that I couldn't wait for the damn practice to be over.

When I got back to my hotel room, totally exhausted, Maddie was gone. And I need to get ahold of her, stat, so that I can prep her for the insanity that is about to break loose in T minus one hour when our plane departs Vegas for Atlanta. We swapped numbers this morning, so I'm praying that she looks at her phone soon.

As if in response to my thoughts, my phone vibrates on the bed. I reach for it with reflexes I barely knew I possessed... and I'm a professional athlete.

> Who, sorry?

> Kidding. What's up, you miss me already?

I snort.

> Nope, I actually want my robe back.

> Which reminds me, are you dressed right now? Because if you're naked again, we probably shouldn't be talking. Rule number two, remember?

> Oh I remember, boyo. And you can breathe easy, 'coz I'm fully clothed. In a turtleneck and long pants.

> Phew. Now that I am no longer suffocating from desire... just thought that we should probably turn up for the plane together. What's your room number? I can pick you up and we can ride to the airport.

> 1301.

> Cool. Also, so you know, everyone knows and they're very excited to meet you.

> WHAT?!

Oh, boy. It's gonna be a long flight.

Twenty-five minutes later, I've collected my wife—who

was full of questions about my teammates' reactions to our elopement—and we are pulling up to the FBO by the airport. Perks of flying private: you can turn up *way* later than when you fly commercial and walk right onto the plane; no lines.

I tip our driver, and then retrieve both Maddie's and my own bags from the trunk. The rest of the guys and the staff are already here, boarding the plane, and all of their heads seem to swivel in our direction at once.

Maddie and I share a long look.

"Ready?" I ask, tilting my head towards her.

"Nope."

"Me neither." I love my teammates, and I love the pressure of performing on the ice with all eyes on me... but I'm not sure I like being the center of so much attention when it comes to my personal life.

Goodness knows what Jimmy's gonna say to her.

We greet the staff and I hand the bags to the ground crew. Then, we walk towards the plane.

With every step, my bravado seems to leave my body, leaking like jet fuel all over the runway, and being replaced by a very unsettling, foreign, anxious feeling.

Can I really do this? Can I really make this look believable— play the part of "husband"?

I'm sweating as I climb the stairs behind Maddie, but right before we step into the cabin, she turns around and reaches for my hands. Her small, slim fingers slip through mine, cool to the touch. I look at our joined hands, then up at her, and she offers me a smile. "Gotta make it look believable, right? Just doing my part."

My eyes widen at how she suddenly takes charge of the situation. While I was enjoying making her flustered this morning, somehow, the tables have turned and she is now the calm, cool, and collected one.

And I'm glad for it. Her composure right now calms me. Reassures me.

This is the right move.

This is how I keep playing hockey, how I keep from letting down the guys currently sitting inside this plane.

Even if it means I'm about to be heckled beyond belief.

"You're confident," I tell her.

She grins. "Confidence is sexy, don't you know."

I look her up and down slowly. Smile. "Agreed. Here goes nothing."

We step into the cabin to a thunderous round of applause and an alarming amount of... Wait, are those penis straws?!

"To the happy couple!" Triple J yells, holding up his drink— *yup, that's definitely a penis straw*—towards us.

"What the...?" I stare blankly at the offending items.

Jake scowls at Jimmy. "I told him these were for bachelorette parties, not elopements, but would he listen? Nooooo."

Dallas, meanwhile, jumps to his feet. "Oh, YOU'RE Maddie! Of course. I should've known something was going on when Seb wouldn't shut up about our new nutritionist."

"Really?" Maddie turns to give me a pointed, cheeky look. "Good things, I hope?"

"The best, my love," I reply dryly, her confidence still rebuilding mine, piece by piece. I surprise her with this comment, and she blushes sweetly. Which actually looks very convincing, indeed.

"I would have hit on you myself actually, but I have a rule about mixing business and pleasure," Dallas continues. "But I guess that all worked out because clearly my man was already in deep."

"That's what she said," Maddie deadpans, and I snort, while Dallas breaks into immediate laughter.

"Y'all are cute." Aaron holds up his own penis-straw-free drink and toasts us. "Congrats."

"I always wanted to elope in Vegas," Colton pipes up. "Figured it would be a perfect thing to do with a first wife..." His eyes widen as he clocks Maddie's amused expression. "Not that I'm insinuating that you're going to be Seb's first wife, obviously. I hope you have a very long and happy marriage and—"

"Shut up, dude," I tell my teammate.

Behind him, Mal—the only person actually *in* on this whole thing—is practically doubled over with laughter. "Hey, Maddie," he calls when he can catch a breath. "It's a pleasure."

"Likewise." Maddie gives an easy smile. "I've been cooking for you guys for a couple weeks now, so it's nice to actually get to know you. Despite the penis straws, of course."

This makes everyone crack up, which puts me even more at ease. I glance at my new wife with something akin to pride.

She's *good* at this.

Maybe this crazy charade will work after all.

As we slide into our seats, Maddie continues to sparkle. She fields my teammates' questions like a pro, and somehow even manages to charm the coaches when they stop by for a chat after we've taken off.

All in all, she's doing way better than I would have. And I've had freaking media training.

Finally, about an hour into the flight—when everyone is either asleep or has their headphones in—Maddie and I get a quiet moment. And I find myself almost bursting to say something. Talk to her. Thank her.

For making this look believable... But also for being so damn easy to pretend to be in love with.

"You're doing incredible," I tell her.

She takes a slug of her ginger ale. "Good to hear because I feel like absolute crap. Last night is catching up with me."

"Get some rest."

"Okay," she replies. And then, before I know it, she's asleep, her head snuggled up against my arm. She looks so peaceful that I stay stock still for the rest of the flight for fear of waking her.

I'm exhausted myself, but sleep evades me.

Because in a couple of hours, my new wife will be moving in with me.

12

MADDIE

December

A couple of weeks after the wild ride that was Vegas, I'm standing in the Cyclones' kitchen in Atlanta when Reagan—the social media and marketing manager—walks in.

"Okay, so I'm thinking a sexy calendar," she says as she slides onto a stool and swipes a bran muffin from the perpetual healthy-muffin-scone-and-pastry tin on the kitchen counter. "Get twelve of them up there, no shirts, holding geese and hens and a freaking partridge or whatever, and title it The Twelve Lays of Christmas."

I practically spit out my water.

"No way management will allow that!" I sputter on a laugh.

"Forget management," Stef snorts. She's back at work now—started back last week—with her thumb healing nicely in a splint, and she manages to open the oven door while expertly balancing a pan of sautéed veggies across her splint. "You're planning to get the guys on board with this *how*, exactly?"

Reagan waves an airy hand before flipping her purple-streaked blonde hair over one shoulder. "Oh, please. Half of them have egos big enough to singularly drive the desire to feature in a half-naked photo shoot. And the other half... I'll guilt into doing it because it's for charity."

I throw my head back and laugh. I know which category Seb will be in—the guy may have a big ego, but I've gotten to know him well enough over the past couple weeks to recognize that sexy photo shoots are *not* up his alley.

Dallas and Jimmy, however, will be all over it. Guaranteed.

It's kind of surreal—not that two of the vainest men who ever walked planet Earth would want to be featured in a calendar shoot, of course—but that I would even *know* such a thing about a couple of the Cyclones' top players.

More than a few things have been surreal since I started this job.

"You're laughing now." Reagan points at me. "But you're the one who's going to have to twist the arm of that husband of yours to be front and center in the pear tree."

I snort with laughter. "As if I have any say in that."

Reagan and Stef join me, shaking their heads.

If you had told me a few weeks ago that I'd be standing here right now, chatting with Reagan and Stef about my hockey player husband, I would've laughed you straight out of the RGM arena's industrial kitchen.

Arriving back in Atlanta after Vegas was a reality check. Because after a whirlwind wedding and life-changing decision, we were back at home, and work, and...

Married. In real life.

Which kinda makes me feel like Sandra Bullock in *The Proposal*. It's not quite the main character Sandra Bullock moment I always hoped I'd have, but Seb's as hot as—maybe even hotter than—Ryan Reynolds, and at least nobody had to go all the way to Alaska in our scenario.

I guess I can hardly complain, though. Because for such a strange situation, it's actually been pretty straightforward, logistically speaking.

Seb went to see Roger, the immigration and contract sports lawyer that the Cyclones work with, and, well... Seb said he was skeptical, at best, but he couldn't exactly refute what Seb was telling him.

Meanwhile, I went straight to Jax's place and packed my things. Thank goodness my brother was still off in the wilderness, sans cellphone, so I didn't have to play twenty questions with him about where I was going. Lying has never been my strong suit, and lying to my brother is next to impossible. I've been avoiding his calls since he got home, opting to tell him via text that I've moved closer to work—which is, in itself, not a lie.

I simply failed to mention that I've moved into the huge spare room of Seb's gorgeous apartment in one of Atlanta's most exclusive residential high-rises. Needless to say, it's a lot more comfortable than holing up on Jax's old—but not half as dirty as Seb implied it was—couch with Rick Astley the dog breathing meatily all over me at 5am every day. I now have a plushy king bed, my own ensuite bathroom, and a beautiful view of downtown Atlanta.

Living at Seb's place has led me to discover two things about my new husband: one, he is a neat freak. To the point where if I leave a bowl in the sink or a towel on the floor, it magically disappears. When he was gone for a few days, playing away games up in New England (Stef traveled with them and I stayed here), I even peeked in his underwear drawer to confirm that, yes, his boxer briefs are ironed and folded to perfection.

Two, he is *definitely* not into decorating. His place, though luxurious, is pretty bare and sterile. For fun, I've added a few colorful throw pillows and blankets and decorative mirrors and pictures to make the place feel more homey. Seb protested at first, but quickly seemed to accept his fate.

I also taped one of our wedding pictures to the fridge as a joke, and for some reason, he didn't take it down. It makes me smile every morning when I'm grabbing my orange juice—me,

Seb and Elvis with our arms around each other, laughing hysterically.

The craziest part is that people actually seem to be *buying* this story (probably because I'm refusing to show anybody said drunken, traffic-cone-including wedding pictures.)

Stefani hugged me when she found out, noting that she'd seen Seb and me in the kitchen together my first day and thought there was something going on. Tony, the head coach, knows my name now. And the Cyclones players themselves have been sweet as can be—they seem to think that Seb being married to someone from Atlanta will make him want to stay more permanently.

If only they knew the lengths he was going to in order to do just that...

But yeah, everyone's been really nice. Aside from Adrienne, who, for HR personnel, really lays on the snide comments.

I figure she's jealous. Which I get.

I mean, have you *seen* my husband?

With a cheesy grin, I pirouette to the fridge, turning up the knob on the radio so that Taylor Swift's "Christmas Tree Farm" fills the room nice and loud. I retrieve milk, eggs, cottage cheese, and chives. The team will be done with their morning skate soon, and a high-protein breakfast is surely in order before Reagan drops her Twelve Lays of Christmas bomb on them all.

A knock on the kitchen door has me looking up from my gigantic pan of scrambled eggs, and a woman I don't recognize steps into the kitchen. She's gorgeous in that off-duty super-model kinda way: tall and slender, with flawless, makeup-less ebony skin, and black hair pulled back in a middle-parted bun that would make me look like a Founding Father but makes her look chic AF. She's wearing yoga pants and a cropped hoodie, along with a dazzling smile.

And I mean *dazzling*. Because I am well and truly dazzled.

"Chantal!" Stef squeals, rushing to the door. "I haven't seen you in forever!"

The woman nods in agreement. "Ugh, I know. The littles are keeping me on my toes these days, but I have the morning off —thank you, grandma—so I decided to drop by and surprise Mal for lunch."

Whoa. This goddess is married to Malachi Holmes?

Chantal hugs Stef and Reagan, and then turns to me with a friendly expression. "You must be Maddie! Mal has told me all about you." She steps forward and touches my arm. Looks down at me, because unfortunately for me, I only come up to her shoulder region. "I was *dying* to meet the woman who stole Seb Slater's heart. Everyone in hockey was convinced that the guy would only ever be married to this sport, and yet, here you are!"

I laugh nervously, sounding vaguely like a car that's having trouble starting. "Yup!" I chirp, gesturing to myself in all my egg-splattered-aproned glory. "Here I am."

Chantal, for some reason, doesn't point at me and laugh, calling BS. Instead, she looks at me kindly. "If you ever want to talk, let me know. Being a hockey wife can be exhausting, and I can't imagine having to work at the same place as Mal on top of being married to him! Much as I love him." She erupts into positively flowery laughter, her beautiful face somehow more striking.

"Well, if you have any advice on how to talk Seb into posing for Reagan's sexy Christmas calendar, I'm all ears!" I say swiftly, changing the subject away from myself.

I'm casual and laughing on the outside, but inside, my imposter syndrome is festering like a stagnant pond.

Chantal giggles. "Tell me more..."

At that moment, the guys burst into the kitchen in a sudden cacophony of yells and shouts and whoops. Seriously, when these men travel as a pack, there's no describing the decibel level they operate at.

"Smells good, Mad Dawg." Dallas sidles up to me and ruffles my hair like I'm his pet. Actually, ever since I officially met the team on the plane back from Vegas, we've become something that feels close to... *friends*.

Guess I'm friends with an entire hockey team now.

"Do we really have to call me that?" I shoot back.

"Yup."

"I'm starving," Aaron—who is quite possibly the biggest man I've ever seen—says from behind his teammate. "Is there any way I could get a protein shake, too?"

I jerk my head in the direction of the fridge. "I whipped up a bunch this morning. Banana, vanilla, and chocolate. They're all labeled in there."

"You're the best." He points at Seb, who's walking towards us. "Your wife is a keeper, Slater."

My husband gives me a silly little smile.

"Don't I know it," he says, coming up and giving me a little shoulder squeeze. "Hi."

"Hi," I say back, my breath catching as I take in the scent of his masculine shower gel and feel the heat radiating from his body. I may be slaving over a hot stove, but I swear that Seb is producing more heat than the burners.

What I have learned about Seb over the course of our very short marriage, is that not only is he an absolutely downright, shameless, incorrigible flirt who can make me feel hot and flustered at the drop of a hat, he's also a man of his word. He toes the line on rule number one like one of those insane slackliners that dangle over canyons, but he never crosses it. To his credit (and honestly, to my surprise), I've only ever seen him flirting like this with me.

Mostly at work, which is where we have to keep up appearances. At home, we don't see each other a lot, what with his away games and busy schedule. And when we do see each other, Seb keeps things very professional. Respectful.

Just like he said he would.

And I'm not going to lie, I find that I almost look forward to his teasing flirtations and his shoulder squeezes every day at work.

Simply because he has such nice, big hands. Adam had pale, little, soft hands, which I've officially decided are my new ick.

The team gathers at the huge oak table at the side of the kitchen, some of them piling onto the long wood bench while others grab a chair. I dish out the eggs and Stef serves up the sautéed veggies she was keeping warm in the oven.

"I don't know why you all insist on eating in my kitchen these days," she grumbles, but she's smiling. "Y'all used to have no problem staying out of my domain and eating in the players' lounge."

"That was before we had an in with the kitchen staff," Malachi jokes, looking right at me and winking from where he's standing hand in hand with his wife. I give him a slightly perplexed smile in return. I like Mal, but he always looks at me strangely... like he knows something. He then turns to his wife with the sweetest expression I've ever seen before announcing, "Okay guys, we're out."

Chantal smiles at him, and then looks at me. "Maddie, you'll be at the toy drive, right?"

I have no idea what she's talking about, so I turn to Seb for guidance. He gives a decisive nod. "Of course she's going."

He then returns to his conversation with Aaron, and I nod, too. Like a puppet. "Guess so."

"Okay, see you then." She sounds genuine. "It was really nice to meet you."

"Likewise," I reply. But honestly, nice as Chantal is, all I can think is that if she's the image of an NHL wife, how on earth is anyone actually believing that I'm one too?

After Mal and Chantal depart, the conversation turns to tonight's game against North Carolina. I cart my pans to the sink, and find myself watching Sebastian as I scrub. He's still speaking with Aaron, head bowed, hands moving fast. I'm pretty sure that the two of them are on the same line—wooo, more hockey speak I learned—and I'm one hundred percent sure that they're talking hockey right now.

Because that's what this is all about: Hockey.

And revenge.

Not marriage. And certainly not thinking that my husband is hot and worrying about what he thinks I look like.

I sigh and wipe my hands on a dishcloth, my eyes landing on the ring I place every day on the sill next to the sink.

I don't wear my ring while I'm working—food prep and jewelry are not hygiene friends. I find I kind of miss it when I don't have it on. Mostly because I never dreamed I'd own anything so gorgeous. For a time, after Adam dumped me, I believed I'd never even *have* a ring to place on my ring finger.

I still can't believe that Seb insisted on letting me keep it. After we got back to Atlanta, I broached the subject of how expensive it was, and he didn't even bat an eye. Said I needed to have a better ring than Elizabeth for the revenge plan to really work, and I could pawn it and donate the money to charity after we're done with our agreement.

Must be nice to be rolling in so much NHL player dough that a freaking diamond sapphire isn't on your spending radar.

Stef putters up behind me, managing to balance a stack of plates on her splint. The lady is an absolute marvel, and I'm happy to call her my boss and friend even after only a few weeks of employment.

"Are you going to the toy drive thingy, Stef?" I ask as I pick up a steel wool sponge to scrub a dirty pan.

"Of course, wouldn't miss it!" She shoots me a quick glance. "Oh, right, this'll be your first one. Every year, the team does something charitable for the holidays, and this year, they're partnering with a local charity doing a *huge* toy drive. The guys have to dress up as elves and everything."

This makes me laugh. "How do they decide what cause to support?"

"Well, they all propose ideas and vote at the beginning of the season. Your hubby was actually the one to suggest the toy drive for underprivileged kids."

Well, if that's not the sweetest thing I ever heard...

"Hey, Lady M." Seb—the apparent philanthropist—is suddenly behind me, empty plate in hand. "Thanks for lunch, it was great."

"Welcome," I reply, taking the plate from him. He still hasn't told me where that stupid nickname came from and I've basically given up on asking at this point.

"You want help with the dishes?"

I shake my head with a smile. Because the thing is, he means it. Seb really would take the time, roll up his sleeves, and start scrubbing if I so much as hesitated. In the weeks I've known him, I've learned that Sebastian Slater is much sweeter than people give him credit for. "You have better things to do with your afternoon. Don't you have a game to prep for?"

"Nah. We have that win in the bag."

"Overconfident, much?"

He leans forward so his face is close to mine, and he speaks in a low, gravelly voice for only me to hear. "Haven't you heard? Confidence is sexy."

I put my hands on my hips. "And arrogance is—"

"Equally sexy," he finishes for me. "So, you gonna be out there rooting for me, Wifey?"

"I don't know," I say with an easygoing shrug as I stack a couple plates to the side of the sink. "It depends what time I get off."

"I requested you get off early so you can be there. There's a spot in the family box with your name on it."

I blink. Turn off the sink and turn to my husband. "Wait, really?"

Seb smiles, but it's a different smile than usual—somehow sweeter. "Yeah, I want you there. And besides..." He lowers his voice. "It's a good look, right?"

I roll my eyes with a little laugh. Honestly, maybe I shouldn't be surprised given that the players' wives and girlfriends are often present at home games, but this is unprecedented for us—an official, public appearance as Seb's wife.

And he *wants* me there.

What I want to do is give him a big, wide grin, and tell him that I'd really like that. But what I actually do is give him a cheeky smirk. "I guess I could make time for it. Have to cheer on my dear husband, don't I?"

He gives me a wink. "I left you one of my jerseys to wear."

"I dunno... I was thinking of repping number 35 tonight. Joining the Dallas Cooper fan club."

All of a sudden, Seb's hands are on my waist and he's jerking me towards him. "I'm a jealous man, Madelyn," he whispers in my ear. "So you'll be wearing my name tonight, or nobody's."

The hot shiver that rushes through me is positively electric. He takes a step away from me, cool, calm, and collected as ever, while I'm a veritable puddle of fluster. Why does my husband have to be so damn sexy? And why does he have to know it?

I can tell that he knows how flustered I am, but he seems to take pity on me, because he simply nods. "See you tonight, Mrs. Slater."

When the puck drops, I feel nothing but pure gratitude to be out here, playing for a sea of maroon and white jerseys cheering the Cyclones on. I'm totally amped up, fueled by the desire to perform for this crowd who have embraced me as one of their own.

I love playing on home ice. And I'm very much aware that the one and only reason I'm still able to call this arena my home is sitting in the family box, cheering me on.

Near the end of the first period, I skate off the ice after a shift and climb over the boards, slapping Jimmy on the arm as he jumps out in my place. As I sink onto the bench, squirting a stream of Gatorade into my mouth, I crane my neck to see if I can spot the woman who made this all possible.

My *wife*.

It still sounds hilarious to me. I never wanted a wife. And if you told me precisely fifteen days ago that I was about to be in possession of one, I would have laughed in your face.

Which is almost what Roger—the Cyclones-approved sports lawyer who has taken on my paperwork—did. Minus the actual laughing part. He's more your stern, professor-y type with elbow patches and bushy gray eyebrows that furrow like twin fuzzy caterpillars as he asks a *lot* of questions about your sudden marriage.

But as Mike reminded him, we'd employed him to fix my immigration status, not question my personal life. And I have to say, I'm happy with how everything has gone down so far.

Right now, I'm on a temporary bridging contract as the team management and lawyers prepare my new one. According to Roger, he'll file the elementary immigration forms for a change of status for me, and once those process, we'll be able to proceed with the interview for my green card. In the meantime, I get to keep playing the sport that my life revolves around and take my team to the playoffs.

It also means getting to watch Maddie blush like a tomato every time I tease her.

I keep reminding myself that I shouldn't flirt with her like that, but my gosh, it's fun to see her react to me calling her "Mrs. Slater."

Plus, I gotta make this thing look realistic, right?

I crane my neck forward and finally spot her. She's seated next to Chantal Holmes and a pretty woman with white-blond hair—Lena, Lars Anderssen's fiancée. Maddie's hair is tied in a high ponytail, and she's talking a mile a minute, clearly not paying much attention to the game. At least she's not talking on the phone this time.

At that moment, she looks down and spots me peering at her. Grins.

"Hi," she mouths.

"Nice jersey," I mouth back. I point to the jersey I'm wearing, and then to the one she's wearing, and give her as good of a thumbs up as I can with my glove on. Even though all the other wives and girlfriends look to be in their regular clothes, Maddie made use of the clean, perfectly folded gift I left for her to wear.

I was mostly joking, using it as an excuse to corner her in the kitchen earlier and get a reaction out of her. The fact that she actually wore it makes me smile, for some reason.

Over the last couple weeks, Maddie has made me smile a lot. She's constantly chatting, full of life and energy and ideas. Just last night, she was telling me about her TikTok channel—Maddie's Creations—and while I've never been into social media, her enthusiasm for her healthy sweet treats was beyond infectious.

In the couple weeks that we've been married, I've been doing my best to keep my promise to her—keep a respectful distance and make sure she feels comfortable and at ease in my apartment. It's been easy enough given that Maddie and I have been kind of orbiting each other outside of work, our dual busy schedules meaning that we aren't usually home at the same time (save for when we're both asleep in our respective bedrooms).

But even when I don't see her, she's everywhere.

There's the sneakers stacked by the doorway, even though there's a perfectly good closet to put them in. And the girl's hair. Don't get me started on her hair... it's on the couch, on the rugs, on the hardwood floors. It's like living with a shedding dog.

But then, there's the fresh flowers on the table. The butter sitting beside the toaster. The orange juice in the fridge, and the bagel crumbs scattering the counters. And sure, I pick up after her, but these little pieces of her, scattered like confetti around my apartment, feel nice and homey.

I've been in Atlanta for just over a year and I've never taken the time to settle in. My only focus was hockey. And yet, in just a few weeks, Maddie's made my apartment feel as much like home as playing for the Cyclones does.

And while things are all professional at home, save for the constant mess she seems to make, it's like when I do see her at work and I get to let my flirty flag fly, I *really* enjoy letting it fly. Almost as much as I like seeing her get all flustered and blushing.

I've decided I quite like my temporary wife.

Maybe quite a bit more than "quite" like...

Now, Maddie gestures down towards her own jersey and blinks innocently before shaking her head. Then, she holds up three fingers on one hand, and five on the other.

35.

Dallas Cooper's number.

No way. She wouldn't.

My pulse jumps and I feel my expression slide into a frown as I try to figure out if she's joking. It occurs to me that my reaction may be a little irrational, but I can't help it.

There's not a chance she'd turn up here wearing his number. His name.

Wait... am I jealous right now?

I startle, a little surprised. Nah. I like Dallas. I'm simply concerned about keeping up appearances, that's all.

Which has been super easy, actually. The guys all like Maddie. After the introductions on our flight home from Vegas, they immediately made an effort to get to know our team's assistant nutritionist.

And then, of course, once they discovered how cool and funny she is—because she is both of those things—I could hardly get them to leave the poor woman alone. The team even eats their meals in the kitchen now, much to Stef's dismay seeing as her previously spotless workplace is now a constant chaotic mess.

Maddie holds my gaze for a few seconds, smirking. Then, she blows me a kiss, stands up and twirls around to show me that the jersey she's wearing is, in fact, number 19 and does say Slater on the back.

Brat.

"Oh, you are in for it later, missy," I mutter as I shake my head at her. Her eyes are dancing as she looks back at me, delighted by her own joke.

"Huh?" Aaron asks as I get ready to go back onto the ice for my next shift.

"Err... just saying that these guys are in for it."

"Riiiight." He sounds sarcastic AF, but still dutifully fist-bumps me with his glove.

As I jump over the boards and skate back out to center ice, I'm suddenly fueled with a bigger drive than ever to perform tonight.

To score.

To lead my team to a win.

To make a certain someone in the crowd proud that she's wearing my damn name on her back.

She's waiting for me when I walk out of the locker room.

And when I say "waiting for me," I mean that she charges at me like a bull to a red flag as I step into the corridor.

"Seb!" Maddie shrieks. Her arms are outstretched, but when she reaches me, she seems to rethink what she's doing. Stops about two millimeters short and hesitates, arms wind-milling as she attempts to balance from grinding to such an abrupt halt.

Half to stop her from falling, half to make this look like a natural hug between a newlywed couple for everyone else in the vicinity, I tug her towards me and wrap my arms around her tight.

I feel her body tense for a moment, then relax, her hands locking behind my neck.

Around me, the other players are hugging their own wives, kids, girlfriends, and/or parents. And it occurs to me that it's nice that I have someone here for me, for once.

"Nice goal." She beams. I scored at the end of the second,

and another goal from Aaron at the beginning of the third was enough to earn us the W.

"So you saw me score this time, then?"

"What?"

"Oh, nothing." I hug her tight for another moment—just long enough that it looks like a loving embrace—and breathe in her cinnamon-vanilla scent before letting go. "You ready to head home?"

"Yup." She fishes the keys to her old rustbucket Jetta out of her pocket.

As we turn to leave, Aaron looks up from where he's been practically eating a pretty redhead's face off and winks at me. "You kids have fun tonight."

I pointedly look in the direction of his arm candy for the evening. "Likewise."

"Later, Slater." He nods at me, then at Maddie. "Later... *missy*."

"Missy?" Maddie looks at me with a question in her eyes as I put my arm around her and guide her down the corridor. "Why missy?"

I sigh, debate lying for a moment, but then decide to grab the bull by the horns and go with the truth. We're still *technically* at work, and so my at-home boundaries of keeping Maddie comfortable don't have to count here, right? "I'm pretty sure he thinks we're heading home to have some wild freaky sex."

"EXCUSE ME?!" Maddie's face is priceless.

"What?" I blink at my wife innocently. "Isn't that what married couples do?"

She gives me a little shove. "In your dreams, Slater."

"In my *wildest* dreams," I confirm with a laugh, tousling her hair. "But I would settle for hot chocolate and a movie when we get home, if you're up for it."

Usually after evening games that go late like this, I want

nothing more than a long, hot shower, my bed, and a baking show in the background as I drift off to sleep. Alone.

But tonight, I'm not feeling my regular routine at all.

Tonight, I'm actually kinda hoping she accepts my request to hang out because I'm in the mood for company. Specifically *her* company. My wifey not for lifey, so we may as well enjoy spending time together while we're in this.

I look down at her, waiting for her response, and she surprises me by smirking. "From freaky sex to hot chocolate? Boy, that de-escalated quickly."

"Disappointed?" I tease. Because that's all this is gonna be tonight—silly teasing and hanging out.

No thinking about how cute she looks, how good she smells...

"Nope." She grins. "Coz I'm picking the movie. And you'd best believe it's gonna be one of Hallmark's very best."

"I wouldn't expect anything less. But there had better be a big city girl who is desperate to change her ways after visiting a small town for the holidays and meeting the local lumberjack, or I'm going to revolt."

She rolls her eyes with a smile. "Dur, that's all of them. You're safe."

"Well, that's a relief." We're in the staff parking area now, her Jetta parked a few vehicles down from my Volvo.

"You'll love it. See you at home, Seb."

"Actually... you wanna ride with me?" I ask on a whim. "That car of yours sounds like it's smoked six packs a day for the past few decades."

"It's not that bad!" she exclaims. But then, she casts a side glance at her rustbucket and gives a resigned tilt of her head. "Erm, okay. It was making some worrisome noises as I pulled in here today. Should probably get it looked at. And besides, I'm dying to know if your car is as neat as your bedr... uhh, apartment."

Even in the dim lighting of the underground garage, I can make out Maddie's latest shade of tomato-red blush. And I can't stop my eyebrows from popping up.

She was in my bedroom?

I don't know why... but instead of making my well-honed stalker alarm bell go off, this thought makes my heart pound. In a good way.

"It's spotless. Like my bedr-apartment," I tell her evenly. "Get ready to take notes, *missy*."

"Nah, I'm just gonna tinker with everything so that it's all *slightly* out of place the next time you get in your vehicle."

"You wouldn't dare!" I reach for her, but she darts around the car and jumps into the passenger side, cackling like a... well, like a madwoman. My madwoman.

I climb into the driver's seat, laughing along with her. And as I start my car, it occurs to me how new and cozy this is— driving home with the wifey.

How domesticated of us.

As we drive out of the parking garage, Maddie kicks off her shoes and tucks her legs up under her. "So, tell me about this toy drive."

"Oh, right." I meant to tell Maddie about this days ago, but the whole orbiting thing got in the way. "The team does something like this every Christmas. Last year, it was caroling in the children's hospital. Which was a terrible idea, trust me. Not one of us could sing a single note in tune." Maddie starts to laugh and I shake my head. "Seriously. Two kids cried."

"Oh my gosh," she hiccups. "That is both hilarious and terrible all at once."

"We will not be doing that one again, believe me. The year before that—before I was a Cyclone—the guys handed out presents alongside Santa at a few different malls. I think that one went over better, but it sounds like Triple J got a little carried away and ended up upside down in Santa's sleigh." I grin at her. "It's a nice concept though, a chance for even the toughest hockey players to show off their sweeter sides."

Maddie nods sagely. "A little birdie once told me that I shouldn't judge hockey players by their covers."

"Hmm." I drum my fingers on the steering wheel. "That birdie sounds incredibly wise and also incredibly smart."

"I also heard that you were the one to come up with this year's idea. A children's toy drive is very sweet."

I lift my shoulders in a nonchalant shrug. "Guess I was the one to pitch it, but the guys all voted to do it."

"It's a great idea."

"I guess I want to make sure that kids whose families don't have much still get everything they want for Christmas."

"That's really kind of you, Seb. Thoughtful."

"Not really," I respond, a little uncomfortable with being complimented for something so nominal. "I grew up pretty poor. My parents worked hard and made a lot of sacrifices so that I could play hockey. And I guess I don't want other parents to have to make huge sacrifices to see their kids happy on Christmas morning."

"Definitely sweet," she responds. "It's lovely that you're doing something to honor what your parents did for you."

The lights of downtown Atlanta sparkle all around us as I turn onto the road where my apartment complex is located—it's only minutes from the arena. But I'm lost in my memories as Maddie's words sink in. "I never really thought of it that way."

"I did," Maddie replies. She waits a beat. "Are you close with your family?"

"I... don't keep in touch with them as much as I'd like to." It's a massive understatement—my days are consumed with hockey, the sport trickling into all areas of my life to the point where I eat, sleep and breathe it, even in the off season. "I want to make them proud. Prove to them that all their sacrifices have been worth it."

Maddie smiles at me softly. "Well, I've never met them, but I'm sure they're proud of you, Seb."

"Thanks." I'm pulling into my parking spot, and it's a natural subject change. "Shall we go watch this terrible, sappy movie you promised me, then?"

"Oh, get ready to be proven wrong on so many counts." Maddie wiggles her eyebrows at me. "This one's a masterpiece."

When we get upstairs into the apartment, I sit almost awkwardly on my sectional couch. This is the first time I've watched a movie with someone at my place. And I find I'm glad when Maddie forgoes the armchair and plops down right next to me. So close that I can smell that cinnamon-vanilla scent of hers. Map the freckles dancing across the bridge of her nose.

"Get ready to have your mind blown!" she announces, reaching for the remote.

"Kill me now," I moan dramatically, miming being stabbed in the heart.

But I don't mean it. Not one bit.

This is... quite nice.

Quite a bit nicer than quite nice.

14

MADDIE

I take a deep breath. Then another. Then another.

Hit the "call" button on my phone, then panic and immediately hang up.

I sneak a peek at Seb, who's in the driver's seat of his SUV, one big hand draped casually over the wheel like he's taking a little drive down an abandoned country backroad, rather than doing 120 on a slam-packed I-85.

It's the day of the toy drive, and we are currently en route to the big event—and I say we, because we've been carpooling everywhere since our trip home from the arena the other night, mostly because Seb was right and my Jetta does sound wheezy as all hell.

Usually, I enjoy our little car rides together, but today, not so much, because of this pesky phone call Seb is insisting I make.

My husband—who's looking particularly hot right now in gray sweatpants, a form-fitting black T-shirt, and a backwards Cyclones baseball cap—looks at me. "Just do it, Mads. Woman up and call her."

"Thank you for not saying 'man up'... and please watch the road!"

He laughs and turns his eyes back to the freeway, but then immediately starts fiddling with the radio, skipping from one station playing Christmas music to the next. "Unlike most men, I am a master at multitasking."

I don't know why, but his words make me blush. Seb can make the most innocent sentence sound innuendo-laden—not unlike Joey "Grandma's chicken salad" Tribbiani from *Friends*. It's a freaking talent, I'll give him that... but it makes for a constantly giggly and squirmy existence as his wife who has never experienced more than a drunken, fleeting kiss at our wedding ceremony.

I shiver at the memory of brushing my lips against his for that split second. The rest of the night might be a complete blur, but that moment is crystal clear in my mind.

Our wedding kiss was warm, tentative, and surprisingly soft. Sebastian Slater has nice lips. Lips that look like they'd be really good at *actual* kissing.

Guess I better engrave it onto my frontal lobe—it's the most physical we will surely ever get as man and wife. Because of *my* stupid rules... but maybe some rules are made to be broken?

Hopefully?

Gahhh, shh, brain. Behave yourself. We are on our way to a freaking toy drive for children right now!

"Call her, Lady M. Rip the bandaid off," Seb urges, fiddling with the vents so they blow warm air in my direction. Thoughtful.

"Watch the road," I chastise again. "And seriously, Seb, why do you call me Lady M?"

He smirks, shoots me a side glance. "Stop changing the subject, Lady Macbeth."

My eyes widen. "Wait. You nicknamed me after a murderous villainess?!"

"You were scrubbing those hands like you were trying to

take your skin off, first time we met," he replies with a laugh. "It was a natural nickname to bestow upon you."

"Well, luckily for you, I never plan to manipulate my dear husband into committing brutal atrocities against his kingdom."

"What a relief." His eyes are twinkling. "You'll just play along with fooling everyone into thinking we're madly in love with each other."

"Exactly." I grin at him. "And hopefully not be driven mad by guilt about the whole thing like Lady Macbeth was."

"Let's hope not," he says gravely. "But if I find you sleep-walking around the apartment, scrubbing those hands, I'll know what's causing it."

This makes me laugh, and I stare back down at my phone, feeling a bit more buoyant than I did a few minutes ago. "I never thought I'd be calling my ex-mother-in-law-to-be to tell her that I'm bringing my new NHL-playing *husband* for the holidays."

"And I never thought I'd be driving my new wife to a work event where I have to dress up and parade around as a six-foot-four, twenty-seven-year-old freaking Christmas elf, but here we are. So, no more excuses."

He's not wrong. He *is* going to be posing tonight as a Christmas elf (the costume is in the trunk) with the rest of the team at the home of Carter freaking Callahan—yes, *the* Carter Callahan, Hollywood A-Lister extraordinaire—for this year's Cyclones charity event.

Apparently, Chantal Holmes is friends with Carter's wife, and when she heard about Seb's idea for a toy drive, she suggested combining hockey and movie star forces to make the event the biggest and most successful yet.

But my excitement at meeting my favorite actor is overshadowed by the call I really *do* have to make.

Seb and I have been talking lately about the logistics of our upcoming little cabin vacation (which I've taken to calling our Christmas of Horrors). I told him that Alicia Plumlee is a nice lady, but my own mom can be prickly. That the dads will likely be more interested in their cigars and business talk than in our relationship. That Jax is my favorite, and he's a bartender at a really cool restaurant downtown that I love. That Adam, in general, sucks.

And while I've been focusing on whether Seb should gift Adam a signed photograph of himself for Christmas (my vote was yes, whereas Seb's was a resounding no), Sebastian has been mainly concerned with letting Mr. and Mrs. Plumlee know that I'd be bringing someone to their cabin because he doesn't want a surprise guest to cause them any bother.

In fact, his exact words were, "I take up a lot of room, Madelyn. And though those people raised an absolute idiot of a son, we will be staying in their house. I was raised to have manners."

Again with the thoughtful. And I know that he's right.

Seb looks at me expectantly and I sigh.

Here goes nothing...

The phone starts to ring and one hand tightens around my cell phone, the other on my thigh. I wince like I'm preparing for impact when Alicia Plumlee's aptly plummy voice says, "Hello?"

Her voice is painfully familiar and painfully far away, all at once. I haven't heard that voice in months. Not since before I dunked her son in a vat of frosting.

I can't do this.

Panicking, I clear my throat. Croak out an incoherent sound.

Cough again.

And then, while I'm frozen with my soundless mouth open like a frog, wondering whether I should open the door and fling myself from the moving vehicle, a warm, strong, solid hand covers the hand that's currently cutting off the circulation to my leg.

Seb gently pushes on my fingers, one by one, until he's released my death-grip. Then, he takes my hand in his.

All while he maneuvers into the left lane around a semi.

He wasn't wrong when he said he could multitask. And it's enough to give me the confidence to find my voice. "Hello, Mrs. Plumlee. It's Maddie. Um, I mean, Madelyn Grainger."

Seb gives my hand a little squeeze, as if to reassure me that, yes, I am speaking somewhat coherent English and not pig Latin.

"Madelyn, so nice to hear from you. To what do I owe the pleasure?" Alicia's tone is more confused than pleased, but I can hardly blame her for that. If Adam called my mother out of the blue, she'd probably have a stroke. And then immediately start planning our wedding.

Meanwhile, my actual husband begins to rub his thumb back and forth along the edge of my hand in a steady, calming, reassuring rhythm.

He's telling me that he's here for me. That I can do this. And I can.

"I'm calling to talk to you about Christmas…"

The toy drive is a totally chaotic scene of Holiday cheer, and the Christmas-lover in me is positively joyful to be a part of this event at the Callahan mansion.

Seb and his teammates have all donned their costumes, complete with pointy hats, velvet tunics, and curly-toed shoes with bells on them. Some of the guys are sporting their elf-wear with more pride than others—Jake Griswold is scowling like an angry racoon, his tights straining around his gargantuan thighs. Meanwhile, Jimmy is wearing a reindeer nose and antlers with his costume, for some unknown reason, and Dallas has gone for a shirtless elf look, foregoing a tunic in favor of suspenders worn over a lot of bare abs on display for everyone to see.

Nice abs, too, if I'm being very honest.

Jeez, these hockey players have *serious* physiques.

As the guys playfully jostle around, sorting the veritable mountain of toys into bins in front of a twelve-foot Christmas tree, Reagan livestreams the scene with glee. I don't blame her—this is A+ content: the laughter in the room is infectious, the guys look hilarious, and Carter Callahan himself is in the middle of it all, sitting on the floor next to his pretty, dark-eyed wife as they wrap gifts.

It's a bit surreal, watching someone I've seen in so many movies exist as a real-life person covered in pieces of sticky tape.

After we've finished the sorting and wrapping, the plan is for everyone to jump on the Cyclones' bus and head to different locations around the city to give out the gifts. It's such a sweet gesture. And Reagan seems happy enough with the team dressed up as buff elves that she's dropped her Twelve Lays of Christmas idea... for now, at least.

I hum along to "It's Beginning to Look a Lot Like Christmas" as I work, curling ribbon after ribbon on the wrapped gifts. I try not let my eyes keep drifting back to Seb, but at this point, it's impossible *not* to look at him. He's accessorized his ridiculous elf costume with a cheeky smirk, and he's currently locked in what appears to be a lively debate with a blonde-haired, dark-eyed little girl who's been prancing around the room since we arrived.

He looks cute talking to kids. I'm sure I'm wearing a dopey grin as I watch him.

Adrienne is watching him, too, I notice. And when she sees me notice this, I bravely stare her down until she looks away.

Back off, HR Lady. That's MY husband.

Wow, this charity toy drive is bringing out the jealous in me. Which isn't exactly charitable.

Or maybe, it's that after our conversation the other night where I learned a little more about Seb's background, it's becoming harder and harder for me not to acknowledge that this guy is the total freaking package. Because while he's obviously hot, talented, and great at making me feel like a flustered mess with his smart-mouthed flirtations, on a deeper level, I'm learning that Seb is *kind*. He cares about the people around him. He's determined to give back.

It's... well, it's sexy beyond belief.

My dopey grin widens as I focus back on Seb and the little girl.

"That's Carter's daughter." Chantal Holmes materializes at my side, holding a clipboard in one hand and about ten rolls of wrapping paper in the other.

"Oh, really?" I peer at the girl, who has her hands on her hips and is squaring up to Seb like he's a ballerina and not a hulking hockey player. "She seems like a feisty little thing."

Chantal laughs with me. "She keeps Carter on his toes, that's for sure."

"She's adorable. I love the sass." I've never really imagined my own future with kids in it. I want them, but Adam never wanted to talk about them. To this day, I have no idea if he sees kids in his future. Maybe he didn't want them with me, but wants them with Elizabeth.

I flinch a little. Six days and counting until I'm face to face with the nightmare I like to call my past, in the present.

The phone call to Alicia Plumlee went okay. Mostly thanks to Seb, who held my hand the whole way through. After I hung up, he folded his hand back into his lap like it was absolutely nothing.

But it meant a lot to me.

Alicia was shocked, to say the least, but accommodating. Especially given the fact that we're due to arrive there in less than a week. I was vague, only saying that I was bringing my new partner. Figured I'd save the H-for-Husband bomb for when I'm there to see everyone's faces. Especially Adam's.

"He looks like he'll make a good dad someday." Chantal nods at Seb, pulling me from my thoughts.

"I dunno, I mean..." I'm about to laugh and make a comment about Seb's only baby being his job, but at the last minute, I remember that I'm technically married to the guy. "I guess," I finish.

"You haven't talked about kids?"

I shake my head and try to look nonchalant. And wifelike. "Not yet. All in good time."

"Of course. Enjoy being newlyweds first." She pats my arm and wanders off, and I refocus on my task: curling ribbon with military precision and trying very hard to ignore Seb's flushed pink cheeks, tilted elf hat, and raucous laugh as he talks with the Callahan girl.

He *does* look like he'd make a good dad someday. You'd have never caught Adam joking around with a little kid like that while wearing a ridiculous costume. It's attractive how comfortable Seb is in his own skin. How unafraid he is to look silly. And sure, he may not be the dad of *my* future kids, but it does make me realize something I want in my next *real* partner: qualities that'll make him a good father.

I'm so lost in my future-baby-daddy daydream that I don't notice Seb approach me, trying his best to balance a gigantic stack of toys that resembles the leaning tower of Pisa in his arms. "Need a hand, Santa's helper?"

I can't help but smile at the sight of him. Those striped tights are a real winner. "Well, I don't know. You look like you've got your hands full."

He winks and expertly deposits the toys into a nearby box. "You're underestimating my multitasking skills again."

"I was more wondering if you or the little girl won that argument. You looked like you were getting your ass handed to you."

"Nah." He laughs and shakes his head. "That kid is a spit-fire, but I won in the end."

"No!" The kid comes running up, waving her arms at me. "For the record, he did *not* win. I just said that girls my age *might* find hockey a little less boring if they got a pink stick for Christmas instead of a stupid gray one."

"Those stupid gray ones cost two hundred bucks a pop!" Seb argues, but he's grinning.

Meanwhile, my mouth falls open. Seb's trunk was packed to the brim when we got here. If he's serious about how much they cost, there must've been ten grand's worth of hockey sticks in there.

"Don't make 'em any less boring," the kid shoots back. She stares at Seb with a slightly terrifying expression, then turns to me, suddenly all sunshine. "Hello, I'm Allegra Liana Donovan Callahan. Who are you?"

"Maddie Grain–uh, Slater. Maddie Slater."

She wrinkles her cute nose and jerks a thumb at Seb. "You married to this guy?"

"She sure is." Seb slings an arm around me, still laughing good-naturedly. "Lucky lady, eh?"

Allegra narrows her eyes. Considers this quietly for a few minutes before nodding. "Maybe... I mean, Sebastian is very nice to buy so many hockey sticks for kids. Even if hockey is really, really boring."

It's my turn to laugh, and I give the little girl a conspiratorial look. "You get used to it after awhile."

"Hey!" With the arm that's still around me, Seb tickles my ribs, making me squirm to get out of his grasp. "Take that back."

"Never!" I shriek, and he holds me tighter, pinning me against him as he tickles my side relentlessly. I'm giggling and gasping for air all at once, while simultaneously being hyper-aware of how tall he is next to me, how good he smells. "Okay, okay! I didn't mean it. I secretly love hockey. Promise!"

He releases me from his death grip. *Sheesh, he's strong!*

"Atta girl," he says with his eyes fixed on me.

My stomach flips as electricity charges the moment so it crackles.

Seb looks like he's about to say something further, but before he can, Allegra crosses her arms. "You look at her like my daddy looks at my mommy. And they're super happy together. So, I'm going to go with yes. She *is* lucky to be married to you."

15

SEB

The night of the Christmas Elf toy drive, Maddie and I drive home together and watch—you guessed it—*Elf*.

The couple of nights after, we watch more sappy Christmas Hallmark movies, and the night after that, it's *The Holiday*. Maddie is clearly a huge romantic at heart, and I find myself hoping that, when this is over between us, she has that perfect "movie" romance with someone. That she falls in love, and has a fairytale wedding when she gets married for real.

She's a great girl, and she deserves her dream love story.

But for now, while still in her temporary situation with me, watching movies together has become our unspoken little routine. Neither of us acknowledges that we're no longer ships in the night, heading straight to our separate bedrooms when we get home. We just... adapt. And I'm a fan of it, I gotta say. It's nice to come home to someone, especially someone who's good company and always has healthy baked goods hanging around. Someone who sits closer and closer to me on the sofa each night, so much so that we're practically cuddling at this point.

The Hallmark movies aren't even that bad. In fact, I've enjoyed them so far—not that I'd ever admit that to any of my teammates. Dallas would never let me hear the end of it.

Before I know it, it's our last night in Atlanta before the holidays. In the morning, we'll fly to Denver, then drive to the cabin in Aspen. Tonight is also the Cyclones' last game before the NHL break for Christmas. Unfortunately, it's a loss to the Philadelphia Phantoms, finishing at 2-1. But somehow, the blow of losing is softened by Maddie in the box reserved for friends and family, wearing my jersey—coupled with a white ribbon in her ponytail. She jumps up and down and screams when I score our team's only goal at the beginning of the third.

When I get out of the locker room afterwards, she's not waiting for me in the corridor this time. And I'm surprised at the twinge of disappointment I feel that nobody's there to greet me. Guess I better get used to it. It's not like my marriage to Maddie is meant to be a forever thing.

The sting lifts a little when I walk through the front door of my apartment... and find a total winter wonderland.

I stand in the entryway for a second, wondering if I've got the wrong place. But no, this is where I live—in an unbridled explosion of holiday cheer, apparently.

The riot of colors and chaos defy all the usual rules of festive decor. Tinsel hangs in unruly clumps from the ceiling, twisting and tangling together in a metallic cascade of gold and silver. Multicolored lights blink erratically from the tree in the corner, which is decked out with ornaments of all shapes and sizes, from shiny baubles and stars to... *are those hockey figurines?*

There's a collection of penguin-shaped cookie jars on the kitchen island, arranged in a semi-circle like they're caroling. Garlands—apparently not having enough space on the walls— have made their way to the furniture, wrapping around chairs and sofas like festive boa constrictors. An inflatable snowman with a missing arm sits at the kitchen table like he's waiting for his next meal.

And speaking of meals, the smells coming from the kitchen are mouthwatering. Sugar and spice and all things nice.

"What the..."

I don't get to finish the sentence because a red-cheeked Maddie is suddenly skidding into the living area in reindeer-socked feet. "Hi!"

She's changed out of my jersey, and into leggings and a ridiculous Christmas sweater that says "Happy Birthday, Jesus!" on the front. Complete with a picture of a festive Jesus in a party-hat, his arm around a Santa Claus sporting sunglasses.

"Sorry I wasn't there after your game, but I had to run home to finish this," she continues in a burst. "Do you like it? Are you surprised?"

"I'm..."

I'm remembering our conversation the other evening as we were watching one of the Hallmark movies. She told me that my —our—apartment looked shockingly unfestive and asked where my Christmas decorations were. I told her that I didn't have any, and the look on her face could only be described as sheer horror. She questioned me about last Christmas, and I ended up confessing that I spent it working out, watching game tape, eating chicken and steamed veggies, and getting ready for the Cyclones' first game after the break. Alone, in my decoration-less apartment.

"Oh, no!" Maddie's face falls as I stand on the spot like a freaking lemon, my words caught in my throat. "You hate it, don't you? I'll take it all down. It was an overstep and I'm—"

"No." I cut her off as I catch her arm. "I don't hate it at all, I'm just... very surprised. You did this for me?"

She looks down, those luminous eyes falling on the spot where my fingertips are gently pressing into her arm, soaking up the warmth of her skin through her sweater. She then peeks up to meet my gaze, carefully taking me in before she eventually says, "I did it for us both." She wrinkles her little button nose.

"Your story about your solo, veggie-eating Christmas day last year was the saddest thing I ever heard. Tonight's our last night before we go to my family's Christmas of Horrors, and so I wanted us to have a nice Christmas to remember, too."

I'm touched beyond words. So I settle for a simple, "Thank you, Maddie."

She perks up. "Well, come on, then. I've baked a bunch of treats that are tailored for your macros... ish." She gives me a little bashful smile. "Figured there was some leeway for the holidays. And I even have *Home Alone* ready to play."

The thought she's put into this is above and beyond. Like someone who really, truly knows me and cares about me.

And that's without her even knowing how much this cheerful, festive scene reminds me of the gaudy and bright Christmases of my childhood, growing up in Canada. The whole thing makes me miss my family, but at the same time, makes me glad that I have Maddie with me for Christmas this year. I make a mental note to check in with my family soon to see if the gifts I sent up there have arrived. I haven't gotten Maddie a gift yet, but I know for a fact that I want to get her something as thoughtful and meaningful as what she's just given me.

"I should get married more often," I say playfully, reverting to humor to attempt to soothe the painful thumping coming from that pesky organ in my chest.

She pokes her tongue out at me. "No other wife would be able to plan something this amazing."

"No," I agree softly. "She wouldn't."

Maddie holds my gaze for a long, heated moment, before throwing a ball of green fabric at me. "Here. Suit up."

I sputter a laugh as I unfurl a sweater with the words "Get Lit!" splashed across the front. There's a huge Christmas tree, complete with actual flashing lights, underneath.

Maddie grins wickedly. "In commemoration of our very lit wedding."

"You are too much."

But she's not. She's exactly the right amount of... everything.

I pull the sweater over my head, and then we curl up on the couch under a huge blanket with bulldogs wearing hats and scarves (seriously, where did she get this stuff?). Press play on the movie as we dig into an assortment of cookies, each better than the last. We wash them down with peppermint hot chocolate, which we *cheers* like it's champagne... but better.

As the movie gets underway, her feet find their way into my lap, and I rest my hands on them. Before long, my thumbs are gently massaging her arches, which makes her groan with happiness.

I don't remember the last time I felt this relaxed. This content. My mind is at rest, rather than spinning through a million different goals and achievements I'm working towards... all hockey-related.

And yet, Maddie seems to be growing more and more tense by the moment. I can see it in the corner of my eye, can feel it radiating off her—her knuckles are whitening on her lap, her feet are suddenly stiff.

I reach for the remote. Hit pause.

She looks at me, her face a question mark.

"I want to check in," I tell her. "Are you feeling okay about tomorrow? You can talk to me if you need to get anything off your chest."

I mean it, too. Maddie is the first person outside of my teammates here in Atlanta that I've actually grown to care for, and I want her to know I'm here for her through the holidays.

She blinks a few times, twisting the ring I gave her—the ring which really does suit her—around her finger. "I'm... scared," she admits. "Scared to see Adam again. Scared of how I'm going to react, of what the family is going to think of me. I've been going to this cabin for Christmas as an unofficial part of the Plumlee family for years, and last December, I remember thinking—this is it. He's going to propose this year. Next Christmas, I'll be back as an official Plumlee to-be. I'll be talking wedding venues and dresses and honeymoon plans."

She sniffs and wipes her nose with her sleeve before she continues, "Believe me, I'm not sad that it didn't end up happening that way. Adam showed his true colors and I know I dodged a bullet. But it seems like... there's so much history there, and somehow, in the space of just a few months, someone else moved into the place I'd been holding for over a decade."

Maddie's fist is clenched into a ball on her lap. I reach over and take her hand, releasing the tension a little.

"I'm angry that Elizabeth is where I thought I'd be this year, and I'm..." She glances at me, and then looks down at her lap again. "Temporarily married to someone else to spite them all. And, I guess I'm also scared that they're going to see right through it, and I'm going to be an even bigger laughingstock."

I bite the inside of my cheek. I have no idea how to help her with everything she's lost. She was with Adam for a long, long time, and nothing is going to change the past and erase that history. It hurts, I get it. And I don't want to downplay the legitimacy of that for her.

But what I *can* do is help her feel a little less achy for a while. Show up for her in a way that Adam obviously didn't. Not gonna lie, the guy sounds like a total prick.

I touch my thumb to her chin to tilt her face towards me. "One: you are not, and have never been, a laughingstock. Two: you're totally justified in everything you're feeling right now. And three: I wish I could somehow make the pain of what Adam did to you go away. I'm sorry I can't. But I *can* promise that, when we arrive at his cabin tomorrow, you've got an ally in me. A teammate. I want to be there for you. Okay?"

"Okay." She lets out a long breath. "You ready to act like a married man, Slater?"

"All over it, Wifey." I smirk, and she swats my arm. "But

seriously, yes I am. I've got your back, like you've had mine. I'll do whatever it takes to get you through the holidays as unscathed as possible." I stroke the tip of my finger over the soft skin of her jaw. "You can lean on me, Maddie. I promise I'll help you bear the weight of this."

Her hand closes around mine, still cupping her face, and squeezes. "Thanks, Seb."

"It's what I'm here for. I'm your husband, remember?"

"How could I forget?"

She says this flippantly, her tone light, but her eyes are still wide, her teeth worrying at her bottom lip. I find myself wanting to make sure that she doesn't have to worry about a damn thing.

"Just... make it look like you're in love with me?" she asks.

I give her my best flirtatious smile—one that I'm hoping will make her smile, too. "Pretty sure I can manage that."

16

MADDIE

We're here.

It's happening.

Lights, camera, action... Showtime.

A shiver runs through me as I stare at the forest-green front door whose threshold I've crossed every Christmas for the past decade. My fingers itch to straighten one waxy holly leaf that's half escaped from the oversized wreath and is currently hanging droopily, ruining the whole, perfect, round formation of the thing. I feel for the little leaf—out of place and making everything messy.

Man, it's cold out here. Is it always this cold?

It's snowing, like it always is. So... probably.

A warm presence suddenly fills the empty, chilly space beside me, and I take in the now-familiar scent of Sebastian—clean and woodsy and manly and delicious in this understated way that makes you wanna breathe in deeper so you can have more.

"Mads?"

I look at him where he stands next to me on the stoop with all the bags he insisted on unloading from the rental car by himself. "Yeah?"

"You okay?" His voice is soft, his breath forming a white cloud in the frigid air.

"Yeah." I give myself a shake. "Why wouldn't I be?"

"Um, because you've been staring at that door for the past five minutes like you want to kill it?"

"Oh." I laugh nervously, whisps of white surrounding my face. "Sorry. I'm nervous to see everyone. Adam and Elizabeth."

"Awh, Mads. Elizabeth ain't got nothing on you."

"How would you know?"

"Instagram, duh. Did some research before coming here."

I blink, surprised that he took the time to do this. "That was... thorough of you."

"Of course. That's *my* rule number one: never hit the ice unprepared."

"Always with the hockey." I peek up at him quizzically. "And do you really mean that—about Elizabeth? Or are you just trying to pump me up?"

"I always mean what I say." He looks down at me and gives me a goofy, soft smile. "And I might be biased, but I know that she isn't half as great as you are. Plus, you have way better boobs."

My eyes go wide and I slap his arm as he laughs, but I'm laughing too. His cheeky teasing helps me relax, and I have a feeling he knows that. "Thanks. I think. If all else fails, I'll just tell myself that."

He looks at me for a moment, and then slides our bags off his shoulders. Puts a big hand on each of my arms and looks me dead in the eye. "In all seriousness, you can do this, Maddie. I'm here for you. I've got your back, no matter what goes down. I'm on your team, remember that. Okay?"

"Okay." I nod slowly, suddenly overcome with happiness that he's here. "Good pep talk, Hockey Man."

"Gotta practice for when I'm captain one day." He gives my arms another squeeze. "You ready?"

"Ready," I confirm.

He picks up the bags again, and rings the doorbell before I can chicken out.

Oh, Lordy.

"And if you feel like killing someone, I'm not above stabbing Adam's gingerbread man with a toothpick."

"Excuse me?"

Seb raises a brow at me. "Didn't you say you have a tradition where you make gingerbread people in everyone's likeness for Christmas? One cookie per person?"

Wow. I mentioned that once, weeks ago. This guy listens.

"Uh-huh," I reply.

"Well, I'm bringing a new tradition." Seb shoots me a cheeky grin. "Voodoo cookies for anyone who upsets my wife."

I don't even get a chance to process how simultaneously unhinged and, well, sweet that is, because the door flies open, and suddenly, I'm face to face with the woman I spent most of my adult life thinking was going to be my mother-in-law.

"Madelyn!" Mrs. Plumlee gives me a quick, only slightly awkward embrace before nodding up at Seb. "Come in, come in. We'll get you out of the cold before we do introductions. Don't want you freezing to death out there."

Seb smiles cheerily, and with the few rogue snowflakes caught in his tousled hair, he looks like he belongs *in* a Hallmark Christmas movie. "No worries, Mrs. Plumlee. I'm from Canada, originally. Used to the cold."

"Oh, is that so?" She peers at Seb curiously as we step into the cabin. I'm hit with a dizzying wave of nostalgia—from the scent of the crackling applewood fireplace to the squidgy, dated red carpet beneath my feet.

"Yes, ma'am," Seb replies, all sweet and polite and angelic all of a sudden as he unbuttons his gray wool peacoat. He hangs it up, then helps me out of my bulky parka. The perfect gentleman. "But I have to say, I like living in Atlanta. Much hotter."

He looks right at me as he says this, his eyes briefly traveling over me before he winks. Alicia gives a short laugh, shaking her head, and when she turns away to hang up our coats, Seb gives me a little thumbs up.

Mrs. Plumlee has us leave our bags by the door, and then leads us down the hallway and into the living room, where I know the rest of the crew will be sitting. Waiting for us. I take a deep breath before I round the corner, knowing that once everyone sees me with Seb, there's no going back...

Season's schemings are officially upon us.

I trail behind Alicia, heart throbbing in my throat, and as I step into the familiar living room, time slows. My eyes travel over the old, overstuffed plaid couches blindly, the myriad of colorful garlands (hung up successfully on the wall where they belong, unlike the attempts I made last night), the fireplace adorned with Christmas stockings. I notice my parents—my brother hasn't arrived yet—and the rest of the Plumlee family.

Finally, my gaze lands on Adam, who's hand in hand with Elizabeth in the corner loveseat.

The gut-punch I'm waiting for as my eyes meet his... doesn't come. It's more like an uncomfortable pinch. I mean, I'm still quivering at seeing him for the first time since *The Incident*, but it's more like getting in a fender bender than a plane crash.

Which isn't a morbid analogy at all.

"Hello, everyone," I say woodenly as everyone gets to their feet.

"Maddie." Adam's voice drips condescension. "Glad you could make it. Mom told us you were bringing a... SEBAS-TIAN SLATER?"

Adam's voice turns into a choked, fangirl-like strangle, and I'm gloriously thrilled to see my ex turn the pasty-white of the ghost of Christmas past as my gloriously handsome husband comes to stand next to me.

Man. Seb looks *good* in that wool sweater.

Adam's blinking his big, round eyes rapidly behind his glasses, looking not unlike a malfunctioning Furby. I have a momentary urge to smash him against the stairs, which is how I fixed (read: permanently silenced) my own broken, hyper-blinking, childhood Furby toy.

Instead, I smile. A big, wide smile. "Oh," I say innocently, looking from Adam to Seb. "Do you two know each other?"

"What's going on, Madelyn?" My mother's face is pinched and her voice shrill.

"I told you. She said she was bringing a new *friend*," Alicia hisses to Mom.

"You didn't tell me that friend was Thor!" Mom hisses back.

Seb, meanwhile, turns to Adam with a friendly, relaxed expression. He's got about six inches and forty pounds of muscle on my ex. I'm not usually so shallow as to judge solely based on appearances, but boy oh boy, am I enjoying this particular observation.

"Sure we do," Seb says confidently. "It's Eugene, right?"

"Eugene?" Adam stutters, apparently still starstruck enough to be entirely dazed. "Who's Eugene?"

Seb turns to me with his forehead wrinkled, but I don't miss the evil twinkle in his eye. "Didn't you say that your ex was named Eugene, love?"

"Love?" Mom and Adam say simultaneously, their faces identical masks of confusion.

"No, it's Adam," I correct Seb happily.

"My bad, my bad. Hi, Adam." He puts a hand out, and Adam takes it. Seb's big, tan, callused hand totally dwarves Adam's pale and soft one, and if I'm not entirely mistaken, I could swear that Adam winces from Seb's grip. "I am Sebastian Slater, yes, but you can call me Seb. And I hear congratulations are in order for you, too."

Seb nods towards Elizabeth, who's come to stand behind Adam. She looks chic as ever in a silk shirt and chinos that emphasize her tall, slim frame, but her pretty face is screwed up in concern as she watches her fiancé practically spontaneously combust.

I, meanwhile, can barely contain my glee.

How did I ever think this was a crazy plan? This is the most fun I've had in months.

"Too?" Adam looks from me to Seb and back again. "I don't understand."

Seb grins like he and Adam are the best of friends, and then steps next to me and puts his arm around me. Draws me close and looks down at me like I'm actually the love of his life and he couldn't bear to ever lose me. "You know. You two getting engaged, and me and Maddie getting married."

A shocked silence falls over the room. I expect it's the calm before the storm.

And man, I've never been more excited for a storm.

I snuggle into Seb's side. "Oops." I spread my left hand over my husband's chest, flashing my ring for the room to see. "Did I forget to mention that Sebastian's my husband?"

17

MADDIE

One very eventful hour later, Sebastian and I are walking into our designated bedroom with the premise of "freshening up for dinner"—which earned a loud guffaw from Adam's grand-mother as she slugged back her fifth brandy of the evening.

The second the door closes behind us, Seb chucks our bags on the ground and falls on the bed, laughing. "Oh my gosh, Mads, that was insane."

I don't reply, because I'm too busy staring at the four-poster bed he's currently sprawled across, his big chest rising and falling as he chuckles to himself. The bed itself is lovely—made of a mahogany wood that plays off the dark wood walls, and the green and crimson flannel bedspread matches the curtains. There are about ten huge, fluffy pillows on top, but they're all mussed up thanks to Sebastian's current starfish position.

I love a good throw pillow, and resist the urge to shoo Seb off the bed so I can fluff them all up and put them back in place.

As I'm paused in the doorway, reflecting on this, Seb props himself up on one arm to look at me. "What? You don't think that went well? I'm pretty sure I made a good first impression."

He definitely did.

After we dropped our H-bomb, Adam ogled us like a gold-

130

fish, and then proceeded to handle the shock of meeting his athletic hero in the flesh—and finding out the guy is now married to his ex—by asking tons of personal, almost intrusive questions, rapid-fire style. All of which Seb answered calmly, with perfect composure, as he played with my hair and pretended to be head-over-heels in love with me.

But on top of that, Seb was slick enough to show up with wine and chocolates for both our host and my mother, and then won all the women over by dropping compliments on literally everything in sight (including the heinous art on the walls). And also by pretending that he thought Adam's tiny, sassy, gray-hair-in-a-bun grandma was his aunt.

Then, as if that wasn't enough, Seb went on to ask my stepdad and Adam's father questions about their lines of work in criminal defense law. In turn, he regaled them with some appropriately hilarious tales about being in the NHL, spending time in the sin bin, and someone named Wayne Gretzky.

I may or may not have thought that Seb was saying Wayne Jetski at first, which is a way better name. Seb was unimpressed to the max with me, because apparently this Gretzky character is a Canadian hero.

Who knew.

But that's not what I'm concerned about right now. Because I'm only now realizing that, as we are a married couple, the guest bedroom Alicia assigned us has only one bed.

Because what newlywed couple sleeps in separate beds?

I sink into a decorative armchair in the corner. "I didn't think about the sleeping situation."

He looks at the flannel comforter, then back up at me. Shrugs. "No big deal. What's a few sleepovers between a temporary husband and wife?"

My brain is misfiring right now—obviously payback for the chaos I caused downstairs.

It may be night one at the cabin, but this new, increased

proximity between Seb and me is making everything I've been feeling of late seem escalated. Elevated.

The problem obviously isn't *sleeping*. The problem is the pesky amount of attraction I'm feeling for Seb. Attraction that's been growing night after night as we sit on the couch at his apartment, talking and laughing and watching movies. And don't even get me started on how he rubbed my feet *just right* last night. Holy moly. I'm beginning to realize I like Seb a bit too much for my own good, and this is something that sleeping next to him is hardly going to quell.

I can only cross my fingers and make a Christmas wish that he snores like a freight train and farts in his sleep.

"Oh, come on." Seb grins at my dithering and pats the bed beside him. "I promise I don't bite. Unless you want me to, that is."

"Stop it!" I instruct, my entire body blushing a vibrant shade of Christmas crimson—the exact shade of red that that frosting *should* have been.

"Relax, I'm *kidding*." Seb rolls his eyes and starts piling up the pillows, making a line down the middle of the bed. "We can build a little pillow wall so you don't come anywhere near me. The Great Wall of Slater. So that no mini Slaters will be made on this trip."

"Seb!"

"Sorry, sorry. I promise I'll stop now." He chuckles and gets off the bed. Stretches out his arms towards me and gives me his sweet, sincere smile, that cocky smirk he was wearing melting away like spring snow. "C'mere."

I step into his hug and relax immediately. "I'm glad you're here."

"Me too, Maddie." He squeezes me tight. "Everyone believes us so far. Eugene looked like he was going to explode. We got this thing."

"Just wait 'til Jax gets here," I murmur. "He's never going to buy it."

I was relieved to learn that my brother won't be arriving until later this evening. Making my ex jealous of my level up is one thing. Lying to Jax is another. And there's no way he's not going to see right through me.

"Don't worry. I can be very convincing."

A shiver runs through me as I lean into his chest, relishing the feel of his strong arms around me as I breathe in his woodsy, sexy smell. He's got *that* right.

"Now," he says as he pulls back with a sly grin. "Be a good wife and cover your eyes so I can get changed."

"We have to find a... pickle?" I frown at Maddie, who's standing next to me looking cute as hell in the outfit she changed into for dinner—a plaid kilt and a cream sweater with a V-neck that shows a tantalizing glimpse of her cleavage. Because no, I was not lying when I told her she has great boobs, and no, I am not being a creep by noticing this. It's just a fact that is impossible for any heterosexual male not to notice immediately.

I *know* Adam's noticed.

That tool has been hovering next to us for the past few minutes, trying (and failing) not to stare at Maddie, and then at me, and then at Maddie again.

Which, on the one hand, I get—Maddie is a knockout. But the possessive side of me wants to tell him to stop undressing my wife with his beady eyes. He had his chance with her and he blew it to smithereens.

The bozo is clearly still in his feelings for her, even if he doesn't know it yet. I almost feel bad for Elizabeth—who's pretty, but like I said, has nothing on Maddie's gorgeous eyes and cute smile and curves for days. But then, I remember that she started dating Adam while knowing he was in a long-term relationship, and I don't feel so sorry for her anymore.

"Yeah, it's a pickle ornament that's hidden in the tree," Maddie replies, her full, pretty lips curling upwards. She's wearing red lipstick tonight, and it's a great look on her. "The game's a tradition for our first night at the cabin."

"I'll explain for the newcomers!" exclaims a very merry grandma Dorothy 'call me Dot, my boy!' Plumlee. As she says the word "newcomers," she gives Elizabeth a hard stare before beaming at me and reaching up to ruffle my hair.

And I do mean *up*, the elderly woman cannot be more than five feet tall. And with her gray hair pulled back in a neat bun, her poinsettia-printed, button-up blouse in the dead of winter, and her ruby red glasses, she could honestly give Mrs. Claus a run for her money.

A bit of a drunkypants Mrs. Claus, mind you...

As Dot drains the last of her mulled wine, she launches into an explanation about how the game of "find the pickle" (a name I couldn't help but laugh at) is a Christmas tradition in Germany, and the family does it every year to celebrate their German heritage. "The first person to spot the pickle-shaped ornament in the Christmas tree gets the first gift on Christmas morning, and will be rewarded with good fortune in the year to come!"

I nod. "Got it."

Sounds insane, but no more insane than anything else that's happened lately.

Elizabeth nods too, smoothing down the tight black mini dress she's changed into for the evening before looking at Maddie and putting her hand possessively on Adam's arm. Adam, meanwhile, is sighing and not-so-subtly checking his cuticles the entire way through his grandmother's explanation.

I note with happiness that the diamond on Elizabeth's ring finger isn't half as awesome as Maddie's ring. Elizabeth's ring looks like what you're supposed to buy for a woman with expensive taste, while Maddie's looks like... *her*. It captures who she is—interesting and unique and sparkly and cool, all at once.

"One, two, three... go!" Dot cries, and everyone starts pickle-hunting.

I swear. You can't make this stuff up.

The Christmas tree is a real Douglas Fir that has to be at least nine feet tall, taking advantage of the cabin's vaulted ceilings. Hunting for a green pickle amidst the branches covered with sparkly, colorful ornaments and lights is actually more difficult than I expected.

It's also much more competitive. Maddie is crawling on the floor on her hands and knees. Mr. Plumlee is literally throwing ornaments around the room in his search. Maddie's prim and proper mother is tangled in Christmas lights and (hilariously) screaming "Dig deeper, Richard!" at Maddie's stepfather.

But hey, I'm a competitive guy—I compete for a living—and I'm not above getting involved in the hilarity. Unlike Elizabeth, who looks like she's stepped in cow poop with the way her nose is wrinkled and her chin's tilted up.

"Come on, Lizzie, get in on the action!" I call out as I use my height to my advantage and start rummaging through some upper branches. She looks like the sort of Elizabeth who doesn't enjoy the nickname "Lizzie."

"Yeah, Lizzie, put your back into it," Adam pipes up, his grabby hands patting the tree up and down.

Lizzie sniffs. "I'd rather not, thank you."

I zone in on a glittery green ornament at the same time as Adam.

Our hands reach for it at the exact same moment.

"Got it!" he exclaims, his fingertips making contact as my hand wraps around the pickle, beating him to the punch. I'm holding the stupid thing, but Adam continues to grab for it, so I decide to let go, stepping back and raising my brows at him as if to say, *really, man?*

"Seb had it first," Maddie points out.

"*I* had it first," Adam grumbles like a child, fingers closed around the pickle possessively.

"No. Your reflexes are too slow, boy." Dot chuckles. "Sebastian beat you. He may have gotten there second with Maddie, but he was first with the pickle, that's for sure. It's Sebastian's pickle now."

I've been at the cabin for just over two hours now, and I am confident that I already have a solid ally in Adam's grandmother.

Adam grudgingly goes to hand it to me, but I stop him. "That's okay, he can keep it," I say, adopting the same gentle tone that I used to talk to Allegra-the-hockey-hating-kid at the toy drive.

"But it's your pickle, Seb," Maddie says with a small smile, like she's realizing that I have the upper hand here and my nonchalance is making Adam look petty as all hell.

I have the urge to make her smile again. Because this guy hurt her and humiliated her, dammit. On national TV, no less. She might be my temporary wife, but nobody messes with the people who are important to me. Ever.

I look pointedly at the little three-inch ornament in Adam's fist. "Nope, that's *definitely* Adam's pickle."

Elizabeth gasps, Adam looks vaguely confused, and Maddie lets out a strangled burst of surprised laughter. Fueled by this, I wrap my arm around my wife and kiss the top of her head. "Now that the game is done, shall we go get a drink?"

Maddie nods, looking at me like I hung the moon as we walk into the kitchen. When we're out of earshot of everyone, she practically convulses with laughter. "That was genius, Seb."

Which is nice to hear and everything, but it also makes me strangely sad. All I did was subtly insult her ex's manhood. Not exactly original or smart. For Maddie, the bar's so low, it's practically rolling around on the floor.

"The guy's a tool," I tell her lightly, filling up two glasses with sparkling apple juice.

She hops up on the counter. "I wish Jax had been here to see that. He never liked Adam. I think he'll like you, though."

"Good," I say, and I mean it. I want her brother to like me—I can already tell that he's the only person in this family that actually seems to *know* Maddie.

"And he'll talk hockey with you. He likes to watch it."

"But you don't."

"Sure I do."

"Yeah right. Wayne Jetski ring a bell?"

"Fine." She smirks at me. "I like to watch when *you're* playing."

The compliment is unexpected. The type of comment that makes you feel warm inside, and then feel like an idiot for feeling warm inside.

But even stranger than those unexpected warm feelings is the fact that thoughts of my marriage have begun to take center stage in my mind. For the first time in forever, hockey is background noise—Maddie is my focus.

I really do like my temporary wife. More than I ever thought I might.

We've only been married for a matter of weeks, but I can already see when she's tensing up. When she needs me to crack a joke to lighten the mood, or hold her hand to give her the confidence she deserves to have in the first place. Because Adam is clearly an idiot for leaving her, and I wish I could make her see that.

She deserves better. And if I can help her get anything from this marriage, it's the realization that she deserves a gentleman who treats her like a queen.

After everything that she's done for me, the least I can do is be the best husband in the world for her.

138

19

MADDIE

The next morning is Christmas Eve, and I wake up to an early Christmas present in the form of a very shirtless Sebastian Slater sprawled out beside me in bed.

And... wow. I *must* be on the nice list this year.

I take a moment to admire his sleeping form. He's dressed in only a pair of gray sweatpants and is lying on his side, one arm flung over the pillow wall, one tucked under his head. His face is peaceful, almost angelic, as he dreams, his mouth ajar and his eyelids fluttering. Which *would* be the cutest thing I've ever seen... if I wasn't so preoccupied staring at the expanse of tanned skin stretched taut over long planes of muscle. There are two freckles to the right of his belly button, decorating one of his ridged abdominal muscles.

I feel weirdly pleased to be in possession of this knowledge.

There's definitely nothing *cute* about Seb's big, manly, athletic body. It's a landscape that should most definitely be appreciated in all its natural glory.

I wonder at what point in the night he ended up shirtless. Not that I'm complaining. When we were getting into bed, he told me that he sleeps hot, but I wasn't really listening. I was much more focused on making sure that I donned my huge, inherently non-sexy flannel PJs, wooly socks, and a sleeping mask. And building the pillow wall between us as high as I possibly could.

Not because I was worried about *him* trying anything... I actually thought that sleeping next to all that hotness—especially after he insulted Adam's, ahem, *pickle*—might make me do something crazy. Like try to kiss him.

He's been such a gentleman about making sure that I feel safe and comfortable. Meanwhile, I'm reeling myself in from jumping the poor guy's bones.

But I'm not sure that it's only my husband's attractiveness that's making me feel this way—I've always thought that he was gorgeous. He's always made me blush with his inappropriate jokes.

This feels... different than simply lust. It's more like an invisible string pulling me into his orbit. The way he knows if it's a hug or a joke that I need to feel better. The way we've been here for only one night and he defends me before I even know I want to be defended. The way that, for the past couple of weeks, I've been excited to come home every night and spend time with him.

I swallow.

Frick.

The last thing I need to do is catch freaking feelings. There is no place for feelings in this marriage. It's strictly business, with a side of ogling appreciation for the particularly spectacular specimen of the male human form that is Sebastian Slater.

That's it.

I swallow and reach for my water bottle on the nightstand. Drain it. Because yes, I'm freaking thirsty right now.

I slip out of bed as quietly as possible. The closest bathroom is across the hallway, so if I play my cards right, I'll be able to creep over there, brush my teeth, do all my skincare and my hair, and then slide back into bed and pretend I "woke up like this." With dewy, plump skin, sleek hair, and fresh, minty breath.

Probably the same way that all the women Seb has shared a bed with *actually* wake up.

But, I'm not going to think about them right now, because it's Christmas Eve. And *I'm* the one waking up next to this glorious sight.

Fa la la la la la la la la.

I tiptoe across the room and let myself out the door. I'm practically prancing across the hallway, high on the beauty of this particularly festive season, when a big, muscled, tattooed arm shoots out and grabs me. Drags me into the bathroom by the buttoned-up collar of my flannel PJ shirt.

"Hey!" I squawk, glaring up at Jax, who's dressed in jeans and a gray T-shirt. His eyes are bright and his cheeks are red from the cold. My guess is that he's been up for hours—by choice—for an early morning hike in the snow. By choice.

Like I said, my brother is a total weirdo who makes very questionable life choices.

"What the hell is going on?" Jax demands, glaring down at me like I'm the Grinch who stole Christmas.

Although, on second thought, he would probably high-five the Grinch—he's a bit Grinch-y himself with his lack of holiday enthusiasm.

"Well, I *was* on my way to brush my teeth. But then, some jerk pulled me into the bathroom and started hassling me."

"Ha ha," Jax deadpans. His face is a mask of complete and total unfunniness. Closer to fury, really. "I got in late last night and found your mom still up, pacing the floors in her nightgown like some kind of Victorian house ghost, and she told me that you're here with your *new husband,* Sebastian Slater. And now, she's upset because you won't try to win Adam back like you planned."

Wow. There is so much to unpack in that sentence.

I start by rolling my eyes. "Like *she* planned."

"What?" Jax hisses.

"*Mom* planned for me to try and win Adam back. I never wanted to win Adam back."

He nods. This is believable to him. He fires the next question, "And you got hitched to Seb Freaking Slater how, exactly?"

I hate lying to Jax. So, I stick to what *actually* happened. "Drunken night in Vegas."

"WHAT?"

"Yup." I try not to smile at how positively flapped my entirely unflappable brother is right now. "Elvis married us, so it was all very official. We woke up the next morning and decided we'd give it a try. At least, for a while."

I mean, it's not *not* the truth.

Jax's face paints a picture of a thousand words—none of them nice ones—but he only utters a single syllable: "Why?"

I shrug. "After all the crap that happened with Adam, moving on and leveling up with a pro hockey hubby seemed like a good option."

My brother's gray eyes narrow to slits. "So, what you're actually saying is that you got *married* to get back at Adam."

"Umm... not no?"

His dark, slanted brows fly up his forehead. "Maddie, in all the absolute..."

What follows is a string of entirely unfestive four-letter curses, interspersed with words like "idiotic," "ridiculous," "harebrained," and—my personal favorite—"preposterous."

Big word for the grizzly barman.

But clearly, he has never tried Revenge Marriage (trademark pending). Which is a shame, because I ten out of ten recommend it. It's very soothing for the jilted romantic's soul.

I yank my arm out of his grip so that I can cross my arms over my chest. "What's preposterous is that you actually give a damn why I got married. You don't even believe in marriage. Or love. So why do you even care why I chose to do this?"

His face softens, his slate eyes lightening a touch.

"Because I love *you*, silly," he says on an exhale. "I care about *your* happiness. And you believe in love so much that it's to your detriment sometimes, I think. Therefore, the thought of you being married for anything *but* love makes me upset for you. Especially with a hockey player who's known for his commitment to nothing and nobody but hockey itself."

"Jax," I say confidently, grabbing his hand. "Put aside all of your feelings about love, marriage, and what you've read about Seb. The question is, do you trust me?"

"Of course. I just worry about you."

I shake my head. "Well, don't. I'm happier than I've been in a long time."

This, at least, is the full truth.

Jax closes his eyes. Breathes in slowly through his nose and out again. "Fine. But tell me, is he being good to you?"

A smile splits my face. "Honestly, he's the best. He treats me *way* better than Adam ever did."

"Good. Because while I will choose to back down and support you in this madness for now, I also have no problem stabbing Sebastian Slater with his own hockey stick if he hurts you. Understand?"

I laugh. "Relax, Michael Myers. Seb is one of the good ones. You'll see."

And with that, I steer my brother out of the bathroom and shut the door in his face.

By the time I exit the bathroom—hair straightened and breath fresh as could be—my "I woke up this sexy" plan is foiled. Because the bed is Seb-less.

Which I totally blame Jax for, by the way.

I get dressed in a cute pair of leggings and an oversized cream-and-black fleece sweater with a zipper. Very cabin chic, I think.

I'm feeling pleased with my choice until I bounce downstairs and the first thing I see is Elizabeth leaning against the kitchen counter looking all svelte-like and catalog-modelly, dressed in one of those all-in-one ski suits with a belted waist and fur-lined hood. It's a mauve color that looks great on her, but would probably make me look like I have cholera.

Her shiny black hair is French-braided and she's wearing the perfect amount of makeup to emphasize her natural beauty while avoiding the freshly-scrubbed and pink look my complexion is currently sporting.

"Maddie." She gives me a tight smile. "You're finally up. We were just talking about today's plan."

As she says this, she gestures to the long, elegant dining table where Mr. and Mrs. Plumlee, Dot, my mom and stepdad, Adam, Jax, and Seb are currently sitting. There's a spread of croissants, preserves, Danish pastries, juices, and cut-up fruit laid out in front of them.

Great. Of course I'm the last person down to breakfast. Seb must've located the other bathroom at the far end of the hall, because he looks freshly-showered and, quite frankly, delicious, in a diesel-blue beanie hat and black Patagonia fleece.

I note with pleasure that he's sitting next to Jax, and Jax doesn't look like he's about to stick a fork in his eye.

I also note with pleasure that Adam is sitting across from them, and has clearly been watching them talk with an expression that's halfway between disbelief at Seb being here, and jealousy that Seb and Jax are talking to each other, and not him.

144

Jax never cared for Adam, and while he was never blatantly rude, his distaste was always somewhat apparent. Which irked my ex to no end.

But my jolt of pleasure is short-lived. As I walk to the empty seat on Seb's other side, my mother frowns at me. "You look tired, Madelyn. Do you need some of my concealer?"

Elizabeth presses her lips together, and the rest of my confidence slides straight into my under-eye bags, filling them up bigger and mauver than ever. Santa's sacks of eyebags.

I slide onto my seat with my tail between my legs, but as my butt hits the cushion, Seb already has an arm around me, pulling me close.

"Morning, my love." He presses a kiss to my forehead that's featherlight and flutter-inducing, then smiles at me before declaring, "You look beautiful today." He turns to my mom and adds, "If she looks tired, Mrs. Grainger, it's probably because I kept her up late. We were having a really interesting debate."

He's giving Mom this endearing, earnest smile that must prompt her to ask, "What about?"

"How effective The Great Wall of China has been for, erm, *border* control." He gives me a secret little look, and I'm sure my entire head turns blistering red.

"I didn't know you were interested in ancient history," Adam says.

"Oh, she's not at all. Maddie's much more interested in *current events*." Seb gives him a jaunty wink. "Told me all about it last night. Three times, in fact."

Adam's normally alabaster-pale cheeks redden and Jax snorts into his water glass. Which is as good a signal as any that Seb has won my brother over, once and for all.

I *knew* that Seb Slater charm would get to him, just like it gets to everyone else.

"Well, I think it's lovely that you two have so much to talk about that you chat into the wee hours of the morning," Alicia

145

says pleasantly, the double entendre of the conversation entirely lost on the old folks at the table (thank goodness). "But I hope that means that you're not too tired to ski today."

I groan inwardly, especially when I see Seb's face light up and his blue eyes sparkle.

This is one of the more insufferable Plumlee-Grainger Christmas Eve traditions. If the weather allows it, the whole crew of us—including the parents and the grandparent—hit the slopes for the day before après-ski fondue.

I like the cheese part. A lot. What I *don't* like is the slipping and falling down a mountain like a graceless idiot with two left feet, while everyone else perfectly, effortlessly carves their way through the snow.

I'd say that I never took to skiing... but it's more like skiing never took to *me*. The whole sport and I have a mutual loathing, and it's been that way since the time I slipped while coming off the chairlift and it whacked me on the back of the head.

I'd much rather curl up in front of the fireplace with a good book, any day.

"It's going to be such fun." Elizabeth sparkles as she spreads a thin layer of blueberry jam on her croissant. "I'm itching to get out there and hit some black diamond runs."

Of course she is.

"Do you ski, Seb?" my stepdad inquires. "Growing up in Canada, I'd assume you ski or snowboard."

"Both," he replies easily. "I grew up near a ski resort, and when I wasn't skating, I spent my entire childhood on skis or a board. I love skiing, but I like snowboarding even more."

"Excellent." Elizabeth's lips curve upward. "We'll have one more expert to join us more daring members of the family today."

Adam gives a jolly chuckle. "Yes. You'll have to come with Elizabeth, Jax, and myself. I'm sure you'll be bored spending all day with Maddie falling on the bunny hill, as usual."

Elizabeth laughs like a tinkling bell at this, and my dislike for her only grows.

"I'm skiing alone," Jax responds immediately, the look on his face communicating that the thought of spending *any* time with Adam is the most repugnant thing he can possibly imagine. Which I appreciate.

Meanwhile, I force my face into a pleasant, neutral smile. "I think I might sit this one out... Seb's right, I didn't get much sleep last night."

I'd much rather impale myself on one of Elizabeth's ski poles than have her laugh at me sliding face-first down the ski hill.

Dot shoots her grandson a *look* before tilting her head my way kindly. "Nonsense, deary. You must come. I can keep you company in the beginner area."

Lizzie and Adam snicker behind their hands. Because while Dot is clearly only trying to help, an eighty-year-old wizened woman with bad hips offering to join me on the bunny hill for *my* sake is... well, humiliating.

"Oh, no. I'll just—"

"Make Christmas cookies with me," Seb supplies. He looks around the table. "As much as I love to snowboard, there's a clause in my contract with the NHL that doesn't allow me to take to the slopes." He grins. "Guess my limbs are too valuable to risk breakages. And Maddie was nice enough to offer to forgo skiing today to keep me company. An offer I very much accept."

"Oh, well in that case, of course. You newlyweds enjoy some alone time." Dot taps her nose knowingly.

Adam looks miffed. At best.

And I feel... like I'm on top of the world.

Because I know that Seb doesn't have a contract right now.

Which means he is choosing me over snowboarding today.

20

MADDIE

The first Christmas after my mom moved us in with my now-stepdad and Jax, I was mad.

Every single cell in my little six-year-old body was protesting—I was upset that Mom wouldn't let me play my Disney Holiday Sing-Along CD in case it gave her new husband a headache, scared in case Santa didn't know that I had a new address and my presents wouldn't get delivered, and angry that I wasn't allowed to hang my old snowman stocking on the front door knob like I used to at our old house. This new house had a fancy fireplace with four matching, white, fluffy stockings adorning it.

My mom was abandoning me, my stepdad was ruining everything, and my new big brother was gross and stinky. I was convinced that it would be the worst Christmas ever. A disaster. Catastrophe. Travesty of the highest order (yes, I was a dramatic child, if you hadn't already gleaned that).

But then, on Christmas morning, little eight-year-old Jax came running into my bedroom at 5am in his Sonic the Hedgehog pajamas with a huge, overstuffed stocking in each hand. Turned out that in *his* house—which was now my house, too—you didn't have to wait for the grown-ups to wake up to open the presents in your stocking.

My eyes grew huge at this news, and the two of us ripped into our stockings with glee. Then, we lay in my bed and stuffed our faces with the chocolate Santas we'd opened. By the time the adults finally got up and we could go downstairs and open the presents under the tree, we were both high on refined sugar and festive cheer, giggling like crazy.

The day only got better: not only did I have a brother to open presents with, but there was also a bowl of Ferrero Rocher we could *just help ourselves to*. Plus, the really big TV in the basement was *way* better for watching our new DVDs than the small TV we had in our old house.

By the end of Christmas day, I crawled into bed happy and content, and with a new best friend in my stepbrother. Everything that had previously felt so wrong—so out of place and different, in a bad way—now felt like it had fallen perfectly into place. The *right* place.

This is what Christmas morning this year feels like.

"You sure you're comfortable?" I put a hand on Seb's shoulder. His big body is positioned in front of me, leaning against my legs on the sofa. He offered to sit on the floor when he saw that there weren't enough seats in the living room for everyone. Thoughtful, as usual.

He reaches up and laces his fingers through mine, holding my hand in place. The simple sensation of his callused fingertips moving over mine draws shivers out of me.

"Definitely," he says as he leans back to rest his head against my legs. His dark blond hair fans out over my tights, and I resist the urge to stroke the strands with my free hand.

Instead, I smile. We're all gathered around the tree, sipping mimosas (well, Seb and I are drinking orange juice—neither of us has touched a drop of alcohol since the hangover from hell after our wedding), and waiting for Dot to distribute our gifts.

"And this one is for... Elizabeth," Dot—clad in a very appropriate red fleece robe, a Santa hat, and elf slippers—says almost darkly as she checks the tag, handing over a robin-egg-blue Tiffany bag.

Diamonds for the black diamond skier protegé. How original (insert eyeroll here).

"Oh, Adam, you shouldn't have," Lizzie says in this breathy voice, fingering her sparkle-clad earlobes as she gazes upon the shimmering pendant necklace laying upon white tissue paper. "You got me these earrings last week."

Adam smiles at her. It's a nice smile. A smile I always liked. But it's nothing like when Seb smiles, and his eyes go soft and crinkly, and his cheeks curl like parentheses around his mouth, bracketing the smile to show it off in all its glory.

"It's Christmas," Adam tells her. "It's my job to spoil you."

Seb's fingers tighten on mine, and I squeeze back reassuringly. Gift-giving was one of the things I was most nervous about—seeing Adam and Elizabeth, happy and in love, as he showers her with tokens of his affection on Christmas morning. Just like he used to do with me. Not that gifts hold much importance to me—I value time and thoughtfulness over material things—but I was still not looking forward to it.

This morning, however, I find that I don't give a flying fudge about what Adam or Elizabeth are doing. He could be composing sonnets to rival Shakespeare's for her, and I wouldn't bat an eye.

Why?

Because honestly, I'm enjoying my time with Seb way too much. The two of us spent all day yesterday baking cookies and gingerbread people in everyone's likeness while we blasted Christmas music. Turns out that Sebastian Slater knows all the words to "All I Want for Christmas is You," is an absolutely terrible baker, and is somehow an even worse cookie decorator. We eventually made an assembly line of cookies that we were able to decorate and arrange in boxes to store overnight.

Seb made me laugh, in particular, when he "accidentally" broke the foot off the Adam cookie and fed it to Dot's scrappy little terrier, Porkchop.

"Skiing accident," Seb told me gravely when I assessed the damage. "He may never walk again."

I grabbed the cookie, bit off the other foot, and declared, "No, he will *definitely* never walk again."

Seb laughed at this, and I inhaled the velvety sound, committing it to memory.

After we finished baking, we went for a walk into the village. The cabin is a couple of miles away from the little mountain town, and it's a beautiful walk to get there, whether you take the residential side streets—the way I like to—or the snowy, twisty-turning, hiking trails through the forest—Jax's preferred route.

In town, Seb and I went to a cozy little cafe, where we sat in front of a roaring fireplace, talking for hours about everything and nothing all at once.

It was amazing.

Once Elizabeth is done cooing over her new necklace, Dot harrumphs and shoves a large square package onto Adam's lap. "This one is from me, for you and your fiancée."

Adam takes the package, without thanking his grandma, and rips it open. He stares at the contents until all of us are staring at him, too. Waiting.

"Well?" Elizabeth demands. "What is it?"

Adam holds up a vintage-y wall sign—one of the ones you buy on Etsy or at craft markets with swirly letters that spell out inspirational quotes.

Only this particular sign says:

~~Live, Laugh, Love~~

Don't be a dick

"Oh!" Elizabeth squeaks, looking scandalized in a Jane Austen sort of way that I must say really suits her.

"Mother!" Alicia exclaims. "That's... entirely inappropriate."

"Thought it would look good on your bathroom wall," Dot declares with a sniff, ignoring her daughter-in-law and staring right at Adam. "Sometimes we need a reminder when we're doing our business."

I smush my lips together in an effort to keep the laughter that's currently bubbling in my chest from pouring out. Seb's shoulders begin to shake and he tightens his grip on my hand.

This might be my favorite Christmas morning ever.

I'm so relaxed and content watching everyone else swap gifts that I let my hand sneak into Seb's hair, running my fingers through it while my mother gifts my stepdad with a new watch, and then opens his gift of a gingham apron. Savage.

Alicia gives us all socks and gift cards—she was even sweet enough to include Seb—and my mom gifts me multiple self-help books. Different than the ones Jax threw in the trash last month because these are themed along the lines of "How to Make Your Husband Stay" and "Don't Screw Up Your Marriage." Which she must have run into the village to grab for me yesterday, because she literally didn't know I was married until I turned up here with Seb.

I thank her with a grimace, shoving away the thought that I will have to tell my mother at some point down the road that my marriage is over, and Seb has, indeed, not stayed.

I'll just blame the stupid book for giving me bad advice.

Sebastian and I didn't discuss gifts—because I certainly wasn't expecting him to buy anything for anyone, including me—so I am both shocked and gratified when he produces VIP tickets to a Cyclones game for everyone, earning heartfelt thanks from Mr. Plumlee, my dad, and Jax, and a half-excited, half-awkward thanks from Adam. He's clearly right where we want him to be: in a pickle over whether to love Seb, the athlete, or hate Seb, the guy his ex leveled up with.

When we're finished with the pile of gifts, I untangle my hand from Seb's and lean back to stretch, like a cat. Next on today's agenda is a Christmas brunch featuring Adam's hand-made confections, which, if history is anything to go by, he will drone on and on about for the entirety of the meal.

"Wait," Dot says as we're standing to head to the dining room. "There's one more."

At the base of the tree lies a long, thin envelope tied with a gold ribbon. Dot squints at it, then says, "It's for Madelyn."

I frown around the circle. Jax and I don't exchange gifts, and I already have my pile of trusty books for the trash later. Or a nice festive bonfire.

My gaze lands on Adam, who's looking back at me keenly. A cold shiver runs through me. Oh no, is this something else designed to embarrass me? A consolation gift for being the ex-at-Christmas?

But Adam blinks down at the envelope like he's never seen it before.

I take it from Dot, slide my thumb along the edge to ease it open... and a key falls out.

Trying not to react—because I still don't trust Adam's intentions right now—I pull out the folded piece of paper inside.

Read the page.

Read it again.

It's the deed to a commercial kitchen space. Rented for the next twelve months to a company called Maddie's Creations.

"I... don't understand." I look at Seb, because I *have* to look at Seb. It has to be Seb.

He's studying me like I'm a textbook that he's trying to decipher.

"So you can grow your business," he says simply, a question mark in his eyes.

"I don't have a business."

"You do now." He nods at me gently. "I got Roger to register it. There's tons of space to make whatever you want and it's set up so you can film in there, too. For your social media audience."

I'm staring at my husband like he's speaking in Klingon, my mouth wide open. I can't say anything. I'm worried that if a single squeak comes out of me, the floodgates will open and I will bawl like a baby.

Because Seb, in a few short weeks, understands me better than Adam ever did. And instead of making a "look at me, I'm so flashy" move with jewelry, he went for something infinitely better: he read my heart's desire and made it happen... without me having to say a single word to him.

He just *knew.*

"Mads?" Seb prompts, looking almost nervous.

I can't speak—the lump in my throat is too big. So instead, I throw myself into his arms.

He catches me and pulls me to him, wrapping me into his chest and holding me there, safe and sound. One big hand winds around my waist, and the other strokes my hair while I hiccup and drool over him like a blubbering baby.

"Thank you," I cry into his chest, any embarrassment at my display being drowned by gratitude.

His hand tightens on the back of my neck, holding me ever closer.

Somewhere in the far, far distance, Dot applauds. "Now, THEY would get a sign that says 'Live, Laugh, Love.'"

21

SEB

I've faced off against veritable Nordic giants. Been slammed into the boards by goons drunk on violence more times than I can count. Had my ribs cracked twice with the jab of someone's stick on the ice.

But I don't think I've ever been more scared or tense in my life than when I was watching Maddie open that envelope. I worried that I'd overstepped. Jumped so far over the line that it was somewhere on the far horizon. I hoped that she would be pleased with the gift, but I prepared myself that she might be annoyed.

What I *wasn't* expecting was for her to literally tackle me, clutching onto me like a spider monkey.

I also wasn't expecting to like it as much as I did.

I liked the way it felt when she was in my arms. Liked it even more when she stepped back and looked up at me with huge eyes, and I swept my thumbs under them softly, brushing her tears away. Liked it the most when she looped her arm through mine, spreading her fingers on my bicep, and then stayed that way as we walked to the kitchen for Christmas brunch.

And all I could think was how happy I was that I'd made

her happy. That I'd be happy every day to make her happy like that.

Now, she's eating clumsily with her fork in her left hand, while her right hand stays firmly planted on me. Adam keeps shooting slightly perplexed glances towards where she's touching me.

And I keep smiling at him. It's great.

"What're you kids up to today?" Alicia smiles around the table at all of us enjoying our mix of eggs benedicts, and waffles with syrup, and tomato and green pepper omelets, and, at the center of it all, Adam's pastries. "Dinner is at 4pm, so please try to be back by then from whatever you're up to."

She really is a nice lady.

Pity about her son.

"Elizabeth and I will be hitting the slopes again," Adam says with a pointed look in Maddie's direction. "It's so nice to have a partner who enjoys the things I do."

"Indeed," Maddie's mom agrees. For some bizarre reason. The way she takes every opportunity *not* to defend her one and only daughter is beyond baffling to me.

But Adam's not-so-subtle dig bothers me to the point that I decide it's time to knock him down a peg or three.

I take a bite of my glazed pecan braid—which is, annoyingly, an absolute pastry masterpiece shaped like a wreath with two freaking turtledoves nesting in it—and wince, acting like it's painful to swallow.

"What?" Adam's eyes are on me immediately, blinking behind his glasses as he studies my reaction to his food.

"Oh. Nothing. It's, um, delicious." I half-gag, then politely wipe my mouth with my napkin. "Super delicious."

Adam eyes me, his face a perfect blend of suspicion and fear. To a guy like Adam—whose entire identity is built on gourmet fancies—serving bad pastries has got to be up there on his top terrors list. Especially when serving them to his favorite hockey player.

Well, his *ex*-favorite hockey player. Which I think—*hope*—I'm well on my way to becoming.

I smile placidly at Adam, then turn to Maddie. "When do you usually give everyone their gingerbread people?"

Her eyes dart to Adam, then back to me. "Later. After dinner."

Right away, I decode this to mean that Adam doesn't like her giving them out during his brunch, so that he's not upstaged. Which, sadly, doesn't surprise me in the least. And I've known the guy a total of three days.

"You should give them out early this year."

"Oh, no," Maddie protests. "Let's do it later."

"I wanna see mine now." Jax immediately backs me up, throwing his own half-eaten pecan braid down on his plate. "I'm hungry for gingerbread."

Maddie looks at her brother like he's grown a second head. "You hate gingerbread. I always make you a sugar cookie version."

Jax raises his eyes heavenward. "Give us the cookies, Mads."

I like Maddie's brother. I can see from a mile off that he genuinely cares about her. And he's made an ally of me because he sees that I do, too. Gives me that weird warm feeling in my stomach again just thinking about it.

Dot starts to demand her gingerbread cookie, too. And Mr. Plumlee joins in.

"I'll grab them." I scrape my chair back and begin to stand, but then I look at Adam with wide, innocent eyes. "That is, of course, if Adam doesn't mind."

Adam looks like he minds. A lot. His face is a mask of frustration and upset, but he can hardly go and *say* that he minds now, can he? Otherwise, he'll look like a total prick.

So, he's forced to nod.

"Great." I jump to my feet to fetch the platter from the pantry.

"I'll help you," Maddie says tightly.

And then, she follows me. Right into the pantry. Shuts the door behind her.

It's a very small pantry.

So small that we're practically chest to chest.

I look down at her, hyper aware of how close we are. The heat of her body. How small she is, yet somehow, she's filling this entire space—her perfume mixing with scents of ginger-bread cookie, her breathing shallow and quick.

The sound of it makes my heart speed up, pounding in tandem with her inhales.

I take a step closer (if you can call it a step), closing the remaining inch between our bodies so that we're standing flush together. I flash her a devious smile. "If you wanted to get this close to me, you could've just gotten rid of that pillow wall in our bed, you know."

She looks left, then right, her cheeks reddening like she's suddenly deeply second-guessing her shut-us-in-the-pantry decision.

"What I want is to know why you're making such a big deal over the damn cookies?"

"Because nobody puts Maddie in the corner," I quip. "I would offer to try the *Dirty Dancing* lift with you to accompany that statement—I think I'd nail the move, personally—but I'm afraid we'd smash the pantry to pieces and people would think we are up to no good in here. Or lots of good, depending on how you frame it."

She lets out a shaky laugh. "What in the name of Father Christmas are you talking about, Seb?"

"What I'm saying is that you should be loving every minute of seeing Adam squirm out there. But instead, you're acting like you're still afraid of hurting his feelings. Like you need to lurk in his shadow so as not to upset him."

Her eyes grow even bigger and rounder as my words sink in. To further convey my point—excellent husband that I'm aiming to be—I reach out and tuck a strand of hair behind her ear, my fingers skimming her cheekbone. This draws a shudder from her that has me continuing on, sliding my hand behind her neck.

"You deserve to be celebrated, Maddie. Deserve to be praised. Deserve to have all of those people look at you and talk to you with *way* more respect. And I'm pulling double duty as your husband to help you get everything you deserve."

She gulps, which I don't blame her for, because it suddenly feels like there's no air in here. Everything feels hot and feverish, and every place our bodies touch feels electric. She's staring up at me, pupils dilated, breath coming shallow through those full lips...

Full lips that are begging to be kissed.

"You're special, Maddie." My voice is so full of gravel, I barely recognize it. "And I'm going to do everything in my power to show you just how special you are." I lean towards her and close the space between us, everything in me suddenly desperate to know how sweet she tastes.

She tilts her face up, eyes fluttering closed, and a little gasp escapes those parted lips.

"Show you how beautiful you are," I murmur as I move closer still, my own eyes closing.

Because she is. My wife is gorgeous.

And I plan on damn well making sure she knows it.

"What're you guys doing?!" The sound of Adam's voice makes the heat in my veins turn to ice and my eyes fly open.

Maddie and I spring apart—not that there's far to go—and I look down at her. She's still wild-eyed and breathy, her skin hot and her expression dazed, and I curse Adam under my breath.

He should *really* follow the advice on the sign Dot gave him and try not being a dick.

With a regretful smile, I run the pad of my thumb over Maddie's bottom lip, drawing a full body shiver out of her. Then, I lean down to whisper in her ear. "Guess I'll have to show you later..."

And with that, I reach past her, grab the doorknob, and throw the door open. I may or may not be hoping to *accidentally* smoke Adam the Absolute Buzzkill in the face with it.

No such luck, though. He's standing a couple feet away, arms crossed.

"Ah, sorry," I say, making sure I don't sound in the least bit sorry. Which is very un-Canadian of me but necessary right now. "We just can't seem to keep our hands off of each other, right, Mads?"

I sling my arm around my wife, who's stepped out of the pantry after me, cheeks the color of my hockey jersey.

"Right," she says. And she sounds like she means it. Which I, again, like way too much.

Adam glowers at us in a way that makes me want to laugh. And with his tacky, jingling Christmas sweater, the green hat that Elizabeth asked him to wear (for "fashion," apparently), and his glasses sitting slightly crooked, he's giving me pretty intense flashbacks to the Whobilation scene in *How The Grinch Stole Christmas.*

"Oops, forgot the cookies." I reach back into the pantry and pull the tray off one of the high shelves, and then, I look straight at Maddie. "Shall we get back to the group, love? Give out the delicious cookies you made?"

Maddie laughs a perfectly sweet laugh. "You mean the cookies *we* made, babe."

Adam's face is redder than I've ever seen it, and for a moment, I'm mildly concerned for his health. But then, he turns on his heel, uttering a supremely mature, "*Hmpf.*"

As we follow him back to the dining room, I'm smiling confidently and Maddie looks half-proud, half-mortified.

"Sorry for the delay, everyone, but I promise that these are worth the wait."

It's cute to see Maddie blush as everyone oohs and aahs over her cookies. They really are spectacular. She's managed to capture the most amazing details—mine is wearing a #19 jersey and skates, Dot's is sporting a blouse and a low bun, Mr. Grainger's is smoking a cigar, Jax's comes complete with arm tattoos and is wielding an ax...

And Elizabeth's has a huge brown blob on her shirt and glitter in her frosting hair. Which may or may not have been my doing.

Maddie looks at the cookie made in the likeness of herself, and traces its mouth. Like I was doing to *her* mouth minutes ago. She looks lost in thought, her eyes glazed and her expression far away.

She must press the cookie a bit too hard because she mutters, "Oops, I smudged my lipstick."

I give her a heated look, and I'm gratified to see those green eyes darken once again. "That's a look I'd like to see more often on you."

22

MADDIE

Just like that magical Christmas when I was six, this one keeps getting better and better as the day goes.

After Seb's sexy little performance in the pantry—there's a sentence I never thought I'd say—I'm filled with renewed belief in myself. Confidence in the way I want, and should, be treated by my family.

So much so that when my mother pulls me aside after brunch, I'm ready.

I'm out on the balcony, sipping on ginger and lemon tea and gazing over the postcard-picture-perfect snowy scene—and reflecting on Adam's hilariously puzzled facial expression when I presented him with a double-broken-footed, Seb-voodooed cookie. And that's when my mom chooses to step outside.

She walks up next to me, leaning on the wooden balcony railing, and follows my gaze. In the clearing beside the cabin, Jax and Seb are chopping firewood.

Wait. Did I say I was looking at the pretty snow?

Yeah, I was lying.

Seb is glorious to watch. Every time he swings the ax, muscles rippling, face angled in concentration, another butterfly escapes my stomach and flutters into my throat. Men don't have any business being this hot. *Nobody* has any business being this hot.

He splits the huge log clean in half, then wipes his brow with the sleeve of his sweater and turns to say something to a flannel-clad Jax. My brother laughs.

"He's really something," my mother says after a few beats of silence. "A professional athlete with a face like that. I'm sure he's a hot commodity."

"He is," I say dreamily. *And he's all miney mine mine...*

Well, for now.

But it's Christmas. Those details can wait until tomorrow.

Mom crosses her arms. "So, Madelyn. What's the catch?"

My eyes reluctantly move from Seb's immaculate wood-cutting form to my mother. She doesn't have a coat on, for some reason, and her lipstick is perfectly matched to her cardigan. Pearls adorn her neck and wrists, and she has heeled pumps on her feet.

She looks perfectly put-together... and poised for battle. I was beginning to wonder why she hadn't ambushed me, but now, I see that she was picking her moment. Both Seb and Jax— my allies in this fight—are out of earshot and otherwise occupied.

"No catch," I say lightly.

"And you expect me to believe that you're suddenly bliss-fully in love and married, when not a month ago, I spoke to you on the phone and you were reeling at the thought of even looking at Adam after what you did to him?"

"What *I* did to him?" I choke.

"Pulling that dreadful, childish move on television, of all things."

"Mother," I hiss. "He humiliated *me*. For the entire country to see."

"Oh, please." She waves a hand. "If you hadn't pushed him like you did, the whole thing with that stupid girl would've been

163

a brief affair that passed in a breath, and *you* would've been the woman with the ring on your finger."

I stare at her.

At first glance, she looks intimidating. A force to be reckoned with.

But my new perspective is allowing me to see past this for the first time in a while. Maybe ever. Now, I can see where her lipstick bleeds into the lines around her mouth. Where her stockings have a snag on the ankle. Where her powder hasn't fully covered the capillaries on her cheek.

My mother is deeply unhappy. She's stayed in a loveless marriage for years, just for the sake of appearances, and is choosing to have Christmas with her daughter's ex-boyfriend's family for the same reason... watching Elizabeth sit in my old place at the table.

It's a place I don't want anymore, but my mother wants so desperately, she'll cling to it until her hands are cold and lifeless.

I feel sorry for my mother, I realize.

"Does Dad cheat on you?" I ask softly, asking aloud for the first time something that I'm sure I've known, deep down, for a very long time. "Is that why you're justifying Adam cheating on me?"

Her laugh is full of mirth. "Cheating," she scoffs. "What an ugly word. I simply turn a blind eye to Richard's wanderings, and in return, I keep my place as his wife."

"You mean his access. Connections. Social circles." *His money*.

Mom sniffs in response, and turns away like she didn't hear me.

"Don't you want to be in love?" I press.

"Don't be so naive, Maddie," Mom says thinly, still looking in the other direction. "Love isn't always what matters most in relationships."

I thought I was ready for this conversation... but maybe I'll never be truly prepared to take on my mother. Her armor is too thick, her battle skills too honed.

All I can do is shake my head. For so long, I worried about what she thought. For so long, I molded myself into what Adam wanted me to be... I hardly stopped to think about what *I* wanted.

My mind flashes back to Seb's words from earlier: *You deserve to be celebrated. Deserve to be praised. Deserve to have all of those people look at you and talk to you with way more respect. And I'm here to help you get everything you deserve.*

I draw strength from his words, from his belief in me, and I turn to face my mother, head on. Stand up to my full height and look her dead in the eye. "Well, Mom, it seems that you and I have very different priorities in terms of what we want in relationships."

Mom sets her jaw, seeming a little taken aback by my response. Which is fair. I can't remember the last time I challenged her like this. "I just want to know when you're going to stop putting on this little *show* with Sebastian, and start focusing on getting Adam to see that you two should be together. "

"Adam and I *shouldn't* be together. The guy cheated on your daughter, and you're somehow defending *him*. I'm never going back to him, Mom. Even if that makes you upset. There's more to life than keeping up with the Joneses—or in this case, the Plumlees—and I feel sorry for you that you don't see that."

Saying this feels good.

I feel empowered. Lighter. *Freer.*

But sadly, instead of listening to a word of my wisdom, my mother sniffs. "Well, don't come crying to me when that hockey player breaks your heart."

"He won't," I insist.

There's a silence before Mom faces me again, an odd smile that I've never seen before twisting her lips. "You think I'm against you, but I'm not. I'm looking out for you. Adam's eyes

165

may have wandered, but he wouldn't have left you if you'd kept your head down and appeased him. Sebastian, on the other hand? He'll leave you when you don't suit his fancy anymore. Don't think I haven't looked him up online—the man is a perpetual bachelor, married to his job. No one can change a man like that. Not even you, Madelyn."

I try not to wince—I don't want to give her the satisfaction—but I'm sure she can see right through me. Some of my Christmas cheer and optimism begins to fade as her words ring true. Because no matter how this all started out, it's pretty clear now that I've let myself develop very real feelings for Seb.

"We're married," I protest, but the little voice in the back of my head—the one that only a few minutes ago was telling me not to worry about the details today—reminds me that she's right. Once Christmas with the family is over, Seb will have upheld his end of our agreement, and once his paperwork comes through, he'll be free to cut me loose.

Mom's face is scornful, yet something in my reaction must get through to her, because I now see some sadness behind her eyes.

"Don't let that rock on your finger fool you." Her voice has softened slightly. "Men like that are all the same. The second something that suits *his* goals better comes along. Look at how your biological father left us."

For the first time, in Mom's expression, I see the truth. That however misguided and warped her advice is, she really *is* trying to look out for me in her own strange way. She's been in my position: she fell for a man who walked away from her and left her alone with a child. She wouldn't be fooled twice, which is why she settled for security over love with Jax's dad. Why she's turned a blind eye to his indiscretions.

Because that hurt less than falling in love and risking another heartbreak.

"Guess it's a good thing that I'm Maddie's husband, and not

her father." The deep voice comes from behind me, and I turn to see Seb standing by the sliding doors to the balcony, his handsome face with a slightly strained smile. "And I also guess it's a good thing your daughter is her own person, and not you," he finishes softly.

Mom actually has the decency to look abashed.

"How long have you been standing there?" I ask, abject awkwardness scraping through me at the thought of his overhearing this screwed up mother-daughter conversation.

"Long enough," he says simply, giving me a quick look up and down—as if checking me for physical injuries—before turning back to Mom. "I'm not going to hurt Maddie," he tells her, his voice slightly thick. "I could never hurt Maddie."

Mom attempts another laugh, but it comes out sounding more like a cough. "You really mean that?" she taunts.

"I always say what I mean, and mean what I say."

His words give me life. His very presence gives me life. Because once again, he's shown up for me without me even having to say anything. He just *knows*.

Seb looks at Mom for a long time, unblinking and unyielding in his stance, and something must transpire between them, because eventually, Mom sucks in a breath through her nose. "Okay."

Seb nods back at her, and then he reaches for me. "Come on, Maddie. We've got a holiday to celebrate."

23

MADDIE

After the showdown with my mom on the balcony, the rest of Christmas Day is much less eventful. We play board games, eat until we're stuffed, and welcome multiple groups of carolers at the front door.

Seb is by my side the whole time, almost protective in the way he holds my hand, slips his arm around my waist, puts a reassuring palm on my thigh under the table when Adam brings up his and Elizabeth's upcoming nuptials over turkey and ham.

But at the same time, there are moments where he's not quite present. He's physically close, but his mind seems to be elsewhere. There's a tension to him that normally isn't there.

I don't blame him—it's an awful lot of high-intensity family time with a bunch of people who are total strangers to him. And he's gone above and beyond for me at every turn. Poor guy probably needs a mental break.

At around 8pm, everyone is cozy in the living room—save for Dot, who's gone to bed early after the day's excitement, and Jax, who's wandered back into the forest to play with wolves or whatever the hell he does in his free time. The parents are playing mahjong around the card table, Adam's waxing eloquent about some new type of confectioner's sugar he's importing from France or Zanzibar or something, and Elizabeth's pretending to listen while playing Wordle on her phone.

Which is the first thing I've found I have in common with her. Two things, in fact—I love Wordle, and often feigned interest in Adam's monologues when we were together.

Seb, though seated next to me on the sofa, still seems far away. His brows are drawn over his eyes and his mouth is twisted down in one corner as he stares out the window.

"Hey," I whisper to him, and he starts a little before his eyes meet mine. "Wanna sneak off and go in the hot tub or something?"

I can't quite believe I'm proposing this. The thought of Seb the Specimen of Human Perfection seeing me, Maddie Grainger, in a bikini, is a little frightening.

But after today, I'm choosing to believe in myself.

His eyes darken at my suggestion, making my stomach fill with butterflies once again. "Hell yeah, I do."

And if that enthusiastic response doesn't quell my worries, I don't know what in the world would.

We manage to creep out of the living room together without garnering more than an annoyed mid-monologue glance from Adam.

Upstairs, I dig two plush robes out of the closet, and then grab my swimsuit. "I'll get changed in the bathroom and meet you out there."

That trademark Seb smirk is back in place. "You can get changed wherever you want, Maddie."

"Perv." I swat him on the arm with a giggle and then duck out to the bathroom.

"Can't a man admire his wife's body anymore?" he calls after me.

This makes me really laugh.

In the little hallway bathroom, I change into my bikini. It's not the sexiest bikini in the world, but it's cute—midnight blue with criss-cross straps on the back and little bows on the sides of the bottoms.

I scoop my hair up into a bun on top of my head, pull on my robe, and pad downstairs to the side deck, where the hot tub's located.

I slide open the door and squeak as the frigid air fills my lungs. Seb's already soaking in the tub, sitting contentedly in the billowing steam and laughing at my current grave peril. "Hurry up, slowpoke! You'll freeze!"

I dart across the deck—skipping as carefully as possible over the icy bits—then throw off my robe and practically jump in.

"Brrrrr," I breathe as the steamy water stings pleasantly on my cold skin. I position myself at the far end of the tub, away from Seb, and sit on my hands. The man looks good enough to eat right now—all wet and shirtless, his hair tousled and damp, his cheeks pink from the heat. I don't want to accidentally maul him like I'm a hungry grizzly bear or something.

Seb catches me checking him out, and smiles lazily. "Hello, Mrs. Slater."

"Mr. Slater." I sigh happily. This is miles better than sitting in the living room. The sky above is a black velvet blanket with a million stars woven across it. The crisp air smells like pine and snow and chlorine. And Seb is looking at me with a heat in his eyes that makes my lower belly feel fizzy.

As the steam clears a little, I catch a glimpse of his swim shorts under the water, and have to laugh. They're canary yellow with pink donuts all over them. He follows my gaze and grins. "My Homer Simpson shorts."

"That explains nothing."

"Okay, if you want the full story... I got them at Universal Studios a couple years back when I was there with my family. I flew them down to see me when I was playing an away game, and I took them to Universal the next day. My younger brother loved the shorts, so we bought matching pairs."

"You have a brother?"

"Two, actually. One's a high school hockey coach back in the little mountain town where I grew up, and the other plays in the European hockey league."

"Runs in the family, huh?"

"You could say that. My dad is obsessed with hockey, but growing up, he could never afford to play. And so, when my brothers and I were younger—and were clearly as hockey-obsessed as he was—he made a ton of sacrifices so we could have the opportunities he didn't." Seb smiles a little wistfully. "My parents are really great."

I put two and two together as I think about how distant Seb seemed all afternoon. "You're missing your family today. Because it's the holidays."

"We actually haven't spent Christmas together in years. Hockey's been my priority for a really long time. I've been lucky to get as far as I have in my career, lucky that I can financially support my parents to thank them for everything they've done for me. "

"But don't you miss being close with your family?"

"I do. I guess family and relationships have just... taken a backseat. I've always been focused on my next goal."

"That sounds stressful."

He looks at me then, and it's a long, loaded look. "I was furious when I overheard your mom talking to you today. The way she puts you down makes me angry. And the way Adam walks all over you makes me wanna punch him in the face. I dunno, maybe I have anger issues." He snorts a laugh. "But I'm so impressed by you, I can't help but go on defense for you. I mean, you showed up for your family Christmas. You could've said no, told them to go screw themselves... but instead, you came. Meanwhile, my family loves and supports me—sacrificed so much for me—and in my trying to prove that it was all worth

171

it... I think I ended up putting hockey first to the point that I hardly ever see them. Or talk to them."

He runs a hand through his hair and tugs on the ends. "I realized today that I've been trying to make them proud, but I think I ended up being selfish in my pursuit of that."

I shake my head. Slide a little closer to him. "You're not. And you know how I know that? Because I initially thought that you'd been distant all day because you needed to mentally check out and take some brainspace for yourself... but here you were, thinking about other people."

He pulls a face. "And how much I suck at keeping them close."

"You can change that." I shrug. "You're a good person, Seb. You're thoughtful. You listen—like, really listen. You care about people. You're already generous and kind with your money, and you just have to learn to be generous with your time, too. Figure out how to make space for more meaningful things in your life than only hockey."

He swallows. Nods. "You're right, Maddie."

"I'm always right. Never forget that."

"C'mere." He wraps his hand around my arm and pulls me none too gently along the slippery seat until I'm right next to him. Like, if I was any closer, I'd be in his freaking lap. "That's better."

"Hey!" I splash him indignantly, glad that the mood lifts as he comes back to the present with me.

He shoots me a devious grin. "I'm making space for a meaningful thing in my life."

My heart jumps into my throat.

That face.

That voice.

Those words.

It's too much for a red-blooded woman to take, I tell you.

"Still!" I manage to force out, trying with everything in me

172

to seem as unaffected as possible right now. "You can't just manhandle me like that, you big—"

"Sexy manly man?" he interrupts, that cheeky grin of his spreading wide. "World-class hockey player? Stellar husband of the highest order, purveyor of the happiest, most satisfied wife in the entire world..."

"I was going to say you big jerk!" I laugh. "But now, I'm changing it to you big, cocky a-hole."

"How dare you talk about your husband like that," he responds with a mocking wag of his finger.

Quick as a cat, I grab said finger and use my other hand to send a wave of water at his face.

He roars like a lion, throwing his head back, and then pounces on me, tickling me as I squirm and shriek and splash around. The hot tub water is flying in every direction and my bun has come unraveled to create a lovely drowned-rat look, but I don't care. He pulls me onto his lap, his chest to my back, and his fingers move over my slippery body for a few dreamy moments before he locks both my arms in one big hand in front of me. But I kick at his shins and he relents, clearly letting me have the upper hand before those arms wrap around my midsection in a bear hug, effectively pinning me against him.

We're still for a few moments, pressed against each other and breathing hard and fast. His skin is hot, and I feel his heart thump against my back. He puts his mouth close to my ear. So close that I can hear the hitch in his breathing, see his words curl like clouds through the night air. "You fight good... for a girl."

Of course, this is fighting talk, and it's immediately on again.

And oh my gosh, who knew that hot tub wrestling with a hockey player was on my sexy bucket list? Not me, I tell you.

But in a matter of moments, it's shot straight to the top.

It feels good to be this close to Seb, this free and uninhibited. I have more fun with Seb than with anyone else, but he simultaneously makes me feel like my heart is ablaze and my veins are pumping full of hot, liquid *want*.

And from the way he looks at me... touches me... I think he might feel the same way towards me. Which is a wild thought in itself.

I whirl around and he catches my hips, pulling me onto his lap once again, but this time, facing him. We're scuffling and wrestling and laughing, our wet limbs tangled, our hands sliding over shoulders and torsos, and the sounds of our laughter filling the night.

Then, a throat clears.

We both freeze—like we're kids with our hands caught in the candy jar—and look at each other before turning towards the noise. That's when I spot the shadowy figures of Adam and Elizabeth peering out an open window upstairs like a pair of weirdos.

Seb sighs with exasperation and touches his forehead to mine. His hands are still on my hips, holding me in place on his lap.

"Guess we were being too loud," he says softly.

"I didn't realize this cabin had quiet hours," I whisper back. "Let's just pretend we don't see them?"

"Deal," he responds immediately, his thumbs gently stroking the soft bare skin of my stomach. "I can't see from here. Are they still looking?"

I check. "Yup."

"I think they're jealous," he mutters into my ear, which makes me laugh and shiver all at once.

"Well, my mom was pretty sure earlier that we were putting on a show," I say, boldly sliding my arms around his neck. "So maybe it's good for Adam to see us together so he doesn't think the same."

"They want a show?" His hands tighten on my hips. "Let's give them a show, love."

And with that, his mouth is on mine. Hot and needy and sexy and oh-so-perfect.

Exactly the way I hoped—okay, *fantasized*—that Sebastian Slater would kiss.

This kiss fills all of my senses, and Adam and Elizabeth are soon entirely forgotten. The only thing I can possibly be aware of in this instance is this.

Him.

The kiss is soft and sweet for a few tantalizing moments, before it turns scalding. I moan into Seb's mouth as his hands expertly move into my hair, one tangling at the nape of my neck and the other dancing down the ridges of my spine. He slants his mouth and deepens the kiss, and when his tongue slides against mine, my whole body arches at the sensation. Prickling shivers run over my skin as I kiss him back with everything in me, completely lost in him.

Our surroundings only heighten everything that's unfolding between us—the cold sting of the wind makes my lips all the more sensitive, the searing heat of the water makes my body feel more on fire. Seb's fingers tighten on my waist, digging deliciously into my bare skin like they're holding on for dear life.

Fueled by this, my hands begin to explore his body, moving over the incredible hills and valleys of his shoulders and chest, my thumb swiping across his nipple and fingernails scratching against his sides, rewarding me with a throaty groan that turns my insides molten.

Who even am I right now?

I have no idea. But I know I've *never* been kissed like this.

His mouth breaks away from mine and a noise of protest escapes me, but it's not for long because his stubbled jaw soon scrapes along mine. He kisses down the column of my throat, his lips fluttering over my pulse for a heartstopping moment before he nips at my skin with his teeth. Soothes the same spot with a kiss.

His fingertips lightly graze over the sides of my bikini bottoms, tangling in the strings, and between kisses and shallow breaths, he murmurs against my skin, "These little bows have been driving me crazy since the moment you got in here. Do you have any idea how hot you are, Maddie? You drive me wild."

I swear I've never heard anything sexier in my life.

I've never *felt* sexier. More desirable. More *wanted*.

Like a woman possessed, I tangle my hands in his hair, attempting to bring his head back up towards me so I can put my mouth back on his. I tug frantically, and he gives a little laugh, looking right into the depths of my soul with those blue-gray eyes of his.

"What?" he teases.

I make an impatient noise in response.

"Is this what you want, Maddie?" He moves to cup my face, and this time, when he kisses me, it's slow and sensual and sweet... and so utterly sexy, I can hardly bear it.

"Yes," I say without breaking the kiss.

"Good," he responds. Holding me tighter. Kissing me deeper in a way that I hope will never, ever end—

"MADELYN LOUISE GRAINGER!"

I spring away, almost falling backwards off Seb's lap, as my mother's shrill and insistent voice lands like a bucket of ice water to the face.

Seb's eyes are a dazed. He swears. "I legit forgot where we were."

I'm breathing so hard, it takes me a moment before I can find my voice. "Me, too. I got a little carried away."

I look over my shoulder to see Mom standing in the doorway of the deck, arms crossed. I'd bet anything that Adam had something to do with her coming out here right now, looking for me. But I'm a grown, married woman doing nothing wrong...

So why do I feel like I'm a teenager, tipsy off a wine cooler and caught making out in the backseat of my car?

Honestly, I feel more drunk than I did that freaking night in Vegas. Seb's kisses have got my whole head twisted.

"Madelyn, come inside this minute. We're starting a cribbage tournament and you are expected to take part!"

"Oh." I breathe a sigh of relief, my eyes flickering back to Seb.

But my Mother Dearest isn't quite done: "And acting like a floozy out here for the entire world to see is not a good look, either!"

Ah. There it is.

Seb chuckles. "Tsk tsk. The *entire world*, Madelyn."

I look around our very desolate surroundings of trees, forest, and snow. Seriously, there's only one paved road leading to this cabin in the woods, and there's not even another building for miles around. "What on earth was I thinking?" I ask, feigning shock.

Seb locks his hands behind his head as he looks at me. "Say sorry to the families of elk in the woods whose eyes you've scarred with your rampant floozying," he says wickedly, quiet enough that it's for my ears only.

I have to laugh. "Sorry, elk."

"Good." Seb's eyes are dancing. "And now, apologize to the bears."

"Wait. Aren't the bears hibernating right now? You're Canadian—shouldn't you know that?"

The look he gives me sears me to the core. "I think we woke them up."

I flush, my mind flashing back to how... *enthusiastic* that kiss was. All at once, I'm embarrassed and excited and hoping we get to do that again ASAP.

"Madelyn, you are being exceptionally rude!" Mom calls again, her voice sharp and impatient.

I cringe. "She's so pissed. She, and probably Richard by extension, are not gonna let us hear the end of this."

"That kiss was well worth their wrath to me," Sebastian responds with a smile. It's a beautiful, dazzling smile—one that signals that he cares not one iota about what everyone else thinks, because he's totally, solely, wholly focused on me. "And for you... worth it?"

I grin back, not even having to think about it. "Worth it."

24

SEB

The morning after Christmas, I'm on top of the world.

It snowed overnight, powdering a fresh sprinkling of fluffy white over what is already a winter wonderland, and my boots crunch in the snow as I return to the cabin with a large takeout cup in my hand. Maddie isn't a coffee drinker—opting for tea instead—and I've noticed that she has a specific preference for peppermint tea. There are no mint tea bags at the cabin, so I walked into the village to get her a cup.

I took the time alone to give my family a long overdue phone call. Wish them a Merry Christmas. Tell them that I miss them and love them. I can't believe I ever thought I had to put hockey above everything else, to the point where it's been to the detriment of my relationships with the people that mean so much to me. I know that my intentions were good, and I wanted to make sure that the sacrifices my parents made were worth it, but along the way somewhere, I became driven to the point that I ended up unnecessarily distancing myself from the people who supported me the most.

I ended the call by promising my mom that I'll come to Canada to see her the next time I get a few days off, and I intend to make good on my promise. I also reminded them all that they're welcome to visit me in Atlanta at anytime, that I'd always be happy to see them.

My priorities have been totally out of whack for awhile now. And being with Maddie has helped me realize that.

Speaking of Maddie, we've planned to hike some of the trails around the cabin later with Jax, and I can't wait to hear what's sure to be a hilarious running commentary about how much she hates hiking and The Great Outdoors.

I'd bet anything she'll look cute as all hell bundled up in her big, fluffy jacket, large snow boots, and thick tuque—*beanie*.

Being in Aspen at this time of year reminds me of being home in Canada. Not just the snow, but the abundance of pine trees, the crisp, chilly air that feels thin in your lungs and makes you want to inhale deeper, the expansive mountain vistas that provide a stunning backdrop for the people skating on frozen ponds.

Skating... Haven't thought much about *that* lately.

In fact, this is the longest I've gone in years without a skate... or a conditioning workout at the gym that's aimed at improving my speed, strength or agility on the ice.

As much as I'm enjoying this time away with Maddie, I'll admit that I'm excited to fly back to Atlanta tomorrow morning. Excited to have my skates strapped on by afternoon for practice. Excited to see the guys and hear all about their Christmases. I'm sure Jimmy, at least, has some ridiculous stories.

And then, I'm excited to come home to Maddie afterwards.

To see that freckle-faced, green-eyed, beautiful girl smile at me every damn day.

I have no idea what the future holds for us, but I know that last night marked something changing. I don't remember ever feeling this way about someone—almost giddy with happiness.

After the wild kiss in the hot tub, Maddie and I spent the rest of the evening acting in a much more family-friendly manner, playing cribbage while I rested one hand on her thigh under the card table. Adam and Elizabeth—who pretty clearly were the ones who sent Maddie's mother to interrupt us—sat stiffly, side by side, across the table. Something certainly seemed to be simmering beneath the surface for my old friend Eugene.

At the end of the night, we went to our bedroom and Maddie tore down the Great Wall of Slater with one fell swoop of her hand. Not wanting to take things too far too fast—and also perfectly content playing that incredible kiss over and over in my mind—I drew her close and just held her. Spent all night spooning her and sleeping curled around her body, listening to the beat of her heart and the stutter of her breaths.

It's barely 8am, and I'm already excited to sleep next to her again tonight.

I walk up the driveway with both of my hands clasped around Maddie's tea to fend off the cold. When I reach the front door, I open and shut it behind me as quietly as possible, in case some people are still sleeping.

Actually, everyone might still be sleeping. The cabin is quiet as can be.

I unlace my boots and am about to bring the tea up to Maddie in bed when I hear voices in the kitchen.

"—none of your business, frankly."

"Of course, it's my business!"

It's Maddie and Adam. I move closer, listening intently, and my fist involuntarily balls at my side.

If he *dares* say even a single thing to hurt her...

"How's that?" Maddie's voice is steady. Calm. In total control. I don't hear a single waver or shake in her voice as she squares up to her ex, and I'm so damn proud of her.

"I wasn't planning on giving Elizabeth the damn ring!" Adam half yells. "And us breaking up on that stupid baking show forced my hand to propose to her before that episode aired, or I'd look like a total fool!"

"Well, then why did you buy her a ring in the first place?!"

I snicker. *You tell him, Maddie.*

"I didn't." Adam exhales heavily. "It's a family heirloom. My mom gave it to me a few months before the show filmed to... give to you."

"And instead, you cheated on me and announced it on freaking television."

"I wasn't happy!" Adam thunders. "Elizabeth was there for me when you—"

Maddie cuts him off with a bitter laugh. "When I WHAT? Supported your business ventures? Was a loyal, committed girl-friend? Tried to help you get more of a fanbase by getting us on the show?"

"You never looked at me the way you look at him!" Adam suddenly blurts angrily.

I set the takeout cup of tea on a sideboard and move closer. I can practically hear her eyes roll. "So this isn't about you and me. It's about Seb. You jealous or something?"

"I'm just a bit confused as to how you made this happen. How someone like *Sebastian Slater* could end up with my sloppy seconds."

I've officially heard enough.

Before I can think about it, I'm bursting through the door and striding over to Adam, who's leaning against the kitchen counter. My blood pounds in my temples and my chest constricts with rage. So much so that I'm almost forgetting I'm at another family's cabin for the holidays, and not facing off against some goon on the ice.

I wrap my hands around Adam's arms and shove him, hard as I can, into the refrigerator, which wobbles as I pin him there. My hands fist in his shirt as I hiss in my most low, vicious voice, "Don't you ever speak to my wife like that again, understand?"

"I-I-I-understand!" Adam spits out.

But I'm going to need more than his understanding.

"Apologize," I demand.

"I'm s-sorry, Maddie."

I turn to look at Maddie for the first time. She's standing there, hair messy, still in her flannel PJs, and staring at us with her mouth open. The sight of her immediately calms me so that I can see through the red haze.

I release my hold on Adam abruptly, worried that I'm scaring her. He loses his balance and stumbles slightly, and he cowers as he looks between us. "I made a mistake, saying that."

I press my pointer finger into his chest. "Damn right you made a mistake. Letting this woman get away was the stupidest thing you could've ever done. But I guess I should be grateful that you're such an idiot. Because if you hadn't screwed up with her, she wouldn't be with me."

And with that, I grab Maddie's hand and march us out of the kitchen, leaving a blubbering Adam in our wake.

The second we're out of the room, she makes a squeaking noise, and I'm scared of what I'm going to find on her face. Horror? Repulsion? Or worse... fear?

But she's smiling.

"Oh my gosh, I think he might've wet himself. Or worse. You, quite literally, scared the crap out of him!" Maddie trails off into peals of laughter and I want to kiss that pretty mouth right here, right now.

"I was worried I took it a bit far," I admit sheepishly.

She wraps her hand around my bicep and squeezes. "Well, you were certainly my muscle back there. I was thinking of smacking him upside the head with a frying pan when he started into that, but what you did was *way* better."

"Are you... okay?"

She shakes her head with a laugh. "Fine. I don't care what Adam thinks anymore or what he says about me. And let me tell you, that is the most freeing thing to happen to me in a very long time. So thank you. You have helped me see that, Mr. Hockey Man."

"You're welcome," I say. With every day that I grow closer to Maddie—get to know all the little details about her that make her who she is—the more I hope that this feels as real to her as it does to me.

Scratch that, the more I *know* that this feels as real to her as it does to me.

I smile as I spot her tea still on the sideboard, going cold. "Oh. I went out and bought you some peppermint tea..."

She throws her arms around me in a hug. "Has anyone ever told you that you're the most thoughtful person ever?"

I lean into her embrace, pulling her closer and breathing in the vanilla scent of her hair. "You did. Yesterday."

"Well, I'm saying it again." She's all happy and giddy when she pulls away. "I'm so glad you're here, Seb."

"Me too, Maddie."

Because somehow, things have shifted and changed. Somehow, since I drunkenly proposed to this incredible, hilarious, minorly insane and totally beautiful woman, she's become one of the most important people in my life. And somehow, in the space of a few days here at the cabin, I know that this marriage is the realest thing to ever happen to me.

Me too.

Okay, so. I would have never, ever said that I was the type of girl to be turned on by macho manliness. Or male dominance. Or violence.

I dated a pastry artist for over a decade, for goodness sakes.

But then, I went and married a hockey player.

And *ho-ly*, I am still tingling hours after the confrontation as I replay Seb's huge, hulking form filling the kitchen doorway. The way his big hand tightened on the frame like he was trying to rip off a chunk of it as he assessed the scene in front of him, then wasted no time throwing down for me with Adam.

The man looked like he was out for blood, and I'm not gonna lie, it was quite possibly the sexiest thing I've ever seen in my life.

Actually, second sexiest thing. First place goes to the way he looked at me after we kissed in the hot tub.

Or the way he stroked my hair last night and kissed the side of my forehead before I drifted off to sleep.

In any case, one thing's for sure: I've got it bad for Sebastian Slater.

"Eeek!" I shriek as I—completely lost in thought and certainly not looking where I'm going—step onto an icy patch on the snow-covered hiking trail and almost go flying into a dense patch of frozen pine trees and pokey bushes.

Seb, who's walking right behind me, has me steadied and upright in moments. So quickly, in fact, that I can't work out if my erratic heartbeat is from my almost-plunge to the ground, or the woodsy, masculine scent coming off his warm, flannel-clad body.

Jax turns and takes in the pair of us with disinterest. "Watch your step."

"You watch your step!"

"Sick burn. Really got me there, Mads."

I kick snow at him. My brother's just bugging me 'coz he doesn't believe in romance (ergo, he's all aloney lonely on our little winter hike today), while I have a knight in flannel to save me from falling on my butt.

"It's becoming more and more evident that you two can't possibly be blood related." Seb points towards Jax—dressed in a sporty (read: mildly insane) waterproof, windproof, everything-proof winter parka and hiking boots with crampons on the bottom—and then, at me—wearing a very cute, very thin pair of slate-gray leggings, ankle boots, and a sweet button-up peacoat whose designer clearly cared more about fashion than warmth.

Meanwhile, Seb is somehow a mix of the two of us, wearing a thick, flannel jacket-shirt with lumberjack vibes, dark jeans, and proper winter boots. Plus, he's wearing his beanie again—which he ADORABLY refers to as a "tuque" in his native language of Canadian—and he looks good enough to eat.

Jax chuckles. "Well, if I can give you one piece of advice to survive being married to my sister, it's to never, ever take the woman camping."

"I sense a story here." Seb smiles as we step off the snowy path and into a clearing.

After a couple of hours spent walking (and, in my case, slipping and sliding) along the hiking trails close to our cabin, we're at the edge of the village now. A little relieved thrill fills me as I make out the distant sounds of laughter and caroling, mingled with the smells of hot cocoa and wood fires.

As we continue our walk towards the town center, my brother, of course, wastes no time launching into a long, drawn-out and entirely *un*hilarious story about how I lost all of my sensibilities and decided to go camping with him one time.

The only time. For very good reason.

I didn't *want* to venture into the backcountry—the Jax life is not the life for me, and I value things like flushing toilets, and running water, and, yanno, having actual chairs to sit on. So, we loaded up Jax's old VW campervan with all of the supplies I thought I could possibly need, and drove up to Cloudland Canyon State Park to stay in a campground. Which was, actually, really beautiful.

Until nighttime came and the campground was pitch black and I was bursting to pee. My phone was dead and I couldn't find a flashlight to walk to the campsite bathrooms, so I decided to do the smart and reasonable thing: creep around the back of the van, and just... be at one with nature.

What I hadn't factored in was the RV parked in the campsite next to us being equipped with a motion sensor light. Which turned on, blinding me entirely, while the occupants came rushing out to find a very full moon shining back at them.

Needless to say, I shall never go camping again.

Also needless to say, Jax loves to whip out this story whenever he thinks I'm in need of a little healthy embarrassment.

See... revenge really does run in the family.

But between my brother and I, at least, it's always good-natured.

Seb is laughing so hard at this point that he's crying, tears leaking from the corners of his crinkled eyes.

"That is absolutely priceless. I am so glad I know this now." He wipes away a tear, grinning at me like a maniac before his eyes grow wicked. "And to return the favor, would you like to hear the story of how Maddie and I met?"

"You wouldn't dare!" I shriek.

"I would love nothing more," Jax says. "Please, enlighten me."

"Well." Seb gives me a look through heavy-lidded eyes that makes my heart pound. "It all started in a men's public bathroom which Maddie happened to be frequenting."

Jax is already howling. I mock-scowl at both of them, leveling my pointer finger. "I'm not sure I approve of this little budding bromance."

But I'm lying. Seeing Seb and Jax get along like this is making my heart soar.

Seb's about to launch into the story, but his phone chimes and interrupts him. He fishes it out of his coat pocket, then frowns at the screen. "I'd better take this, it's my agent. I'll meet you guys at that cafe on the corner?" He gestures in the direction of the sweet little bakery and coffee shop where he picked up my tea this morning.

"Sounds good."

He gives me a lingering smile before swiping his thumb over his phone screen and walking away, his posture suddenly rigid.

I watch him walk away (believe me, it's a pretty sight) until Jax waves one gloved hand in front of my face. "Hello? Earth to Maddie."

I snap out of my butt trance. Which is, apparently, now a thing.

"Sorry. Was..."

"Admiring the view," Jax supplies wryly.

I shove him.

We walk into the coffee shop and join the line, and my icy cheeks begin to defrost. And after a few minutes, I realize that Jax is staring at me.

"What?" I say, my hand rising to my cheek. "Is there something on my face?"

"No, I..." Jax sighs. "Ugh. You know I'm no good at this serious, heart to heart stuff, but I'm just... happy you're happy. With someone who's not Adam. Someone way better than Adam, actually. Like, not even in the same league as Adam."

"Thanks, Jax." I'm oddly touched. "I *am* happy."

In fact, I don't remember the last time I was *this* happy.

"I'll admit. I was very, very skeptical at first. But he looks at you like... like everything you say is the most interesting thing in the world."

"Really?"

Jax raises his eyebrows cheekily. "Yeah, I don't get it either."

"Har har," I drawl, crossing my arms.

Jax holds up his hands in surrender. "I just mean that he's clearly crazy about you. And I know you've always been a romantic. And misguided as I believe that to be, I'm glad that you've found someone who truly loves you. Weird as the whole sudden-marriage thing still is."

I glance through the window of the coffee shop at Seb, who's still on the phone and pacing. A blush crawls up my face. *Could that beautiful man out there* really *be crazy about me?*

The notion floats through my mind, sweet and fluffy as cotton candy. I don't have the words to reply to this (actually really sweet) sentiment from my love-hating brother, so I give him a spontaneous little hug. He squeezes me for a second before letting go, and I'm left feeling entirely warm and fuzzy inside, like I've curled up in front of the fire in my pajamas with a cup of cocoa and a good book.

"Not weird," I tell my brother. "And you should try it sometime."

"What, marrying a hockey player out of the blue?"

I shove my brother. "No, you goon. Finding someone special."

189

"I don't need anyone special, I already have Edna."

"I am going to be entirely unsurprised if I turn on the TV one day, and you're on that show about people who fall in love with their cars."

"Edna's a van, not a car. And that would then make *two* of us in the family who've been embarrassed on national television." I glare at him and he relents. "Too soon?"

I bite my lip, considering this for a few moments, then shake my head. Because the whole *Incident* that inspired this little revenge plot couldn't be further from my mind.

In fact, the revenge plot itself couldn't be further from my mind... all I'm thinking about right now is Seb.

"Sorry, sorry." As if he could sense my thoughts, Seb suddenly appears, lighting up the room with his smile. There's an energy about him that I can't quite read. "That took forever."

"Everything okay?" I lean towards him, tilting my head so that it rests on his shoulder.

"Everything's great." Seb gives my arm a little reassuring squeeze. "Let me get this one. Jax, what're you having?"

Jax takes a step backwards. "Actually, I'm gonna bounce. Go for a real hike and let you two have some quality time together."

"You sure?" I ask. Seb echoes the sentiment.

Jax nods and rubs his hands together. "Definitely. You kids have fun."

And with that, he's gone.

"He okay?" Seb asks, looking after him.

I shrug. "The mountains were calling, I guess."

"Your brother's a bit of a lone wolf, huh?"

"That's one word for it."

Seb laughs and wraps an arm around me. "Well, I'm not complaining," he says in a low voice, his breath warm by my ear as he pulls me close. "Because this means I get you all to myself for the rest of the afternoon."

Like I said, this Christmas keeps getting better and better.

"This can't get any *worse!*" I groan a few hours later, as I take another frozen step forward and stumble. My teeth are clacking together and my socks are soaked in my boots. It feels like hypothermia is about to set in at any second.

"I mean, it could." Seb smirks, putting his hand under my arm to steady me. I have no idea how he's still in good spirits—I'm two missteps short of curling up on the ground in the fetal position and waiting for the bears to find me when they wake up next spring.

Which might sound dramatic—fine, *definitely* sounds dramatic—but ho-lyyy it's cold out here. Even with Seb's coat over mine. Which he insisted on giving me, thoughtful guy that he is.

"You're right," I mutter. "Maybe those families of elk and bears and moose and whatever else lingers in the woods will come out for revenge because we disturbed them last night. Snowstorm be damned."

It came out of nowhere. It was so pleasant when we walked to the village with Jax earlier—not a cloud in the sky and the sun shining warm on our faces.

After getting a couple of hot chocolates at the cafe, Seb and I wandered around the village for ages, ducking in and out of candy stores and handmade gift stores and bookstores. Stopped so that Seb could sign autographs for a bunch of pre-teen boys who recognized him. It was the sweetest thing ever, watching him interact with his fans. Not only was he patient and kind, posing for a bunch of pictures, but he showed interest in each of the boys, asking what hockey positions they played.

It was a perfect afternoon, which faded into a perfect evening. So perfect, in fact, that we decided to have dinner at a cozy little bistro together. It was a long dinner, complete with dessert. We really wanted to make the most of our last night in Aspen sans Adam and the family drama.

But it all went wrong after dinner.

Though it was already dark, we decided to walk back to the cabin along the forest trail instead of taking the main road, like normal, logical people would.

Which was fine until it started snowing. And snowing. And snowing. Add some howling wind and exceedingly diminished visibility resulting in a wrong turn or three, and you've got yourself more of a *Blair Witch Project* vibe than a Hallmark *Snowed Inn For Christmas* feel (double N intended, because there's ALWAYS an Inn when it's a Hallmark holiday special).

Now, Seb must sense my plummeting optimism, because he applies a little pressure to my elbow, halting me in my tracks so he can hug me close. "Don't worry, Mads. I've got you. We can't be far now."

"I thought I knew where I was going," I say dully with a shake of my head. "Thought I might have gleaned something from having an absolute mountain man of a brother..."

He takes my hand. Squeezes. "One step at a time, love. We'll get there. We're fine."

I feel entirely responsible for this. Yet Seb is the one comforting *me*. And he doesn't even have a freaking coat on.

And so, we trudge on. Hand in hand, me stumbling every so often. My phone battery died not too long into using the flashlight, and we're down to 15% on Seb's phone. Seb also doesn't have the number of anyone in my family, so it's not like we can call and let someone know what's happened.

They probably think we're still in the village, all cozy-like in front of a fireplace, drinking hot apple cider...

I think my toes have frostbite.

But Seb is my anchor in the storm, steadfast and unwavering and making light of the situation to keep my spirits up. I have no idea if he's internally freaking out, but if he is, he's doing a perfect job hiding it. If he wasn't here right now, I'd be terrified instead of just angry as a pissed-off trash panda whose trash has been taken away at my dumb decision to take the road less traveled. Which anyone who has studied the poem knows is not necessarily the better choice.

Finally, after what feels like an eternity, the trees seem to become more sparse.

And then, I see it!

A little light, in the distance.

"Aghhhhhhhhh," I gargle like a gargoyle, my mouth practically foaming with excitement.

"We made it!" The relief in Seb's voice is palpable—maybe he was more worried than he was letting on.

We turn to each other, and his blue eyes glint in the faint light, before he scoops me into his arms like a groom carrying his new bride over the threshold for the first time. He breaks into a jog and I fling my arms around his neck, squealing and protesting that I'm too heavy, but he's totally surefooted as he runs, holding me like I weigh nothing.

By the time we get to the front door of the cabin, we're both breathless and laughing with relief. We step inside, and it's warm. Oh so warm. And quiet.

"Everyone must've gone to bed?" I wonder aloud as I slip off my wet boots and double layers of coat. My hands and feet are like blocks of ice, and my nose and ears hurt like hell from the cold.

Seb stops unlacing his boots for a moment and glances at his phone. "I guess it is after 11pm."

"What?! We were lost for freaking ages. We can never, ever let Jax know about this. He'd probably enroll me in some terrible wilderness survival course that would end up killing me."

Seb's mouth twitches in quiet laughter, then his eyes move over me for a few moments, the corners crinkling in concern.

"Come on." He reaches for my hand. "Speaking of not keeping you alive, we need to get you warmed up as quickly as possible."

Seb leads me to the kitchen, grabbing a blanket from the hallway closet as we go. He wraps me in the blanket almost tenderly, squeezing me tight before pointing to a chair and ordering, "Sit."

"Bossy much?"

"Woman, do you want hot tea or not?"

"Want!" I immediately relent, dropping my butt into the chair.

We grin at each other for a moment, and then I grab for the candy bowl in the middle of the kitchen table and tuck into the Lindor truffles. All the while watching Seb busy himself with filling the kettle and placing it on the stove.

"Aren't you cold, too?" I ask around a mouthful of chocolate.

"Canadian." He shrugs. "We handle the cold much better than you wussy southerners."

"I would protest, but I think you might be right. You're a veritable yeti."

"The sexiest yeti that ever was," he responds blithely, turning back to the stove.

I reach into the candy bowl, grab another truffle, and throw it at him.

Without even turning around, he puts a hand out and catches it. Unwraps it and pops it in his mouth without missing a beat.

"How do you do that?!" I gasp.

"I keep telling you, Maddie. I'm an excellent multitasker... among other things."

The smile he gives me makes me feel meltier than the truffle in my mouth.

"I like being your wife, Seb," I find myself saying. Because I

194

do. I love seeing him like this, learning all the secret sides of him that nobody else gets to see.

"And I love being your husband, Maddie," he replies simply. Casually. Like he didn't just seamlessly weave a four-letter word into that sentence that makes my heart thump in double time.

When I meet his eyes, the heat blazing in them is enough to scald my entire body.

I am beyond smitten with everything about Sebastian Slater.

Seb pours two steaming mugs of tea and I wrap my fingers around my mug until my palms are tingling. Seb, meanwhile, takes a seat across from me at the kitchen table, letting one big hand rest on my thigh. It might be the contrast of cold to heat, or the adrenaline from almost spending the night as elk food, but the place where we connect feels almost painful with electricity. We don't say much as we sip at our drinks, but I'm blisteringly aware of him, of how hard my heart's beating, of where his eyes pass over me as though to make sure I'm warming up and doing okay.

After a couple minutes, Seb's blue eyes meet mine, and there's a flicker in his gaze that doesn't look unlike stoking a fire. "Should we head to bed?" he asks quietly, in this low voice that probably isn't meant to be nearly as sexy as it is.

All I can manage is a nod.

With our mugs half-full, we creep up the stairs, and once we're safely in our room, I flick on the bedside lamp as he sets the mugs down. He immediately sheds his sweatshirt, which is damp from the falling snow. His shirt comes off with it, leaving him bare chested.

Our eyes catch.

Suddenly, I don't feel cold at all anymore.

Instead, I notice the pebbles on his taut skin and I take a step towards him. Run my hands up and down his arms in an attempt to warm him up. Just as he tried (and succeeded) at warming *me* up.

"I don't know what I would've done out there without you, Seb. What I would've done without you on this trip." I shake my head. "I believed that being here would be unbearable, but you made it... okay. Made everything okay. Helped me see things that I've never noticed before, especially in myself. I don't know what I'd do if you weren't here."

He tilts his head slightly and there's a beat of silence as his blue eyes meet mine. "I don't know what I'd do without you in general, Maddie."

His voice is low and husky, and his eyes become hooded and hungry, as his hands move to my waist. He wraps them around my middle possessively, pulling me close.

And I'm suddenly so overwhelmed—with what I feel for him, with his comforting, sexy scent, with the feeling of his strong arms around me—that I can't hold it in anymore.

"Sebastian..." I say, and his name comes out like a plea as his mouth finds mine. His lips are cold at first, sending shivers through me, but as we kiss, the heat builds between us like a fire set alight. It's a perfect kiss, soft and slow and deliberate, yet just as passionate—maybe even more so—than our makeout in the hot tub last night.

Something about this feels... deeper. More meaningful.

He's got me.

One of his hands moves to caress my face, the back of his knuckles dragging over my rapidly flushing skin. "Madelyn," he murmurs, barely breaking the kiss, and my name sounds sweet on his lips.

He kisses my jawline. My neck. His hands slide under my sweater and across my stomach, sending a million butterflies coursing through me as his mouth returns to claim mine again, sweet and sure and entirely incredible. I want to live in this moment, in this sensation, forever.

I pull back from the kiss and run my hands over his bare

torso, gratified to feel him shiver beneath my touch. The trail of goosebumps that now follows my fingers.

"I want..." I start, my voice shaky. Unsure.

His eyes darken as he waits for me to find my words, and the sight of him—lips swollen, hair tousled, eyes focused on me like I'm the most precious thing in the world to him—makes me entirely sure of what it is I want to say.

"I want to be husband and wife for real tonight," I confess, my cheeks reddening.

I can see on his face that he wants this—wants me—too, and his hands tighten slightly on my hips as if he's restraining himself. He hesitates.

"Are you sure?" His voice is ragged and his eyes are a dark pool of longing that I want to dive right into.

"Always with the thoughtful," I say through a smile as I throw myself into my husband's arms. He picks me up and my legs circle around his waist as he holds me close, kissing me and kissing me and kissing me while carrying me to the bed.

"I'm assuming that's a yes?" he murmurs as he presses an open mouth kiss to the base of my neck, sending a bolt of heat all the way to my stomach.

And I realize I have never, ever wanted something more than I want my husband right now.

"Yes, yes, a thousand times yes," I reply.

And it's all the assurance he needs for tonight.

26

SEB

The cold, circulated air is thick with the scents of rubber and ammonia, along with a touch of sweat and leather. With the sound of skates scraping over freshly Zamboni-ed ice and sticks clashing against pucks. The buzz of Coach's yells over the rink, rising over everything else.

Today is our second post-Christmas team practice, and I'm back in my happy place.

Well, up until very recently, I would've considered it to be my one and only happy place.

Until Maddie came along and rearranged everything.

Now, my happy place isn't a *place*, per se.

It's waking up to my wife's brown hair spread over my white pillows, her breathing short and hiccupy as she snuggles her face into my chest. Which is the cutest damn thing. It's having this woman to return home to at the end of a hard practice. It's my apartment still bursting with ridiculous, over-the-top Christmas decorations that make it clear that the people who live there actually *live* there, instead of just showering and sleeping there after a long day of workouts and game tape and ice time.

Since we got back from Aspen a couple days ago, we've

fallen back into our pre-holidays routine of coming home together, cuddling, and watching movies—including lots of Hallmark romances.

The only change from before Christmas is that Maddie now sleeps next to me. In my bed.

Well, *our* bed.

After all those nights in Aspen, sleeping next to each other, why go back to sleeping separately when we are, indeed, man and wife? Especially given how magical that last night at the cabin was. How much I was able to express to her without having to say anything at all... It was perfect.

She was perfect.

And I want her next to me every night so that I can touch her, hold her, kiss her until she's breathless.

We haven't really discussed what happens next. When Mike called me on Boxing Day, it was to let me know that he'd set up a meeting between Roger and me for this afternoon. He was cryptic with the details, but insisted that I'd want to be present for it.

I have no idea what he's going to say, but I do know that whatever it is, it doesn't change the fact that I want to be with Maddie.

I love being her husband, paperwork or no paperwork—this marriage is no longer about anything but *her* to me.

I grin, lost in memories of Maddie and me in the kitchen last night, making dinner together but mostly making out. The chicken we ended up eating was bone dry, but neither of us cared about that at all.

"Dude." Colton Perez gives me a little shove. "You're up."

I look over to see my teammate inclining his head at a red-faced Coach Torres screaming from across the ice.

"Slater! You get hard of hearing over Christmas or what?" Coach bellows.

"Sorry, Coach!" I call back, still feeling sunny as all hell as I get into position for the shooting drill.

The coach's whistle blows, and I shoot forward, skates slicing across the ice, puck dancing against my stick. My eyes flick to Lars' backup goalie, Randy Allen, and I attempt to read his body language as I gain on him. I zero in on the net's corners, and I take the shot, reveling in the satisfying *thud* the puck makes against my stick before it sails in a beautiful line of precision right at its target, evading Allen and hitting the back of the net neatly.

"Nice shot, Slater," Coach grumbles. "Almost makes up for you being in La La Land today. *Almost.*"

I'm still on top of the world when we skate off the ice at the end of practice. Tomorrow night, we're facing the Tampa Storm, here at home, and I'm feeling pretty optimistic that we can beat them if we keep playing the way we have been at the last couple practices. Although, to be honest, I'm pretty optimistic in general these days. Hard not to be with Maddie in my life.

Tonight, I'm taking her to a little sushi place in West Midtown that I found a few months back. Apparently, she loves the stuff, but Adam hated it so she hasn't been on a sushi date since... well, ever.

I'm more than happy to change that. And then take her home afterwards.

The team pours into the locker room and it's quickly filled with a cacophony of laughing and teasing and banter as the guys all grab their stuff and head for the showers. Meanwhile, I'm rooting through my gym bag for my phone before I bother to shed any of my gear.

My grin stretches wide when I see that she's texted.

> Stef gave me free rein with today's lunch menu, so steak tacos are up. I plan to make up for that dreadful dry chicken we ate for dinner yesterday.

200

I settle down on a bench and start typing out a text back to her. Flirty, of course, because I like to imagine her down the hallway, blushing in the kitchen.

> I dunno. I'd say you more than made up for that last night ;)

> Sebastian Slater! This is a workplace. Am I going to have to call HR on you?

> Sure. You can tell Adrienne about how skilled I am, both on and off the ice.

> *GIF of Jake Peralta saying "I have no idea what you're talking about right now"*

> *GIF of Jake Peralta saying "I love your face and I love your butt"*

> SEB!

> Oh, please, you know you love the NSFW comments.

> You're right. I really, really do.

I laugh out loud. This woman...

The fact that she can get behind my ridiculously suggestive banter is just a plus on top of a million pluses that make up Madelyn.

I'm typing out a response when a throat clears above my head. Loudly.

I look up to see a towel-clad Malachi Holmes staring down at me with a dark eyebrow raised. I'm still sitting on the bench in full gear, giggling at my phone like a pre-teen girl. And only then do I notice that the locker room is totally empty—the guys have clearly all traipsed off to the showers already.

The captain folds his arms. "Slater—or at least, I *think* you're still Sebastian Slater, I'm not convinced that your body hasn't been invaded by aliens and I'm speaking to one of Earth's new overlords... What is going on with you today? And yesterday too, for that matter? It's like you came back from the Christmas break a whole new person."

I shoot Mal a sheepish smile. "Well, Captain, it's that... I think I might have accidentally fallen in love with my wife."

❋ ❅ ❋

After a huge feed of steak tacos, wild rice, guacamole, and the ever-present sautéed veggies, I tell Maddie that I'm heading out and I'll pick her up for our date as soon as her shift ends. It's actually now turned into a double date, seeing as a gleeful Mal invited himself and Chantal along because he wants to "witness this for himself."

Luckily, Maddie loved the idea.

I give her a quick kiss goodbye. Then, it's time to see Roger.

It's a pleasant day, and I drive with the windows down, breathing in the winter breeze. As much as I love snow and ice, that's one thing about non-Canadian winters that I have to appreciate—not freezing your tail off every time you step out of your house.

I follow my GPS to the shiny law offices on Peachtree Street, and pull into the underground parking lot. I'm making my way to the elevator when someone behind me calls my name.

Expecting a hockey fan looking for a photo, I turn around with a warm smile. Instead, I'm totally thrown to see Richard Grainger striding towards me. He's wearing a three-piece suit and has a leather briefcase in his hand. Which is a very different look from the fuzzy and expensive, various-shades-of-gray cashmere sweaters he donned over Christmas, always paired with pressed slacks and an ever-present snowman mug that smelled of hot cocoa and some sort of liquor.

"Richard. Hello," I say warmly. No matter my wife's family's eccentricities, I still want to be polite when it comes to her parents. Unless her mother's insulting her or her choice in a husband, of course.

"What a surprise." He extends his hand and gives mine a hearty shake. "What brings you to this neck of the woods?"

"My new lawyer works in this building," I tell him.

"Let me guess..." Richard says, pointing a finger at me. "Mitch Goldman? Or Roger Delaney?"

I'm surprised—this is a huge firm. But I nod and say, "Yeah, Roger."

Something flickers across Richard's expression, but he steps into the elevator before I can tell what it is. He presses the button for Floor 21. "You're going to want to get off here, then."

"Thanks. How do you know Roger?" I inquire.

"I'm a senior partner at the firm he works at." I love that he emphasizes that he's a partner, whereas Roger is merely *working there*.

"Wow. Small world."

"Yes. As we spoke about at Christmas, myself and Paul do criminal defense law, whereas Roger works in immigration law. Specializing in representing professional athletes..." Richard's glinting brown eyes roam over me shrewdly. "Mitch is the only other pro-athlete specialist we have, but he works more with brand deals. Not immigration." He pauses for a beat. "I believe Alicia mentioned you're Canadian?"

I give a nod, resisting the urge to shrink back from his steady gaze. "Roger's helping me sort out some stuff with my green card, as well as my contract for the Cyclones."

"Ah." For some reason, this response feels loaded and the atmosphere in the elevator suddenly becomes a touch suffocating.

Finally, the doors open and we step into an opulent, marble-floored lobby, complete with floor-to-ceiling windows with city views that put the ones in my apartment to shame. The office is literally buzzing with activity as well-dressed people move to and fro, and phones trill noisily. And yet, the silence between Richard and me feels almost painful.

"Well. It was good to see you, son." For some reason, the way he says this makes me bristle. But I guess I literally am this man's son-in-law. "Take care."

"You too."

Mr. Grainger shakes my hand once more and marches on his way. I stare at his retreating figure for a moment, feeling like I've somehow said too much.

Richard and I didn't spend a lot of time alone at the cabin. In fact, I hardly remember having a single conversation with him, and only him. I assumed that Maddie's mother would be the difficult parent to deal with given how blatantly and shamelessly she would put down her own daughter. But something in Richard's demeanor—the keen, sly look in his dark eyes—has put me right on edge.

I don't have much time to dwell on this, though, because as soon as I inform the secretary that I'm here to see Roger, he immediately escorts me into a lavish office. The bushy-browed man is seated behind a behemoth pinewood desk littered with piles of paperwork, waiting for me with the same stern expression I remember from the last time I met him.

"Mr. Slater. I trust that you spent a merry holiday season." His mouth twitches upwards at the corner, but I definitely wouldn't call it a smile. I open my mouth to respond—confirm his not-a-question—when he dives right down to business. "Your paperwork has been filed, and we are moving onto the next step in the process."

I blink in full surprise. "Wow. Already?"

Roger tsks as he rearranges some of the mess on his desk.

"Yes. Someone high up in the immigration office must enjoy your hockey or something because you've been given an interview appointment for your green card." He gives me a pointed look. "The *joint* interview."

"Oh. Sure." I rub the back of my neck, feeling my unease radiating around the room.

The lawyer props his elbows on the desk and peers at me. "In this interview, you will need to convince a USCIS officer that you and Ms. Grainger are man and wife."

"Which we are," I say.

Roger nods stiffly. "Which you are." He then shoots me a look that says a whole lot with absolutely no words. "But if the officer gets a hint of a whiff of a rat, I should warn you that the repercussions are... severe. Separate interviews, further questioning, possible fraud charges..."

He trails off, his watery eyes locked on my face. Meanwhile, my jaw sets. I see what he's getting at here: he's not sure he believes me, but he obviously can't come out and *say* that, so he's trying to make sure that I'm aware of how badly this could go.

"I understand," I say.

He pauses for a long beat. "You're sure it's worth it, Mr. Slater?"

"Yes," I answer immediately. "And, by the way, my wife goes by Mrs. Slater now."

"Okay." Roger frowns. "But I wouldn't be doing my job if I didn't make both you and *Mrs. Slater* aware that there may be another option..."

27

MADDIE

Chantal Holmes eats sushi as elegantly as she does everything else. She has mastered the art of using chopsticks, and she's managed to get by without spilling even a single drop of soy sauce on her pristine white halterneck top.

She pops another piece of sashimi in her mouth with finesse while I fight with my own chopsticks so I can clumsily pick up a California roll.

Damn Adam and his unreasonable dislike of most Asian foods—AKA some of the best food in the world. Due to a serious lack of sushi dates over the years, my chopstick work is subpar, at best.

"Doing okay over there?" Seb interrupts his hockey talk with Mal to look at me with these dorky, soft eyes that make me feel a whole lot of something in my (currently very empty, thanks to said chopstick incompetence) stomach.

"Fabulous," I say. And I mean it. Because I'm happy as a little clam right now, sitting here with Seb, and his lovely team-mate, and his teammate's lovely wife.

Since we've come back from the cabin, I've been in total wedded bliss with my extremely flirtatious and loving and sexy to boot husband, who seems to be as obsessed with me as I am with him.

We've had the best time together the last couple of days, both at home and at work. And he also took me to visit the brand-new, out-of-this-world wonderful, create-space he gifted me with for Christmas. It's somehow exactly what I dreamed of, without actually realizing it's what I wanted. If that makes sense. It's spacious and flooded with light from big windows, boasting metal countertops and a huge stainless steel fridge and so many appliances, I've spent literal hours just trying to catalog it all.

And now, I'm actually looking forward to being back in the family box at tomorrow night's game, wearing Seb's name on my back like the proud wifey that I am.

Turns out he could—and did—make a hockey fan of me, after all.

As for the hungry thing... I can always use my fingers to retrieve food when nobody else is watching, right?

"I love sushi," Chantal says, all smiles as she expertly secures another roll. "Maddie, we should totally organize watch nights for the wives and girlfriends when the guys are playing away. But instead of beer and wings, we'll have sushi and champagne."

"I love that idea!"

She leans forward, as if conspiring with me. "I also think it'll be a good way to help us girls get through the playoff season. Because that's looking more and more likely now."

"Hell yeah, it is!" Mal holds up a hand towards Seb, who willingly smacks it. "Playoffs, here we come!"

I have to laugh at their unabashed enthusiasm before turning back to Chantal while also attempting to stab yet another sushi roll with my chopsticks. "What do you mean, help us get through the playoff season?"

"Well, being married to a hockey player is a big enough commitment in itself, and it's *way* more intense when the playoffs start. The guys spend more time on the road, more time at practice... they basically eat, sleep and breathe hockey. But making the playoffs this year means the world to Mal. They WILL make it, and I will support my husband one hundred percent." Chantal sighs sweetly, gazing at her husband. "But... I can't say I'm super upset that he's retiring at the end of the season. We'll get to spend more time together, even if he pursues coaching or sportscasting or something." Another smile. "In the meantime though, I thought starting a wifey support group slash lonely hearts sushi club would be a nice project during Mal's final season."

Chantal picks up another piece of sashimi and pops it into her mouth contentedly. Meanwhile, I've given up on my sushi stabbing for the minute as I process her words. Playoffs have seemed so far away... but I guess they're happening in just a few short months.

Seb, who apparently checked back into our conversation at some point, chuckles deeply. "That's quite the catchy name. You should get T-shirts made."

Chantal rolls her eyes at him, laughing, too, and the conversation soon turns to New Year's Eve. Apparently, it's a tradition for the team to have a huge party that night. A party at which Tony Torres *always* lets his hair down.

Mal's telling an extremely enthusiastic recounting of last year's party when, after a few too many, Coach Torres sang a "You're The One That I Want" karaoke duet with Triple J, and I think I might burst my appendix from laughing too hard.

"I can't wait!" I wheeze at the thought of stern Coach Torres pretending to be Danny from *Grease* on stage.

"You'll have to make sure that Seb enjoys the party too, Maddie," Mal says to me with a wink. "Last year, he only made a quick appearance before going home at 9pm because he had an early morning personal training session. On New Year's Day!"

"It was important!" Seb protests.

I give him a playful jab in the ribs. "This year, we'll make sure we're *both* there 'til at least midnight. I love New Year's Eve, it's my favorite!"

This draws a chuckle from my husband. "Of course you do, it's full of the ultimate Hallmark moments—the glamorous parties, the countdown, the kissing at midnight..."

"Well, you both better enjoy it." Mal reaches for the soy sauce and tops up his little dish. "Because that's gonna be the last chance for us to have fun until we get through the season and postseason, and win the whole damn thing."

The glint in Mal's dark eyes is steely and determined. He's going to throw everything behind this singular goal.

I recognize that look... I've seen it on my own husband many times. These guys are going to do their damndest to win the Stanley Cup this year, and while I'm honored that I get to be the woman behind the scenes, supporting Seb's shot at victory, Chantal's right: it's a big commitment to be married to someone so dedicated to their sport. To their goals.

I pluck a tuna avocado roll from the tray with my fingers and put it all in my mouth, chewing furiously to try and quell the strange sensation suddenly brewing in my stomach.

The holidays were amazing, but Seb has a championship to win. And while I know this, I find that I'm greedy for him—for his time, his attention, the different ways he looks at me like I'm this glorious puzzle he's having a blast figuring out. I want to spend all my time with him... But I also have to remember that I'm a hockey wife. And though Seb has been balancing his priorities differently lately, his life is still built on hockey.

The glint in Mal's eyes? That same fire burns in Seb's every time he talks about what it's going to take for him to help lead the Cyclones to glory this spring.

And isn't that why we're married in the first place? So that he could keep playing hockey and help give the Cyclones a chance at dominating in this year's playoffs?

Hockey needs to come first for Seb for the foreseeable future. And I *will* be okay with that.

I take a long gulp of my water and am relieved when the topic changes again to how successful the toy drive was. Chantal drops gossip that Carter Callahan's wife was puking in the bathroom all evening, fueling rumors that she might be pregnant.

"Wow, that's great!" I exclaim happily—and I am happy for them.

But I'm also very aware of the spot on my thigh where Seb's big hand rests. His wedding band glints on his ring finger, and I find that I can't wait for dinner to be over so I can be alone with my husband. Safe in our little bubble where I can just think about how I'm falling for him, and he's falling for me, and forget all about reality.

28

MADDIE

"Oh, wow. That makes everything feel very, very real."

I prop myself up on one elbow to look at my husband laying beside me. In the background, a Food Network show—*New Year's Baking Bonanza!* (because, apparently, the second one holiday ends, we are onto the next)—plays on TV.

Seb swallows, his blue eyes searching my face. "I wasn't expecting it so soon."

"Me neither," I say softly. He's filled me in on his conversation with Roger this afternoon before our double sushi date, effectively popping the "avoid reality" bubble in which I was hoping to float off into bliss tonight. "Roger said that we need to prepare for the interview?"

"He did," Seb says. Then, he hesitates for a moment. "He also said that if the interview doesn't go well, there could be a ton of repercussions. For both of us." His face is dead serious, his body tense as he looks at me.

"I know," I say simply.

He rubs the heel of his hand against his eye, looking almost lost for a moment. The expression makes him appear younger, more vulnerable, than the man I've gotten to know so well. He bites his lower lip, his gaze trained carefully on the TV. "Well,

Roger *did* say that there could be a different way to do this... One that doesn't involve you having to be my route to a green card. I could look at getting you out of this if you're not feeling comfortable."

My stomach twinges as I look at him, wondering what's going through his head right now. Why on earth would he even be looking for another way when we're already in the middle of executing this plan?

Is he getting cold feet about the green card? About staying married?

No. Surely not.

"I'm comfortable," I tell him. "It's what we agreed on, and I always stick to my word. I *want* to stick to my word."

I'm gratified to see his entire body relax at this. His demeanor changes. And I know I'm right in saying this—he's looking out for me, considering other avenues. Being thoughtful, as usual.

"You're the best wife in the world." He smiles suddenly, running a finger along my forearm and pulling a shiver out of me.

"I know." I stretch out on the luxurious sheets. Seb has the most comfortable bed in the history of all beds, and taking my place in it has been wonderful. I really do love being married to this man. For more reasons than just his sheets of course. Though they certainly are a plus. "So, as a most excellent wife, do tell me how we can start prepping for this thing?"

"I can think of a few ways." Seb's voice takes on a husky quality as his eyes roam over my stretched-out body, the previous tension in the room now evaporated and replaced with tension of a whole new kind. The good kind. I'm wearing plaid pajama pants and a Little Miss Chatterbox T-shirt, yet he gives me such a heated look that I momentarily feel like I'm dressed in some kind of sexy negligée.

This is one of the things I love most about Sebastian—he seems to be into me for exactly who I am, the way I am.

I blush and giggle as Seb sits up, bare-chested and magnificent, and makes a move to kiss me.

"After," I caution him, forcing myself to duck out of his reach while everything in me screams *Nooooo, you idiot! Kiss the beautiful man!* "Interview prep first, then—"

"I give you the night of your life?" He grins cheekily.

I hit him. "More like I give you *yours*."

"I cannot argue with that." He scoots closer to me and wraps an arm around me, pulling me close so that I can lay my head on his shoulder. He smells amazing, as usual, but his scent is even better now than it was at first. Because not only is it incredibly sexy, it's now also familiar and comforting. "So what do we start with, my beautiful wife? Your favorite color?"

"Blush pink," I say immediately. "You?"

"Green." He tilts his head to meet my eyes, his gaze smoky. "The exact green of your eyes."

And I'm immediately in half a mind to throw all interview prep out the window and jump on him.

Luckily (or unluckily), he presses on. "Food?"

"Pizza, the thin-crust, Italian kind. You?"

"Steak. So rare that it's bloody."

"Ew," I respond, wrinkling my nose. "Okay, umm... Favorite flower?"

He blinks. "I dunno."

"Oh, come on. Everyone has a favorite flower."

Seb laughs. "Can't say I'm a big flower guy."

"The correct answer is peonies. Or freesias. Or calla lilies."

"You've really thought that one through."

I blush. Because I have, kind of. When I thought that Adam was going to propose, I started to look into what I might want for a wedding—flowers being one of them. I wasn't too bothered about wedding planning, but I loved the idea of a pretty dress and gorgeous flowers, followed by a big party.

Now, I'm so glad that none of that happened, simply because Adam was the wrong man for me. And even though I always wanted a romantic wedding, I'd take a drunken trip to a chapel in Vegas with Seb a million times over a fairytale wedding with Adam.

We still haven't talked about what'll happen with our marriage once Seb actually gets his green card, but I think it's because we don't have to. It's obvious that both of our feelings have changed, and we will cross those logistical bridges when we come to them.

Seb isn't Adam. And I'm confident that he will never, ever blindside me like my ex did.

I smile at my husband, who's now got his phone in his hand and is looking up flowers, his brow furrowed as he studies them. "These all look the same!" he squawks.

I shake my head with a laugh. "Absolutely not. And you call yourself observant."

"I'm observant of *you*," he says, throwing his phone to the side and pulling me back up against him. "Now, for the next question..."

Seb has a game tomorrow night and really should get some rest, but we end up continuing our interrogation of each other into the night. It doesn't get boring because I find myself wanting to know every little thing about Sebastian Slater.

After we're done talking, we let our bodies take over.

And he makes good on his promise to give me the best night of my life—like every night with Sebastian somehow manages to be.

29

SEB

"You know that we wouldn't usually do this on a game day, Seb, but time really is of the essence here."

I nod at Tony, who's seated across the table from me, flanked by Roger the lawyer and Dennis Lieberman, the Cyclones GM. Up on the wall-mounted TV to our left is a slightly blurry image of Mike, who's been conferenced in for the meeting.

I shift uncomfortably in the plush, entirely comfortable leather chair I'm currently sitting in, and eye the papers on the table in front of me.

Otherwise known as the contract of my dreams.

Apparently, the "other option" Roger was talking about yesterday was a five-year agreement with the Cyclones with a salary increase and a larger bonus, as well as both a no-trade clause and a new work visa for the duration of the agreement— and the promise of a team pursuing immigration matters of a permanent nature for me during this time, which wasn't even on the table before. With the new year coming up in just two days, there will be a whole new quota available for special interest visas, and Roger is confident that we can get one expedited.

I should only have to miss a couple of games in January, max, while the paperwork processes. And with our team performance of late, Tony's not too concerned about a couple of potential losses affecting our chances at getting into the playoffs.

And I say "potential" because I know the team is capable of winning without me. I realize now that I'm one piece of the unit as a whole. And I'm glad of it. There's no need to be a hero... I want to win as a part of the team I love.

But perhaps best of all, I'd be applying for my green card independently. Which means that Maddie would no longer have to go through the arduous interview process with USCIS.

Or is that perhaps worst of all...?

Of course I want to stay with her, no matter what, and whatever way I end up filing my paperwork won't affect that... but I don't know how Maddie would feel about my signing this contract without talking to her. I don't want to put her in an uncomfortable situation that can be avoided, of course, but we've made it clear from the start that we're doing this together. I don't want it to appear like I walked away from something that we started because a better offer came along.

Like that jerk Adam did to her.

A throat clears, and I look up to see Coach watching me. I realize I've been spacing out like crazy.

"I'm honored," I start hesitantly. "And I want to make it clear, first and foremost, that playing for the Cyclones is my priority."

"But?" Tony prompts gruffly, his gray eyes appraising me slowly.

"It's a great offer, Slater..." Mike's tinny drawl cuts in over the speakers before I can say anything.

The undertones in my agent's statement are clear as day: *just sign the damn thing, Slater.*

But I can't say yes. Or no.

Not until I talk to Maddie.

Tony seems to sense my hesitation, because he claps his hands, all brusque and coach-like all of a sudden. "Look, you've got a game to get ready for tonight, so why don't you sleep on it. Think it over. We'll get a copy couriered to your apartment so you can read it through again, go through the fine print with your agent, if you must."

"But remember, Slater," Dennis Lieberman cuts in, his dark eyes shrewd. "This offer isn't going to be around forever. In fact, with a new year a couple of days away, I'd say we're looking at a pretty imminent expiry date on this."

"I understand."

"And bear in mind, our next offer might not be so generous."

"Sleep on it," Torres says again, firmly this time, as he casts a side glance at Lieberman. "We'll be expecting your answer imminently."

"Thank you, Coach." I meet his eyes, trying my hardest to convey my genuine gratitude. Communicate that he isn't looking at the same player who put his own aspirations before the team's with his initial contract last year. I've matured, and this hesitation is for different reasons that have pretty much nothing to do with me and everything to do with a beautiful green-eyed girl who has captured my heart.

I think he gets at least some of this, because as we file out of the room, he stops me. Claps a meaty hand on my shoulder. "Go with your gut, kid. That way, no matter what you choose, it can't be the wrong decision."

30

SEB

You know that old saying, everything that can go wrong *will* go wrong?

Murphy's Law, they call it. Murphy being some old Irish guy who was probably (not) Triple J's ancestor.

Well, that's what happens the second we take to the ice on Thursday night.

From the moment we skate out there, it's an absolute gong-show. Twelve seconds into the game, Tampa scores. Complete fluke, but it sets the tone for the rest of the ugliness that unfolds.

In the middle of the first, one of Tampa's D-men gets called for slashing, and takes two minutes in the box. I'm ready to use this to our advantage, but our opponents run an insanely effective penalty kill, blocking our every opportunity, and earning an insanely colorful stream of language from Dallas, who's playing on my left.

Later in the period, the same jackass smashes into Aaron from behind again, sending him flying against the boards. It's an ugly hit, totally uncalled for. So of course, next thing we know, Aaron's gloves are off, and it's on.

"HEY!" I scream as I skate up, fast as I can, from my position behind the net.

I grab the first blue jersey I see and haul a player who's trying to muscle in on my teammate out of the way. He stumbles on his skates, then turns and swings for me. I catch his fist in one of my gloves, swing with my other. At this point, half the guys on the ice are brawling. Some out for blood. Curses and filthy insults and streams of blood spew from multiple mouths, as the refs get involved and shove us all apart, blowing their whistles frantically.

"That's enough, that's enough!" one of them hollers as he pushes me away from the guy I'm on, his arm a barrier across my chest. Which gives me a moment to assess the carnage on the ice.

And I do mean *carnage*.

By the time the refs separate us all, Aaron and I are hauled to the Cyclones' penalty box, while the jerk who started it all slinks off to Tampa's. 4 on 3—power play, Tampa.

I throw my hands up in frustration as I make my way off the ice. I can only watch as our penalty kill strategy dissolves into thin air and Tampa scores again in just under a minute.

The rest of the game follows the same kind of pattern. Brutal, often ugly. Hard to watch. Perez sneaks in a shot at the start of the second. Another two minutes later. But it's not enough.

Final score when the buzzer sounds: Tampa—5, Atlanta—2.

We got our asses handed to us.

I'm frustrated with how badly we played. How that one player in blue clearly had it out for Aaron. How, no matter how effective my stick handling, I couldn't sneak anything by the opposing team's goalie for the entire sixty minutes of play. My head wasn't in the game like it should've been.

Feeling lower than low, I start to skate off the ice with my stick in the air as a salute to the poor fans who paid to watch that trash.

But then, I hear my name. And I look up and see Maddie,

standing right behind the home bench, her hands pressed up against the boards. I can't hear what she's yelling, but simply seeing her lifts my spirits.

Her eyes meet mine, and the realization hits me like a gut punch.

No matter what happened on the ice tonight, *she* was here. And she's going to come home with me, win or lose. Because hockey may be important to me—it's the career I love and have dedicated myself to... but at the end of the day, it's just a game.

Maddie is my WIFE.

And even when presented with the perfect contract that fulfills all of my hockey dreams and aspirations, *she* was the one giving me pause. For the first time in my career, I put something other than hockey first. Wasn't selfish...

Because I'm in love with her.

She's shown me how much more my life can be, and how much better it is with her in it. How I'm more than just a hockey player... I'm a teammate. A son. A brother.

And a husband who's ready to risk it all for her. I'm all in on this thing between us.

Hockey may have been my top priority in the past, but things have changed. Now, I'm a married man and Maddie comes first. She's home to me. My career will revolve around my marriage—not the other way around.

I blow my wife a kiss, and then make my way to the locker room with a smile on my face—one that *she* put there.

31

MADDIE

He was smiling.

Even after that loss, that bloodbath of a game, he still found something to smile about when he saw me. And though I feel bad that he lost the game and can only imagine how hard he must be taking it, it feels good to know that I could be there for him. That he clearly found some solace, even for a moment, in seeking me out in the crowd.

Because that's what we do. We're there for each other.

The thought has me practically running out of the arena. I can't wait to find my husband.

Hug him.

Remind him that there's always the next game. And the one after that.

And I'll be here for all of them.

I round the corner to the crowded concourse, which smells of stale popcorn and spilled beer and body odor, and start fighting my way through the sea of maroon jerseys towards the players' area.

I shouldn't have left the comfort of the family box... but on the other hand, I'm very glad that I did. I wanted to make sure that Seb saw me on his way into the tunnel. Knew that I was there for him.

Like I said in my vows—for better, and for worse.

And yes, I'm pretty sure I hiccupped my way through that line and Elvis had to thump me on the back until I could speak again, but that's neither here nor there.

I'm racing against the crowd, weaving in and out of human traffic, when a very familiar figure appears in my peripheral. Two, in fact.

"Dad?" I blink in surprise, waving at him. "And Mr. Plumlee. Hi."

I forgot that the VIP tickets Seb gave them for Christmas were for tonight's game. Pity about the game's outcome, but those were great seats, at least.

"Hello, Maddie." My stepdad offers me a thin smile and a little pat on the arm, while Mr. Plumlee gives me a quick grin that doesn't reach his eyes. I notice with some relief and more indifference that Adam doesn't seem to be lurking in any dark corners alongside them. "Nice to see you. And it was good to see your... husband out there tonight."

Is it me, or did his voice tighten on the word *husband?*

He's probably just hoarse from yelling during the game. Or more likely, he's making an allusion to the Cyclones' unfortunate—and in my entirely hockey uneducated but very biased opinion, totally unfair—loss.

I give them both a placid look. "Did Jax come with you?" I ask mildly. Hopefully.

"He came with a friend. Left already."

Phew. If Jax brought a friend tonight, it means that Adam must've given up his ticket. Which means that my ex didn't show. Which means that he may very well be an official ex-Cyclones fan now. Ha.

Mischief Managed, as Wathwart would say.

"Oh. Pity." A beat of slightly strained silence hangs in the

222

air, and then, I wiggle my All-Access Pass in the air like a weirdo. "Well, I better run. I want to catch Seb when he comes out of the locker room."

"I saw him the other day," Richard says mildly.

I pause mid-step. "Oh?"

"Sebastian," he confirms. "He was at our law offices, visiting Roger." He quiets for a long second. "Roger specializes in immigration for professional athletes."

Of course Seb's lawyer would work at Richard's firm.

It's almost laughable how predictably annoying that is.

"Oh." I purse my lips. "Yes. Well, as you know, Seb's Canadian and we're getting his green card sorted out. You know, now that he's a married man and what have you," I waffle, suddenly wanting to stick my tongue out and run away like a bratty six-year-old.

Unfortunately, Richard's staring at me with such an intensity that I feel a single movement in the wrong direction might have him turn his nose all the way up at me like I'm an unruly bug traipsing across his lawyer-y desk.

"Oh I know," my stepdad says. "I stepped in to see Roger after Sebastian's appointment, and he informed me that you two are headed for your interviews with the immigration officials soon."

I nod. "Yup. We have an appointment booked."

Richard smiles thinly again. "He was *also* able to inform me that there's a new contract in the works for Sebastian that would mean he's able to apply for a green card of his own merit. Play hockey here for as long as he desires, without being tied to the conditional green card he'd obtain by filing the spousal application with you, Maddie."

A strange chill runs through me as my stepdad's words fall heavy on my chest.

Is this the "other option" that Seb was hinting at last night? Is there another contract that would allow Sebastian to get his own green card, and if so, was he planning on telling me about it?

"It's especially ideal given that Sebastian's work visa expired so suddenly last month." Mr. Plumlee fixes me with a *look*.

It's a look I do not like.

Defensive, I put my hands on my hips and glare at the pair of men. "Should Roger have *really* disclosed all of this? Isn't there such a thing as client confidentiality?"

They both laugh indulgently, like I'm a petulant child demanding candy. "Sure there is, Maddie," Richard says. "But there's also such a thing as basic research in the public record."

"Oh." I don't know what else to say. I wish Seb was here—he always knows what to say.

"I find it.... interesting that you two tied the knot so quickly when Sebastian was having visa trouble," my stepdad adds. And I know now, for a fact, that I didn't imagine the emphasis on the word *husband* before—he just did the exact same thing with the word *interesting*.

He's lawyerspeaking me. Accusing me without uttering a single accusatory word.

He's good at it, too. No wonder he brings in the big bucks keeping white collar criminals out of jail.

Mr. Plumlee is looking at me knowingly. "Interesting, indeed," he echoes with a smug tone that tells me Adam's going to be hearing all about this.

Maybe he already *has*.

But honestly, I really don't care what he thinks. What any of them think.

And on that, I really don't want to listen to another word they have to say.

I have a husband to find. A husband who's done nothing but be loyal and kind to me. Who defends me and supports me, but also helps me stand on my own two feet and face the people who've hurt me.

And I realize I don't *need* Seb to be here with me right now with all the right things to say. Because he's already taught me how to stand up for myself. For us. And our marriage.

Which is very, very real to me. And I know it's real to him, too... whatever the damn paperwork ends up looking like.

I look up sweetly at the man I've been calling "Dad" for most of my life. "Actually, Richard, what's *interesting* is that you have a totally loveless marriage, and so you assume that everyone else must, too. But guess what? I love Sebastian."

Saying the word out loud makes me feel shaky. But it's the damn truth, and I'm here to speak my truth. All of it.

"And Paul." I turn to my ex's dad. "What's also *interesting* is that your son had a totally loving relationship that he abandoned to chase someone who could further his career. And so you must assume that the next man I fall for would be a self-serving narcissist, too. But Sebastian's nothing like Adam." I smile. "Thank the Lord. So, Merry Christmas and a Happy New Year and Screw You Very Much."

With that, I skip away into the crowd, feeling two sets of shocked eyes fixed on my back—which bears the name Slater, of course.

Fa la la la la la la la la, indeed.

Later, Seb is shaking with laughter as I recount my run-in with Tweedledee and Tweedledum.

"You absolute badass," he cackles. "I wish I'd been there to see it."

"Too bad. You're just gonna have to imagine it, instead." I smirk across at him. We're in his SUV, driving home from the game, and I'm really glad that my story seems to have lifted his spirits. He's only mentioned losing the game in passing.

"In my mind, it's all very sexy—you laying down the law like that." Seb glances at me, his eyes suddenly heated.

"I feel like everything in your mind goes back to sex."

"What can I say? I'm a red-blooded male with an extremely sexy wife who looks extra sexy right now in my jersey."

The ridiculous words are laced with both teasing laughter and a certain gravely heat that makes my stomach swoop. My husband, the charmer with the arsenal of spine-tingling flirty comments... and I love every damn second of it.

I don't think I've ever loved anything more.

"Plus, I can always go see security and bribe them to give me the tape," he adds with a cheeky smile.

I attempt to hit him, but he easily catches my hand and laces his fingers through mine, letting our linked hands rest on his lap as he drives.

We're silent for a few minutes, the Christmas music on the radio filling the comfortable silence in the vehicle, until I finally say, "You know what, though?"

He glances at me, waiting for me to continue.

But I frown, wondering exactly how to phrase this. The whole green card confrontation with Richard and Paul is still buzzing around my head like a pesky mosquito, despite my best efforts to squash it. I know I need to do the mature thing and communicate. Tell Seb how I'm feeling and ask for clarity— because this is a healthy relationship that means the damn world to me, and I'm not going to do that smoothing-over crap I did with Adam when an issue comes up.

Seb is worth every difficult conversation, even if the outcome isn't what I want to hear.

"It's funny... I told my stepdad off, but he was kind of right, in a way," I start hesitantly. "This thing between us started as something we got into to benefit each other. And it still kinda is, with the green card application and whatnot."

Seb's face contorts a little, like the thought is unpleasant to him. "I'm sorry that it started that way. It's certainly not like that anymore."

"If there's another way to do the paperwork, Seb, I'd support you in that. If that was what was best for you," I reply carefully.

"*You're* what's best for me, Maddie," he says simply. His hand tightens on mine and he casts me a lingering, sideways look. "I was hesitating before because I didn't want there to be any negative repercussions for you... but then, I realized that we wouldn't actually be lying in our interview at all. Because this is the realest relationship I've ever been in, and I could talk about how great you are for days to the USCIS." He grins a little. "They won't be able to shut me up."

I smile, too, but I have to be sure. "We got into this for your hockey career. If this isn't the best way for you to move forward with that, then..."

"I don't care. You come first. And I wanna do this with you. Prove that I'm in this for you, and for us. We're a team now, you and me. That comes with both risk and reward... and you're worth risking everything else for."

The affirmations are all I need to feel safe. Secure. A balm to my soul, healing every lingering ounce of doubt that my past scarred me with.

"A team," I echo. "The best team ever."

"Exactly. And while I don't love how this all started out, I'm also glad of it, because it brought us together."

I nod. "Me too. I was always the romantic in the family, always dreaming of this fairytale wedding for love. I grew up in a home where my parents' marriage might've started out with love, but for so many years, has been for pure convenience. And then, I ended up in a relationship with a man who *I* was with for love, but he eventually left me for a woman who could further his career." I give a shrug. "It's ironic that you and I got together for convenience and ended up..."

"With love," Seb finishes softly.

My head swivels so that I'm staring at him; processing what he's just said. And as I do this, I read the signposts outside the vehicle, and realize we're going the wrong way.

"Seb? You missed our turn."

"No, I didn't."

He's got a mysterious glint in his eyes as he drives in, quite literally, the opposite direction from his apartment. But it isn't long before he pulls up at...

"The Atlanta Botanical Gardens?" I ask, frowning. The gardens are known for their insanely beautiful after-dark Christmas light display, but it's 10:30pm, and there's barely another vehicle in the parking lot.

"I know that Christmas is technically over, but 'tis still the season... so I thought we could go look at some lights."

I smile wide, my insides turning to goo again, as they often do around this man. "That's so sweet, Seb. I love that idea... But isn't it closed?"

Seb gives me a hint of that cocky smirk of his. "Not to us, it isn't."

I gape at him and his expression turns almost bashful. "We'll just call it one of the perks of being a pro athlete. Opening hours don't necessarily apply when I want to take my wife on a date."

"This is insane," I breathe, looking towards the entrance to the gardens, then back at Seb. His eyes are soft and crinkly and he's doing that *thing* again where he's looking at me like I'm the most precious thing in the world.

"So, is that a yes?" he asks quietly. "Will you go on a date with me, Maddie?"

"Of course it's a yes!"

His smile broadens and he climbs out of the car, comes around to my side, and opens the door. Offers me his arm. "Right this way, then."

We breeze past the night-time security guards, and the lone

teller left on-site unlocks the gate. I notice Seb slip him a bag that I'm almost certain contains a signed jersey.

How my other half lives...

Stepping through the gate and into the Gardens, it's like I've entered a literal fairytale. The sky above is inky black, but we're engulfed in the glow of a million twinkling lights.

I clutch my gloved hand on Seb's arm as we walk. The night is cool, the air calm and still and crisp, and in the background, soft music plays. We walk through a tunnel made entirely of sparkling lights, and over a bridge rimmed with shimmering, silvery ropes, and into a treed area where thousands of lit teardrops hang from each of the branches.

It's beautiful. And the fact that Seb and I have the entire place to ourselves makes it all the more amazing.

Then, Sebastian stops under the canopy of a sparkling tree and spins me towards him. His handsome face is lit by a million glowing lights as he lowers his lips to meet mine, and I realize that this is, by far, the most romantic thing that has ever happened to me.

And it suddenly doesn't matter at all, whatsoever, in any iteration of the universe, that our marriage started out as temporary. Because I love this man with all my heart, with my entire being. And I fully believe that he loves me with his, too.

By the time we pull apart, we're both breathless and flushed.

"Is this date up to the lady's standards?" Seb asks with a quirked brow.

"Blew all my expectations out of the water," I say, standing on tiptoe so I can wrap my arms around his neck and hug him close. "I can't believe you planned all this for after the game."

"I planned it right after Mal and Chantal crashed our sushi date." He looks down at me. "I realized I'd never taken my wife on a proper date, and that needed fixing. Immediately."

His tone is so sincere, so sweet, that my eyes prick with tears.

Seb's forehead creases and he takes a small step away from me, even as he reaches for my hand. We get to walking again, following a path over a pond, and I can clearly see that Seb's frowning. I tug his hand slightly so that he comes to a stop next to me. "What's on your mind?"

He chews his lip for a moment. "It's just... you've always wanted romance and a fairytale wedding, but you didn't get those things with me. I don't like that."

"I don't care about those things anymore." I shrug. "I'm with you, which is what matters."

He pauses for a long moment, his eyes searching mine. "I love you, Madelyn."

His voice is full of emotion as he stares down at me, and I practically choke, my throat raw. "I love you too, Sebastian."

And then, under the glowing, ethereal lights of the Botanical Gardens, Sebastian Slater gets down on one knee. His hands are still holding mine, and my chest is so tight, I feel like I can't breathe.

What is happening right now?

"I love you so much," he says in a low voice. "And I know that I can't go back and give you the fairytale beginning, but I *can* give you the ending you've always wanted. We've done this whole thing backwards, but one thing's for sure: you come first. No matter how this started, from here on out, we are in a marriage based on nothing but love."

My heart flutters wildly as Seb takes a deep breath and meets my eyes. One of his thumbs rubs over the ring already on my left hand.

"I can't exactly ask you to marry me, but I *can* ask you to date me. To let me keep getting to know the amazing person you are. I want to send you flirty texts and take you to nice dinners and surprise you with peonies and freesias and calla lilies, just because. I want to laugh with you and cuddle you and care for you and make love to you every night for as long as I live."

By now, a mixture of tears and laughter are pouring out of me as I look down at the man that I love. My husband.

"Madelyn Louise Grainger Slater... will you make me the happiest man alive and do me the honor of continuing to be my wife?"

"YES!" I practically scream through my tears. "Yes, yes, a million times yes!"

Seb is on his feet in an instant, and he picks me up off the ground and crushes my body to his as he twirls us around.

"She said yes!" he bellows, the sound echoing through the trees in a perfect concoction of pure laughter and happiness. Around us, the lights twinkle their applause.

I've never been happier. This is all I want... for us to be together, just like this. And I want us to have the choice to keep choosing each other, every day, just like this.

So I know what I have to do.

I pull slightly back from Seb's embrace to look at him. "On... one condition."

EPILOGUE

SEB

On the morning of December 30th, my wife—I'll never get sick of those words, *"my wife"*—drives me up to the players' entrance at the stadium, and then proceeds to throw her arms around me, climb into my lap, and kiss me 'til I'm half considering saying "screw the game!" and driving us back home.

But then, Dallas walks by and smacks the window of the car, catcalling and whooping and plummeting me back to reality.

"Yas! Get in there, Slater," he yells, pounding on the window.

"Screw off, Cooper!" I holler back, but I'm laughing. Then, I turn to Maddie, giving her one last kiss. "I'm going to miss you. First night we've spent apart in a while, huh?"

"We've been sleeping in the same bed for, like, a week."

I grin. "Feels like forever. I can't imagine it any other way now."

The Cyclones have an away game in Tennessee tonight against the Warriors—a good old-fashioned back-to-back to round out the calendar year—and I'm not sure I'm ready for it after the pounding we took from Tampa last night. On top of that loss, everything, physically, is still aching. I'd kill to just sit in an ice bath all day today.

But then again, I'd kill if I couldn't be at this game with all my teammates.

As it's a quick trip up across the state border and we don't really need a nutritionist traveling with us, Stef decided that she and Maddie should both take tonight off. And Maddie, surely overcome with a sudden delirium or fever, decided to take Jax up on his offer when he asked her to try camping with him again.

I think being in love is making her a little loopy.

She nuzzles her nose into my shoulder. "Don't go propositioning any new wives at hotel bars, you hear me?"

I tug gently on the ends of her hair. "Never. I'm a one-wife kinda guy."

"Good." She laughs. "I'll pick you up tomorrow."

"Should be back here around midday." I fix her with a look and mimic her tone from earlier. "And don't get lost wandering in any woods, you hear me?"

She sticks her hand out and her little finger loops around mine. "Pinky promise. Now, go win that game for me."

"I'll call you when I get to the hotel tonight."

"And I'll answer... unless Jax takes me to some weird off-grid place with no phone service and I'm bear fodder by then."

"Ain't no bears in Georgia," I reassure her.

"Yeah, there are." She peers at me, crossing her eyes. "Are you sure that you're actually Canadian? Because your bear knowledge is pretty appalling."

"You're pretty appalling, missy!" I swat her on the butt, and she laughs and gives me one last hug.

I tear myself reluctantly away from her and she hands me the thick manila envelope that's sitting on the center console before I hop out of the car and practically sprint to the bus. I'm not technically late, but I *am* the last one to board.

For a pack of generally unruly guys, the team manages to be pretty timely.

"Sorry, Coach," I mutter when I reach the vehicle.

Torres, who's standing right outside the door, nods at me, his dark eyes steady. "A word, Slater."

We step away a few paces, and Coach looks me dead in the eye. "I'm not going to beat around the bush here. Your head wasn't in the game last night, and I believe the pre-game meeting we had about your contract is to blame."

"*I'm* to blame, Coach." I meet his gaze respectfully. "But I've sorted my head out, and I'll be on it again tonight."

He raises a dark brow. "Does that mean that you've come to a decision?"

"I have. And I would like to accept. In fact, here you go." I pass him the manila envelope. "Signed, sealed, delivered."

Those brows pull together. "Well, I have to say that you've surprised me, Slater. At the meeting yesterday, I wasn't sure how this was going to go."

"My hesitation yesterday has nothing to do with the team or the contract itself, sir. I'm all in with this team."

Like my wife is all in with me.

I can't help but smile as I think back to our conversation in the gardens last night. At first, I wasn't super pumped to hear that her "yes" came with a condition, but when she explained her reasoning to me, it just made me love her even more.

She doesn't want us to continue with the spousal green card, because then, our marriage will always be linked to my career. And to our original agreement. But my new contract with the Cyclones will give me US immigration status of my own accord, and so, we can continue our marriage driven by nothing but our love for each other.

Choosing each other, every single day.

I never considered myself to be much of a romantic, but let me tell you, that was the most damn romantic thing I ever heard.

Torres considers my words for a few moments, and then nods. "You wasted no time coming to that conclusion, Slater."

I grin at him. "You have my wife to thank for that."

This earns me a chuckle. "Whatever she's doing, tell her to keep it up."

"I will, Coach. I'm glad to still be a Cyclone."

Coach offers me a rare smile, one that makes his lined face look ten years younger. "And we're glad to have you, Sebastian. Now get your ass on that bus. We've got a game to win."

❀ ❄ ❀

I step onto the bus to a chorus of whoops and cheers—apparently, word travels fast when it comes from the mouth of Dallas Cooper. Although the story of what he witnessed between Maddie and me in the car has devolved into something considerably more debauched than what was really happening.

"Watch it! That's my wife you're talking about." I smack Colton upside the head as I walk to my seat—retaliation for a particularly lewd comment.

After everyone finally calms down from acting like a bunch of fourteen-year-old hormonal man-children, I sink into an empty row behind Aaron, who's engaged in his usual pregame ritual. His tongue pokes out the side of his mouth as he attempts to wield a delicate crochet hook in his huge hands.

"Whatcha working on today, Marino?" I ask. In response, he holds up a crocheted pattern of a puppy in a basket. I grin. "Nice."

Way back in high school, Aaron helped his grandma with a crochet project the same day as an important game... and then proceeded to have the game of his life. It's been his ritual ever since, and he swears by it. Hockey players are generally known for their crazy superstitions, so everyone takes Aaron's crocheting in their stride, and would never dare make fun of it.

While I respect other players' little oddities, I've never been superstitious myself. But I can certainly think of a few pregame rituals I'd like to adopt that involve Maddie...

I spin my wedding band around my finger, thinking about the conversation I just had with Coach.

Whatever she's doing *is* working. I can feel a change within myself. And last night, she showed me how much she believed in me, believed in the best version of me when she convinced me to sign my contract.

But the whole thing has got me thinking. Because in doing this, she's effectively given me everything I ever wanted... and more. Now, I know that I wasn't ever actually searching for the perfect contract, I was searching for *her*. Hockey is just the icing on the cake, the extra.

She's the actual entire freaking recipe.

There were so many things she wanted, when it came to falling in love, that she didn't get because of the way things happened between us. We met and were married before we even really knew each other. And it was only after we were married that we had the whole romantic experience: the flirting, cuddling, dating, exploring each other...

One thing she never got was that dream wedding.

I turn around in my seat to face Lars Anderssen, two rows back.

"Hey, Lars! How's the wedding planning going?"

The goalie grins, all big white teeth. "I have no idea—Lena does all of it. I turn up for suit fittings, and when she asks my opinion on something, I agree with hers."

Randy Allen, another married guy on the team, laughs. "That's a good strategy. Happy wife, happy life, I say."

"I don't know," Triple J says with a sigh from a few rows up.

"If I got married, I'd want to help plan the whole thing. Little pigs in blankets, an arch made of white roses, and those centerpieces on the tables with floating candles..." He trails off as the entire bus breaks into peals of howling laughter. Up at the front, in the bus's rearview mirror, I see that even Coach Torres' mouth is twitching.

"What?" Jimmy demands. "What'd I say?"

"Just wondering... were you planning on wearing white?" Dallas asks with a smirk.

"Well, I haven't thought about the color scheme, yet," Jimmy replies thoughtfully, clearly missing Dallas's joke. "But I think I'd go for a tuxedo with a top hat. And my future wife would wear one of those poofy dresses with the laces on the back, maybe wear a matching top hat..."

At this, everyone dissolves into a fresh bout of laughter, made all the funnier by Jimmy blinking and saying "what?" repeatedly, genuinely not understanding what's so funny.

It's almost too much, and I'm clutching my sides by the time it all dies down.

Then, Mal looks at me with a smug, knowing smile. "Why all the wedding questions, Seb? Wanna get something off your chest?"

"I was actually thinking that I'd like to give Maddie a wedding, seeing as we eloped and didn't really have one," I admit. I don't care if the guys label me a simp for this comment, it's just true.

I'm amazed when Colton nods encouragingly. "You should."

Aaron looks up from his puppy crochet disasterpiece. "It's a great idea."

"Does Mad Dawg like surprises?" Dallas asks. "You could throw a surprise wedding."

"Do you really have to call her that? And who ever heard of a surprise wedding?"

"Duhhh, they're, like, a thing on TikTok."

"You think I should throw a surprise TikTok wedding for my wife," I repeat dumbly.

"We could plan it!" Jimmy pipes up. "Do you know what she likes?"

I think back, and suddenly remember all of our interview prepping.

Of course I do. I know her favorite food, color, flowers, places...

"Damn right I do," I tell him, a strange excitement building in my stomach. Is this really going to happen?

Jimmy's already got his phone out and is taking notes. "First thing's first: when do you want to have it?"

"I don't know." I frown. "Soon, I guess. How long does it take to plan a wedding?"

"Years, apparently." Lars sighs tiredly.

"I'd say you could do it pretty quick," Mal pipes up. "You'd just need to give everyone a task."

"So..." I blink around at my teammates, who are all sitting up straight, alert, and peering at me like a pack of meerkats. "Are we really doing this? A hockey team is planning a surprise wedding?"

"Looks like it," Jake Griswold grumbles from the back of the bus. "Dunno how you're all gonna keep your mouths shut and not ruin the surprise, though."

Up at the front, Coach Torres stands. He winks at me. "I know how. Because we'll do it tomorrow night. New Year's Eve. The wedding can be in lieu of the party."

New Year's Eve is Maddie's favorite holiday.

A fresh new start for a fresh new year.

I stare at Coach. "A New Year's Eve wedding..."

"And we can do the heavy lifting," Jimmy pipes in. "Work together to get all of Maddie's favorite things."

A loud, communal holler and cheer resounds around the

bus as my team, my dysfunctional pack of brothers, all indicate that they're in.

This plan is so freaking insane, it might actually *work*.

MADDIE

It might be New Year's Eve—one of my favorite holidays—but I'm uncharacteristically annoyed. For many reasons.

First, camping is really, really boring. As well as sucky.

We spent all day yesterday cooking things over a fire, and chopping wood for said fire (well, Jax chopped and I supervised), and peeing in an outhouse. This was followed by a long night of tossing and turning while owls hooted obnoxiously in the background and I had vivid, disturbing dreams of bears peeping on me whilst I peed. So this morning, I insisted that Jax and I abandon the campsite—and the alarming bag of dehydrated "scambled eggs" he brought—early and drive to civilization for breakfast.

I was beyond thrilled to find a cute little roadside cafe.

And it would've been a real mood lifter, except for the fact that I haven't heard from Seb this morning. Not even a single text through the night. I'm also already finished with my bagel (and tucking into Jax's untouched one), and I'm now even *more* bored than before because Jax has barely looked up from his phone.

In fact, he's been on that thing *all morning*.

Usually, this wouldn't be a big deal. But today, I have leaves in my hair and I'm pretty sure a fire ant bit me on the butt. So, let's just say I'm a little more cranky than normal.

I'm definitely finishing off this wildly chaotic year with a bang... though I'm not sure it's a great bang.

All I want is to get home, shower, nap, and then get myself all made up for the Cyclones' NYE party tonight. Which is sure to be a whole lot less boring than this.

"JAX!" I say again, my patience running paper thin. "What's going on?!"

He lifts his eyes for, like, a millisecond. "Get yourself a second bagel instead of eating mine."

"Who're you texting?" I ask through a mouthful of cream cheese. "Is she pretty? Can I meet her?"

I may or may not be asking these questions solely because I know that they'll get Jax to talk to me out of annoyance. What I don't expect him to say is, "I'm texting your husband. Who is quite pretty for a man, I guess."

"WHAT?" I'm double outraged. One, because my other half is talking to my brother while not texting me back, and two, because Sebastian is not *pretty*—he's insanely hot.

Jax sets his phone down and levels stormy gray eyes on mine. "Seriously, give me my bagel back. And before you explode, your better half has a surprise for you, and he was just asking for my help."

"Ooh! Well, why didn't you say so!" I clap my hands. "Consider my mood lifted. And sorry for eating your bagel," I add as I cram the last bite in my mouth.

This earns me an eye roll of epic proportions. "You are such a brat. Now, come on. We've got an appointment to get to."

❀ ❄ ❀

A long drive home followed by an even longer shower later, Jax is shepherding me back into his car like I'm a rogue lamb and he promptly drives us downtown. There's a lot of squinting at the Maps app—which is open on his phone on his lap—and a series of wrong turns, accompanied by swearing and mutterings of "Slater, you owe me big."

Finally, we pull up at a nondescript white building with a mint green front door and a gold sign with swirly lettering I can't quite make out. Jax looks from his phone to the door and back again, and then nods. "Think this is it."

I open my car door, but then look back at him, still sitting in the driver's seat with his seatbelt on. "Aren't you coming?"

My brother laughs and shakes his head. "You're gonna want your girls for this one."

"My girls?"

As if in answer, there's a knock on my window.

I look out to see Stef, Reagan, Chantal, my cousin Bethany, and three of my best friends standing outside the car. They're holding white and gold balloons, and bottles of champagne.

I'm convinced I'm hallucinating, so I turn to Jax, who smiles broadly. "Oh, and one last thing..."

He holds his phone out to me, and hits Play on a video.

"Mad Dawg!" Dallas Cooper's face fills the screen. "Seb told us that you love New Year's. And you love parties. And you love stupid, gushy Hallmark romances. Which I'm willing to overlook, because you're super cool otherwise."

"Get to the point, dude!" someone yells off-screen.

Dallas gives the person the middle finger, then turns his eyes back to the camera. "Anyhow, I made this video for you because, apparently, it's bad luck for the bride and groom to see each other on their wedding day, which I think is dumb, because these are pre-recorded videos and—"

"Get on with it!"

"Oh-*kayyyyy*. Jeez. Anyhow, Maddie. My boy Seb was all

bummed that you didn't get a big romantic wedding like you wanted, so we all decided to throw you one. Tonight. Instead of the New Year's party. Be there or be squa—"

Dallas's face suddenly disappears and there's a huge tussle off-screen, coupled with a lot of yelling. I'm still attempting to process what on earth is happening. And then, a new face pops up.

My husband.

The sight of those blue eyes makes my heart leap to my throat.

"Mads." His voice is soft. "I love you, and I want you to have the romantic wedding you always dreamed of. Tonight seemed like the perfect time to do it... I want to ring in the new year with a celebration of falling in love with you. The guys keep telling me that it's bad luck if you see me on our wedding day, but I don't care. We don't need luck. I already got luckier than I could've ever imagined when you became my wife, and now I want you to be my bride, too. So I hope you enjoy every moment of today, and I cannot wait to see you at the altar tonight."

The video ends, and I look up at Jax in shock. "You knew about this?"

"Briefly."

"Is this"—I squint at the sign with the swirly lettering above the mint-green door. All my best girl friends are standing, waiting outside—"a wedding dress boutique?"

"Yup."

I shake my head in absolute wonderment. Sebastian, once again, has gone to every length to make sure that I know he loves me. That I'm cherished.

I'm at a total loss for words, so I just hug my brother. He actually hugs me back.

"Today's your wedding day, little sister." Jax's voice is gruff as he ruffles my hair, and the reality of the moment washes over me. A whole jumble of emotions—excitement and love and anticipation and abject happiness—tangle in my stomach.

"Will you walk me down the aisle?" I ask him, looking up at my brother with a hopeful smile.

"It would be my absolute pleasure."

His voice cracks slightly on the words. And all at once, I get the sudden and unexpected sense that there may just be hope for his future love life, yet...

"Now, get out there. All those screaming girls are waiting for you."

So I do. And we have the entire boutique to ourselves, and I feel like I'm in one of those dressing room montages they always show in movies.

My proper, real life, main character Sandra Bullock moment... *Finally*.

After trying on a few options, I fall in love with a scalloped lace fit n' flare dress with a dramatic plunging neckline that my mother would hate, but that I love.

Seb's always said that I have great boobs, and he's right—the dress fits like a glove and accentuates my curves perfectly. The girls all cheer and hold up signs with "Perfect 10" written on them when I emerge from the fitting room, and I shed a little tear or two when I see my own reflection.

I'm a bride.

Sebastian Slater's bride.

With the help of my girls, I pick out gorgeous, satin peep toe heels and some teardrop earrings. And when I try to pay for my selections, the lovely store owner assures me that it's all been taken care of.

A literal dream.

There's a limo waiting when we get outside, and we're whisked to a beautiful five-star hotel, where we're ushered up to a set of grand doors belonging to a suite.

Before we go in, Stef hands me her phone.

This time, it's Aaron who pops up on the screen. "Hey, Maddie. Uh, I guess, by now, you'll have your wedding dress... gown? Wait, what's it called?"

"I dunno, I think either is fine," I hear Mal say off-screen, right as another voice—which I think is Triple J—yells, "Tell her she better have gotten a cathedral-length veil to go with her dress!"

"What the hell is that?" Aaron demands with a frown.

"Focus, man." That has to be Dallas, clicking his tongue. "Sheesh. And y'all thought *my* video was bad."

On-screen Aaron rolls his eyes. "Uh, anyhow, Seb wanted you to know that he hopes you found the dress—or gown or whatever—of your dreams, and that you feel like a bride. When you're seeing this video, you should be at the hotel, and if you hear noise from down the hallway, it's just us guys getting ready in our suite. Seb—well, Jimmy, actually—picked out gray..."

"It's called charcoal, dumbass," off-screen Jimmy yells, earning another Aaron eyeroll.

"Fine, *charcoal* suits, 'coz he thought you'd like them and they'd match the flowers or something." He makes a face, his eyes darting to the side as he asks, "Am I done now? Is that it? I'm good?"

He looks back at the camera, his face relieved. "Cool. Well, see ya later, Maddie."

The video ends, and I'm laugh-crying.

Stef grins and squeezes my arm. "You okay?"

"An entire NHL team planned a surprise wedding for me," I choke out.

"Wait 'til you see what's next..." She opens the door to the suite, and I, quite literally, gasp.

Not only is the suite absolutely stunning, but along one wall is a selection of blush pink bridesmaids dresses arranged on hangers. On the table, there's a selection of bouquets, made up of—you guessed it—calla lilies and peonies and freesias.

A huge makeup and hair station are set up to the side of the room, with a freaking fleet of makeup artists and hairdressers waiting.

"This is insane!" I squeak.

Reagan laughs. "I wish someone loved me the way that man loves you."

I'm the luckiest woman alive.

SEB

Ten...

The countdown to the new year has officially started, and there's got to be at least a hundred people gathered on the makeshift dance floor of our wedding reception venue.

Jax somehow managed to secure the super-cool, modern bistro where he works at the last-minute. Sure, I ended up forking out compensation for all the reservations that had to be canceled, but it was totally worth it. I just hope that Jax won't have to deal with too many disgruntled customers as a result of this.

From what I could see, only one petite brunette showed up to complain, but at the sight of her knocking on the front door, Jax muttered "oh, *she's* back" and sent one of the other bar staff to talk to her.

Nine...

Somehow, my teammates and I managed to pull off a miracle. The hotel ballroom the perfect high-end winter wonderland for the ceremony, while the reception here at one of Maddie's favorite restaurants has been awesome and low-key.

The entire bar is decorated in twinkling fairy lights, candles, and Maddie's favorite flowers. Authentic thin-crust Italian pizza

—my wife's favorite—was served to the guests for our meal, followed by a cake topped with a hockey-playing gingerbread man standing next to a smiling gingerbread lady. Which was perfect.

Eight...

In fact, it's been the perfect day from start to finish. And it's definitely not due to my dumb jock brain's lack of vocabulary that I'm unable to find another descriptor... it's because "perfect" is the only word for it.

Because the sight of Maddie walking up the aisle in that white dress earlier, her eyes fixed only on me, is an image that's going to be burned into my memory forever.

Seven...

This time, we did it right. Personal vows, promises that we intend to keep.

Because I mean what I say, and say what I mean, and I'm going to love Maddie for eternity—mark my words.

Coach Torres officiated, which was both bizarre and amazing. A consolation prize for him not getting his karaoke moment at this year's New Year's party.

Six...

It meant the world to me to have my family fly down at the last minute to join us. Both of my brothers stood up for me as my groomsmen, joined by Colton and Malachi—my two teammates on my line.

Blood family and found family, side by side.

Maddie's mom and stepdad were there too, along with Alicia and Paul Plumlee. While I know my wife's relationship with her parents is complicated, I figured that she would want them there. Thought it might be good for her mom to witness it all, anyway.

I have hope that, in the future, she'll change her outlook on marriage when she sees how Maddie and I work together as a team, how we support and love each other. Which we intend to do through everything.

When we said "I do," both of our moms cried.

Five...

After the ceremony came to an end, we took photographs this time that involved no traffic cones.

Well... maybe one. I got Jimmy to steal one from a construction zone so that we could have a little re-creation from our night in Vegas for the wedding album, amidst the other beautiful portraits. Sadly, we couldn't secure an Elvis impersonator, but Jimmy did a rendition of "Hound Dog" for us to bridge that gap.

Four...

And speaking of the Cyclones, when the dinner and speeches were through, I gathered my teammates and the coaches to give them an extra thank you for everything they've done for me, especially over the last two days. We somehow planned an entire wedding *and* won a hockey game in the span of 24 hours— a feat that I'm sure no other NHL team can lay claim to.

Mal also took a moment to officially announce his post-retirement plans: he's going to go to Arlington University, his alma mater, to coach the D1 team there. I have a feeling that he's going to lead that team to many, many victories.

And in the meantime, playoffs are hovering on the horizon, a few short months away, and our team is united on one thing: this year, the dry streak WILL end, and we will be there with bells on, playing our hearts out.

Three...

We've been dancing for hours now, the celebrations going strong. Dallas even requested the DJ play "Cyclone" by Baby Bash, and it was almost alarming to see how Jimmy very much moves his body like a cyclone.

I can't remember the last time I laughed so hard.

And now, I'm standing at the center of it all, holding my wife in my arms, and she looks more beautiful than I've ever seen. Her green eyes are glowing, her cheeks are pink, and multiple light brown strands have escaped her complicated, braided updo and are falling all around her face.

She looks like a Disney princess—one of those new badass ones who don't need a man to swoop in and save them, because they're awesome at kicking ass and taking names all on their own, and the prince is just lucky to be by their side at the end of the story.

So lucky.

Two...

I run my hands down Maddie's back, calluses skating over her bare skin as I soak in this love-drenched moment. I love her in this dress. I never want her to take it off... but I also want to throw her over my shoulder and march her back to our hotel suite so I can take it off her immediately.

One...

And the most beautiful thing about all of this, when it comes down to it, is that there's no rush.

We have all the time in the world. Tonight and every night after.

Together.

"HAPPY NEW YEAR!"

The entire bar explodes in cheers and yells as balloons and confetti fall around us and the opening bars of "Auld Lang Syne" swell. All across the crowded bar, people begin to embrace.

I pull Maddie close. "Happy New Year, Mrs. Slater."

She stands on her tiptoes, arms wrapping around my neck, and she pulls herself towards me so she can kiss me with so much fervor, I almost topple over. Our first kiss of a new year, and I'm already excited for many, many more.

When we finally break apart, I'm hot and bothered in the best way.

"It is a *very* Happy New Year," Maddie murmurs as she catches her breath.

And as I look down at my wife, I know that it's going to be the best one yet.

Thank you so much for reading Seb and Maddie's holiday love story!

Want to keep in touch? Follow me at @authorkatiebailey on Instagram or @authorkatiebailey on TikTok.

A NOTE FROM KATIE

Ahhh! Happy Holidays and a huge thank you for reading this festive little book! I hope you had as much fun reading Seb and Maddie's feel-good love story as I had writing it, and that it brought a smile to your face.

Unlike so many of my other books, this one came pretty easily to me, and I didn't spend *too* much time rocking and crying in a corner. But still, despite the relative ease with which this book baby was born, there are still so many people that this couldn't have been possible without and that I very much have to thank:

SJW, my main girl, thank you for all of your help and advice and suggestions and your endless patience with me and my wild whims, and your diligence with actually forming cohesive story-lines that make sense. As always, I genuinely couldn't have done it without you.

And to the real life Madi Louise, thank you for all of your effort on making this story so much better in the end, and for fitting me in around your insanely busy schedule. You are an angel!

A huge thanks also to my launch team! This was so much fun to do with you all and I can't wait to do it again in future.

Thank you for being along for the ride and helping me get the word out about this book.

To Dawn, Bethany, Abby, Megan, Nikki, and Suzan—my typo and grammar squad. Thank you so much for doing what I (quite literally) could not. You're the best.

Thank you to my wonderful ARC readers, for taking the time to read this book and review it!

And to Jen, who has made my job so much easier. You're wonderful.

To Cindy, who came through for me on a very last-minute request in the most awesome way by bringing Seb and Maddie to life. You're amazing, and I still believe you can read my mind.

Leah, my lovely—thank you for telling me to shut up, stop whining, and just go for it with this book (not in those words, but this is how I interpreted it, and it was the best thing for me). I'm so happy my Cyclones could face off against your Eagles :)

To the Sh*t Sayers. I love you ladies. Thank you for all your support and your friendship, it means the world to me and brings me so much joy.

And last but definitely not least, Jesse. Thank you for gladly answering every single last one of my (many) questions about very niche NHL specifics. Go Flames!

Love always and wishing every single reader out there a very bookish and merry Christmas,

ALSO BY KATIE BAILEY

The Quit List

Donovan Family

So That Happened

I Think He Knows

Only in Atlanta

The Roommate Situation

The Neighbor War

Holiday Hockey Rom Com

Season's Schemings